CALLOUSTOWN

CALLOUSTOWN

GEORGE SINGLETON

DZANC
BOOKS

DZANC BOOKS

5220 Dexter Ann Arbor Rd.
Ann Arbor, MI 48103
www.dzancbooks.org

Designed by Steven Seighman

Some of these stories appeared originally in *Agni, Arts and Letters, The Baffler, Best of the Net, Boulevard, Carolina Quarterly, Epoch, Five Points, Glassworks, Kugelmaas, New World Writing, The Normal School, Oxford American,* and *River Styx.* The author is grateful to the editors.

Library of Congress Cataloging-in-Publication Data
Singleton, George, 1958-
 [Short stories. Selections]
 Calloustown / George Singleton.—First edition.
  pages ; cm
 ISBN 978-1-938103-16-2 (softcover)
 1. City and town life—Fiction. 2. Southern States—Social life and customs—
  Fiction. I. Title.
PS3569.I5747A6 2015 813'.54—dc23

                                                              2015015294

First U.S. Edition: November 2015

Printed in the United States of America

10 9 8 7 6 5 4 3 2 1

For Ron Rash, and in memory of William Gay

CONTENTS

When It's Q & A Time

Although they lived in a giant hole, the Masseys didn't hail from a tribe of cave-dwelling Vicksburg ancestors. They weren't West Virginia coalminers relocated to Calloustown, South Carolina, who longed for happier times. None of the Masseys suffered from syndromes or diseases or allergies or phobias. They merely lived underground, as blithe and relentless as anyone else in Calloustown. My father didn't like or trust them, probably because my father built brick walls and walkways, plus the occasional foundation, and the Masseys needed no barriers or welcoming entrances. I never went to art camp, so I can't draw a picture of my best friend Lincoln Massey's abode, but it's like this: you walk about a half mile south from my parents' house, take a right into the woods, and when you see a door on the ground with a knob sticking out, you're at the Masseys' place. The door might be covered in leaves and pine straw, just like the flat shingled roof, if it's between October and March. To knock on the door, you plain stomp a foot. The whole reason I know Morse code and rudimentary tap dancing emanates from going over to Lincoln's place most days, bored with a simple bang-bang-bang.

Before I was born—and before Lincoln was born, too—from what I gathered later on in life, Mass Massey had a normal, wooden, one-story cottage with a six-hundred-square-foot bomb shelter built below the garage. The house burned down. My father always said two things about this occasion: "That's what they get for not having a brick house," and "Too bad I didn't have my homemade fire tower built at the time or I could've gotten a good view of the flames."

Five or six years after I was born and discovered the door-knob in the ground, seeing as I could wander the woods and fields with little or no supervision, I heard the true story: Lincoln's father and mother moved into the undisturbed bomb shelter, he got ahold of a jackhammer, and through industrious hard labor and obsession he had a two-story, then a three-story house, lined with cement blocks, those blocks painted or covered in fabric. There were a lot of lamps, of course. There was a toilet and shower up on the first floor, but I didn't go to plumbing or engineering camp, either, so I don't know how those things worked. And I guess I exaggerate somewhat about the knob poking out: If the Masseys were home, there was a car and S.C. Dept. of Transportation truck parked right before the roof.

Mass Massey couldn't have stood more than five-two or weighed over 130 pounds of pure muscle. He appeared to be coiled at all times and didn't blink his close-set, agate marble-like eyes. With his shaved head he looked more unforgiving spider monkey than husband and father, and after I tap danced on his door I stood back always, thinking he might pop through the annulled threshold like a jack-in-the-box at the end of its song.

His wife Evelyn, though, was either nearsighted or pious. She stood four inches taller than Mass Massey, wore tight sweaters, and played the role of my pillow when I was thirteen years old and needed a better cushion than my mattress had to offer groin level.

"Be careful of the moles and snakes at night, Reed," my father said to me whenever I went over there to spend the night. "Don't think about earthquakes, cave-ins, or worms." To my mother he said things like, "Mass Massey doesn't sound much like a commie name, but they got to be communists, what with their wanting to dig a house all the way to China."

Secretly, my father loved having Mass and Evelyn Massey living nearby, because it made him seem normal. A man who strove to build the tallest fire tower in the state—for no other reason than to prove that he never should have been denied a job with both the forestry commission and the fire department straight out of high school—seemed normal compared to a family of underground misfits.

I always said, "Their house is nice," seeing as it didn't have knife-sharpening grinding wheels set up in the den or a disassembled window unit air conditioner on the kitchen table. "You should go over there and see it. Mr. Massey's got a gigantic collection of arrowheads and spearheads and hatchet heads."

"That's good. Maybe he can use those things for ammunition when he digs one foot too deep and opens up a door to Satan's minions," I heard my dad say more than once.

My mother said, "Shut up, Dwayne. You're going to give Reed nightmares."

"I tell you what gives a kid nightmares—sleeping in an underground house where yellow jackets might come out of the walls at any moment. Or dead people buried nearby, when their graves slide through fissures. Dead people have abnormally gummy teeth. As does Mass Massey. All gums."

"Go over there and have fun, Reed," my mother would say. "Be polite. Don't go telling the Masseys all these things your daddy says. As a matter of fact, try to keep Mr. Massey from talking. He might have a stutter, thus his name."

I don't know exactly what the psychological phenomenon might be called, but there has to be a label for how a child—or at least a boy—will almost always tell a neighbor something that he, the boy, was counseled to keep quiet. And then there's the opposite: what a boy should tell his parents about the neighbors he forever keeps locked inside until, say, twenty-five years later when he's on a psychiatrist's couch or, in my case, stuck in stalled traffic with my then-wife June until a coroner showed up to put sheets over the bodies of a dead driver and his passengers up ahead on W. Ponce de Leon Drive. A close, lifelong neighbor can touch a boy's pecker and take him on weekly convenience store holdups, say, "Don't tell your mom and dad," and the kid will turn into a compliant mute until everyone involved trades logic for dementia. That same boy can watch his father throw a dinner plate against the wall out of desperate angry boredom, divinely hear, "It's a sign of weakness to lose one's patience and temper, I promise not to act thusly again, don't tell anyone," and that boy will practically rent a billboard to announce his father's weakness.

I sat behind the steering wheel, taking my then-wife June to a lecture over at one of those satellite campuses because she and I were about to give up on our marriage—though we never talked openly about it—and somehow we chose confronting new ideas instead of getting drunk daily as a way to repair our increasingly miserable cohabitation. This particular lecture was open to the public, offered by a female scholar from Mississippi who gained the trust of some Native American potters in New Mexico, where she learned how to build coil pots and fire them in dung. We didn't know that the wreck ahead involved a dead threesome of migrant workers, two of whom got thrown from the cab of their truck, two of whom got ejected from the bed, one of which was only scraped up miserably and knocked unconscious. I looked at the lane next to mine and noticed a foot-deep pothole and said, "Indirectly, when I was six to twelve years old or thereabouts, I ruined a number of rims, hubcaps, and axles."

"When it's Q-and-A time, I'm going to ask that woman if the Hopi Indians were the first to make shallow oval casserole dishes with lids. I think I read somewhere that they were the first to make them, and that Corningware stole the idea."

People ahead of us began honking. I didn't mention how it had always been my experience that the people who asked questions at the end of the evening cared more about letting everyone in the audience know how stupid they were instead of needing a valid answer.

June said, "Wait. What did you say?"

My mother had won an Honorable Mention in the Upstate Fair's craft competition for an egg basket she wove out of kudzu and honeysuckle back in 1972, and for the remainder of her time in Calloustown she concentrated on discovering new homemade dyes and patterns that rivaled "man in the coffin" or "peace pipe" or "snake on the loose." She wasn't paying attention to anything I did. My father drove around

most days in between jobs, making a list of people who chose
wooden fences and gravel paths over brick so he could make
a point of shunning those people in public later. I can't remember for certain, but I think I might've spent the night in
the Massey hole for entire weekends without my parents even
knowing I was missing.

And maybe those creatures did come out of Lincoln
Massey's house at night. I wouldn't know, for we never stayed
there. As soon as it got dark outside, Mass Massey loaded up
his son and me in the truck, and we took off all over Graywood County, and sometimes right on over to the edge of
the Savannah River, probably fifty miles away. Like I said,
Mass Massey worked for the South Carolina Department
of Transportation. He foremanned a road crew. And I guess
with gas prices going up, inflation on the tilt, and the Office
of the President being somewhat tenuous most days, Lincoln's father feared getting laid off. This was the late seven-
ties, both before and after the Iranian hostage crisis.

We got in his truck after supper—and I was glad to get
out of their underground house, for the Masseys seemed to
eat a lot of fish and the odor of cooked fish forever hovers in-
terminably below the earth like stymied clouds. Maybe they
were Catholics. There wasn't a Catholic church within fifty
miles of Calloustown, or a synagogue for a hundred. I never
asked anyone's religion, seeing as I feared a conversation that
would include the question of my denomination. My father
told me to tell people our preferred denomination was hun-
dreds, then punch their noses if they didn't laugh.

So we ate fish, waited for nightfall, then emerged from
the bunker. Mr. Massey checked the bed of his truck and
said out loud, "Shovel, pick, pick." He touched his temple,

looked at us with those beady eyes, and said, "Map." And then we drove off, found quiet country roads with little traffic until teenage drinkers and dope smokers came out, wary and trustful that highway patrolmen stuck to more traveled stretches of blacktop, got out of the truck, and invented potholes where otherwise good asphalt existed.

"My daddy has to do this in order to keep his job," Lincoln said each night, like I didn't remember. "He says when the world runs out of potholes, he'll run out of paychecks."

Lincoln and I remained friends throughout our time in Calloustown, then he went off to college and, from what I heard last, worked as a lobbyist in D.C. Fortunately for him, he looked a lot like his mother, though I tried not to think about that when my pillow groaned beneath me on those confusing and hormone-ridden nights.

"Don't tell anyone about this, Reed. You know that, don't you? One day you'll want people to keep your secrets, and they ain't going to do it if you tell on me. That's how it works. I'm not sure how or why, but that's the way things go."

I never planned on telling anyone about the potholes, especially my parents. I didn't want Mass Massey finding out, then springing toward me one day from his trapdoor.

June rolled down her window. This was in April. The night before we'd gone to a lecture at the Georgia Center for the Book given by a man who published a memoir on his childhood, living with a manically depressed mother and a skeptical father. Personally, I had sat there mostly unmindful. I had caught myself trying to think of anyone I knew in Calloustown who wasn't depressed or skeptical, and how perhaps a memoir of an exhilarated and gung-ho family upbringing might offer an obsequious and prurient reading experience.

June said, "See? This is what I'm talking about. How long have we been together? I can't believe you've never told me this story. You're not making this up, are you?" And then she stuck her head out the window and yelled, "Goddamn it to hell, move! Drive! Somebody pull onto the side of the road!" To me she said, "This isn't one of those stories you heard from one of the barefoot people, is it?"

June never understood how or why I would work for the nonprofit Shod America, or find both joy and meaning in talking shoe companies into donating their products to poor Appalachian people. My wife, I feel certain now, envisioned herself going from food writer to editor of the Lifestyles section of the paper, then trudging forward from there. June, at this point, liked nothing more than to accept assignments from the paper to cover meaningless black-tie fetes of the unworthy, and then write, in my opinion, insipid narratives of how the chocolate fountain was the hit of the night. She wrote about or how the Pyramid of Cheops ice sculpture coupled with the monoliths of pâté formed to recreate Stonehenge seemed destined to live together at every social function.

When we sat at lectures and demonstrations that were supposed to strengthen our unrevivable union, I thought about how she no longer criticized our state's politicians or the president. She no longer blurted out things about home-school parents, and in the afterlife I'm going to ask someone in charge if my ex-wife voted libertarian.

"It's a real story from my life, June," I said. We didn't move. A black man walked by on the sidewalk, and June rolled up her window and clicked her door lock. I said, "What the hell's happened to you?"

"Fuck you, Reed. I would've locked the door if a white guy came our way."

I didn't say "Bullshit," but I thought it. In the afterlife I'd hunt June down and say, "Liar."

How come I had never told my wife of the Masseys? Because when we got along, I didn't want her to make some kind of unqualified leap in logic, which was how this entire conversation would end. Perhaps in some kind of passive-aggressive way it's how I wanted our relationship to finally end. Maybe I'd gotten tired of June saying things to me like, "You've never had any ambition! What's the next big career move for a man who doles out new shoes to poor people? Belts? Are you going to move up the ladder and start handing out neckties?"

When we met I had plans for graduate school in anthropology. I'd been accepted into two of the best programs there were, but June had that meaningless degree in journalism and had taken a job in Atlanta because their last food writer died—get this—when her gall bladder exploded. June had said to me, "I am not moving to Michigan or Chicago. How many columns can I write about bratwurst?" Before Shod America, I worked in the Textiles and Social History collection for the Atlanta History Center, receiving and cataloguing more than ten thousand pieces. June had said to me—though she was drunk at the time—"What's your next step, plastics and social history? Something and anti-social history? You don't have any sense of drive or accomplishment."

I don't know when the transformation took place within her. In the beginning we got along. I don't want to make any presumptions, but she might've thought that my family name—Reddick—meant that I was related to the Reddicks, the ones who made their money in oil, then in newspapers. June drank a bunch for the first few years of our marriage, as did I, so maybe she kept forgetting when I told her I was from the Calloustown Reddicks. Maybe she thought I lied, that I paraded an anonymity-prone nature. I don't know. From those early years I can only recall June looking like she emerged from a shower with Modigliani, and that she pitched a Sunday column called Bar Naked to her editor, which would include the mastery of mixology coupled with True Weird Tales from real-life publicans. The editor said it might work in Portland, Seattle, or Laramie, but not in the South. June quit drinking. I drank more, haunted daily by quilts and samplers on my job at the museum, then by wingtips and cheap canvas boating shoes when I got to Shod America.

I turned on the radio and tried to scramble past evangelists, country singers, and rappers—who all, oddly, seemed to comment on the same topics—trying to find the Road and Weather Conditions station. June looked at her watch. She said, "There's no way we'll make it to the lecture. Damn it. I wanted to learn more about kilns. I'd like to learn how to cook something in a horno, then write about it in my column."

"Kilns get hot," I said. "They get hot enough to turn dirt into a brick." I couldn't pass up the perfect segue, or what in my wet-brained mind I understood to be perfect and serendipitous cause and effect. I said, "You never met my father, but he knew how to turn clay into bricks, and bricks back into ground, kind of."

So I had driven around on weekend supply-and-demand forays with Mass Massey and Lincoln, and when I came home on Sundays my mother looked up from her baskets to ask, "What did y'all do this weekend? Did you go fishing?"

"Who names their kid Lincoln in the South?" my father would bellow. "I'm not saying anything racist, but you'd think that more black people would name their kids Lincoln. If I were black, you'd be named either Lincoln, Harriet Tubman, or Brown Versus the Board of Education."

And then I'd ask, "How come you named me Reed?" knowing all along—because my grandfather got drunk and told me—that I'd had a brother named Ed who died long before my birth, and that in actuality my name was Re Ed.

"Never mind that. It's a good name. In those baby books, it means, 'cleared land,'" my mother would say.

"And it means something that grows near the water. So you got it either way, either cleared land or something growing on the land," my father said.

We went through this incessant charade for, I guess, about half the Sundays of every year for three or four years. And then one rainy day I returned from school to find my pure and patient mother crying. My father was to have driven her somewhere with her baskets earlier—she'd improved to the point of people asking if she had nimble-fingered Cherokee blood in her background, had three craft galleries carrying her work in towns where people had money to buy baskets that didn't hold green plastic grass and screw-top eggs filled with cheap chocolate—and she carried them on her lap. She didn't want them in the back of the truck, seeing as it rained. My father hit a pothole, she lurched forward, the baskets got crushed, and she broke two ribs.

She didn't blame him because, for once, it wasn't his fault. The particular pothole—and I remembered shoveling it out while Mass and Lincoln Massey picked extra hard, out near the center of the blacktop—must've been eighteen inches deep. The hole disappeared once rainwater filled it up, at least to an unsuspecting and non-prescient driver.

My mother's ruined baskets ended up reparable, as did her ribs. But my father took it as a sign: that he'd been punished by God because of his own shortcomings, failures, and mean-spirited acts that he wouldn't divulge completely. I remember only his getting home, having me help him try to bang out the damaged left front rim of his truck, and saying, "There are some incidents for which I need to atone." I remember all of this because it came out so grammatically correct and biblical. "I'll probably need your help."

My father fixed his wheel as best he could. He checked in on my mother, fetched aspirin and ice packs, asked if she wanted any gum, and handed me a ball-peen hammer. Out back, below the homemade fire tower that at this point stood eight or ten feet high, my father kept a stack of broken bricks. He retrieved a washtub and two old stumps for us to sit on like ancient narcissistic whittlers. He stood up and stared at an outbuilding, told me to go fill up a wheelbarrow with some sawdust he had piled up in case I ever decided to be-come a pole vaulter or high jumper, and came back with a bag of cement. I said, "There's no way we can glue these pieces of brick back together."

"No," he said. "No, we're doing the opposite." And then my father told me to break the bricks up further and transfer any pieces smaller than dimes into the washtub. We worked hard together, and played a guessing game with our plink-plink-plinking. "Three Blind Mice" was easy to make out, but not so songs like "What a Friend We Have in Jesus," or "Back in the U.S.S.R." My father mixed the brick crumbles, sawdust, and cement together, and three hours later we loaded the heavy, impossible mixture into the back of his truck and took off with a hoe, two broken shovel handles, and a dozen plastic jugs of water.

I said, "Why don't we just call the South Carolina Department of Transportation? Why don't we go over to Lincoln's daddy's house and tell him about the potholes? He works a job telling people to fill the things in."

My father didn't say anything about Mass Massey being communist, Catholic, atheist, or werewolf. He said, "Mr. Massey has enough things to do besides having someone outside of his work tell him he doesn't have enough things to do." And then, mostly beneath his breath, he said, "I need to do this in case there's really a Heaven."

Was he feeling guilty about naming me Re Ed, and dooming me to live up to my unknown dead brother's prospective reputation? Had he wronged my mother more than what was perceptible? Was my father feeling guilt for never living up to my grandfather's expectations? I never learned the truth. We found the first overt and culpable hole, filled it up, poured water on top, and mixed it together into a foul ashen sludge. Drivers slowed and veered.

"How long will it take for this to dry? Maybe we should borrow some of those orange cones and put them around this thing so people don't drive into it," I said. "I know where to get some. Mr. Massey keeps a bunch of cones in the back of his work truck."

My father stretched his back and groaned. He said, "I didn't think about that. Huh. Damn, I didn't think about that, Reed. Good thinking. It'll stay gummy too long for us to hang around waiting."

I stood there alone while my father drove to my best friend's underground house. He tied a red oil rag to one of the broken shovel handles and said, "Stand in front of the hole and wave this around. If it looks like someone's not going to slow down or move over, jump."

It all worked out well. People saw me and they slowed. A few drivers asked if I was okay, I explained the situation, and they thanked me. One guy said there should be a Boy Scout badge for such community-spirited causes. My father returned, we put up two cones, and we drove onward to the next potential disaster.

"Did your father explain it all to Mr. Massey?" June asked me in the traffic jam. An ambulance, driving on the sidewalk, passed us with its lights on but no siren blaring.

"I have no clue. I asked him, he said I asked too many questions, and that was it. He said it might be best if I never brought this up to Lincoln's daddy, so I have a feeling he plain stole the cones," I said.

"You come from a fucked-up place," June said. I looked forward. The driver in front of me put on his left-hand blinker and crept slowly ahead. June said, "First off, you could've potentially killed people with the potholes, and then your father could've gotten you killed—or kidnapped—leaving you there in the middle of the road."

I didn't argue with her. I didn't mention how Calloustown wasn't the kind of place, back then, where hit-and-runs or kidnapping occurred.

When we got to the site of the wreck, June rolled her window down. She said, "Is everyone all right?" to a highway patrolman who brandished an unlit flashlight.

He said, "Mexicans. Three dead, one unconscious. One of them might be all right, unless the emergency room doctor does the right thing. Maybe they'll send him back before he wakes up." I had never known a highway patrolman to offer the results of a car wreck to passersby and wondered if he'd committed some kind of misdemeanor.

My wife laughed.

I looked at her and said, "That's not funny. What has happened to you?"

June said, "Give it a break, Reed. I'm only interacting with another human being."

I thought, mass murderers might say the same thing on a witness stand. Rapists might do the same, and child molesters.

She said, "At least I didn't break my mother's ribs."

When we got to the lecture, people filed out of the auditorium. June and I took a different route back home, and we didn't speak, that I remember. In the kitchen, later, June looked at a calendar she kept on the side of the refrigerator. She mentioned that we had a cooking demonstration the following night at six o'clock over at the farmer's market, that the chef and author would be using kale in every recipe, and that nutritionists worldwide now touted kale as one of the new organic wonder foods, filled with vitamin A and calcium. June told me that vitamin A was all about eyesight and asked me if I cared to see well for a long time, or if I'd rather live in the dark like all my old friends in their underground lairs.

I might've shrugged. I squinted to look at the calendar, but thought more about which vitamins best kept livers thriving. I thought about Lincoln, which made me think of emancipation. I wondered if there was a vitamin for foresight. We have all kinds of lectures and demonstrations to attend to straighten our lives, I almost said. And then I thought about those sadly doomed people born with holes in their hearts, on edge, I imagined, from impending merciless misfortunes.

Static, Dead Air, Interference, Memory

My wife's some kind of medical fluke, has a nerve running from her tear ducts to her pudenda. She can be out in the kitchen chopping an onion and the next thing everyone in the neighborhood's wondering what's got Mella ululating like a mournful Syrian. Back when we dated, and even for a few years after we married, I'd make sure one of those Feed Our Children telethons was on TV and begin to undress as Mella walked through the room, caught a glimpse of a peckish smudged-faced toddler, then cried until she neared climax as I found inconspicuous ways to pull off her panties. I don't want to say that I'm lazy, but after twenty-six years I feigned the cable being out some nights when I knew that nothing aired save *Old Yeller*, *My Dog Skip*, *Born Free*, or any of those other sad movies. Maybe I'd tired of the bombardment of reminders that I couldn't give Mella the satisfaction that, say, actor Tom Hanks could give her when in movies he spoke to a volleyball, or his wife Jenny died and left him with that bastard child, or he opened up a big soulless bookstore and forced that woman out of business, or that gigantic prisoner's pet mouse got smushed, or he decided he didn't want to be big anymore after talking to that mechanical fortune teller, or he came back to Normandy and talked at a grave marker.

I'll give Mella this: She learned to mask her public orgasmic outbursts into sounding like something else. In a movie theatre she could make the noise of a rusty film reel spinning, for example. At a New Year's Eve party, when that big ball's going down and everyone's crying, Mella sounds like champagne corks exploding. She's an Amazonian bird in that way. She's like nothing else in all others, though.

She got disability early on, of course, even though a qualified doctor finally signed her off as having some kind of rare chronic pain syndrome because he knew he'd be laughed out of the medical community if he wrote down somewhere on an official document, "She can't work seeing as every workplace is sad and sadness makes her orgasmic," blah blah blah. Between marriage and age thirty Mella worked as a high school English teacher who never gave less than an A, seeing as she couldn't take the kids flipping out saying their parents would kill them or that they wouldn't be able to get into college. I met Mella in college—we went to a place that had a perennial 0–11 football team, and let me tell you I got lucky every Saturday night after the autumn games. Hell, I thought every woman was like Mella and wondered how come the boys on my hall had such trouble getting laid—"Take them to a football game," I said. "Then when you get back to your room, bring up something about how the quarterback got a concussion, which meant he'd probably be suffering from dementia later on in life. Go ahead and start taking off your clothes at this point while putting a Tom Waits album on the turntable."

Anyway, Mella "retired" from the workplace and diddled around, so to speak, until eBay showed up. I had a regular job doing regular things that brought us a regular paycheck.

I'm an actuary. An actuary! I'm supposed to be able to predict how long people will live, and whether my company can make money off of them. It's more complicated than that, certainly, but not by much. Let me say this: I have professional friends in the business that I see daily. If I had to predict, and that's what I do, how many times they have a meaningful, productive, non-reproductive, sexual experience with a woman, I'd say the odds were something like, oh, infinity-to-one.

"Oh, Jesus Christ Almighty motherfucker that was good, Tank."

She rarely called me "Tank," but that's how good it was there, pulled off on a dirt road outside Calloustown, South Carolina, on a Saturday morning, driving around aimlessly in search of small boxable items she could sell on eBay—advertising ashtrays, for instance, or first-edition books, or silver salt spoons. My father understood that people named Henry got called Hank. He wanted to name me "Tank," my mother said no, and he somehow convinced her that he had an old uncle named Tenry: "I want to name our first son after my old Great Uncle Tenry," he supposedly said.

"Tenry!" my mother said there on a bed after her water broke. "That's different! With a name like that, he won't be something everyday."

Like an actuary.

My father called me Tank, my mother called me Tenry, I went to college, and I met a beautiful woman who should've been a Sioux named Mella-Who-Cries-and-Seizures-Loudly.

We had pulled off on the dirt road some seventy miles from where we lived and thirty miles from our destination because I'd made the mistake of putting the radio station on NPR on a Saturday morning before Car Talk, and there was this goddamn piece about an ex–opera singer who had at one time sung that sad "O Mio Babbino Caro" song in some kind of production in Tampa, which is sad enough without the story of this ex-opera star having fallen upon such hard times that she had to eat cat food because she didn't have money, and her leg had some kind of nerve damage that made her foot flop around, and a daughter of hers died from a Lortab overdose, and her faithful husband died in a boating accident that involved two manatees, and then the bank finally foreclosed on her house because she'd missed a mortgage payment by several minutes.

"Oh, Jesus Christ Almighty motherfucker," Mella said, and I got back in the driver's seat in order to take us onward. She put her seat back up. "I'm sorry. I needed that. I couldn't handle it alone. Thank you. Thank you, Tank."

I said, "Uh-huh." I'd been preoccupied, up until that point, with the odds of a man living to the age of seventy-six after he'd been in cancer remission since the age of forty-five. What with all the new drugs and experiments and treatments, it wasn't easy.

We drove back down the highway. I turned the radio off. I said, "You got anything special you're looking for?"

My wife said, "Something's wrong with the car."

I thought we'd been hitting potholes, that maybe my eyes failed to discern changes in the macadam. I said, "Calloustown seems like the kind of place where you'll find some old syrup containers, or singletrees, or metal Pepsi signs, or turkey calls, or battery-operated clapping monkeys, or Underwood typewriters, or arrowheads, or

Edgefield pottery, or Vietnam-era Zippos, or confederate money, or dinosaur bones, or…" The car hopped onward, sure enough. And then that temperature needle flew up, showing that we overheated. I knew if I drove much longer my engine wouldn't live another day. I said, "I need to pull over."

Mella started crying.

I'm not sure what kind of so-called qualified town wants to have a funeral home as the first business after the "Welcome To" sign, but I eased into the parking lot of the Glymph Funeral Home and put it in park. I said to Mella, "This is not sad. This is one of those things. Do not make a scene, please. We're all right."

I got out and opened the hood, as if I knew what I was doing. Well, I did know that every damn belt shouldn't be snapped and dangling from its water pump, alternator, power steering, and A/C compressor pulleys. I looked down into the mysterious cavern of my car's innards, saw what seemed to have sprang, and yelled out to Mella, "Look what we did at our age! We're fifty! We killed us some rubber gaskets and whatnot, is what I'm saying. Goddamn. You and I were humping so hard we broke everything."

The front end steamed and pinged and tick-tick-tick-tick-ticked to the point where I could do nothing but close down the hood for fear of getting shot in the head by a rod. Mella nodded inside the car, then patted the driver's seat. She said, "I've seen this happen on TV. It'll be all right. I saw this happen one time in a movie that involved these two guys having to drive through the desert."

I remembered the time she'd watched that movie—a lizard died, and Mella started crying, and the next thing you know I had her backed up against the bookcase. I remember it well, because Mella was the reader in the family, what with her English teacher background, and while I had her there I got to looking over the titles and thought, I really ought to read *Of Human Bondage*, and *Wuthering Heights*, and *Ethan Frome*. That's what I thought back then. But here I said, "We need to call Triple A."

She said, "If I call them, and they come out here to help us, the next thing you know our rates will go up."

There were no clouds in the sky. I reached down at my slightly wet balls and jerked my khakis left and right a few times. I said, "Don't do this again, honey. Please don't do this."

One time we had a hailstorm that damaged our roof and cars mercilessly, but Mella wouldn't call the insurance agent seeing as it would jack our bill.

She cried. She got out her cell phone, though, and flipped it open. "I don't know Triple A's number," she said. "Here."

What did I know? I punched up my buddy Aaron the actuary, seeing as I knew his number, but I learned that we were in a place with no bars. We were stuck in a "fuck you for trying to contact the outside world" kind of place.

"Man, we need to find a payphone or something." I thought, when's the last time I saw a payphone? I thought, Mella ought to buy up payphones and sell them on eBay. I said, "Please don't cry. I'll go inside."

"I'm not going to wait out here in the parking lot of the dead. The parking lot of people who wait to go see the dead. The parking lot."

I doubt I have to go into much detail or speculation about what might happen to an orgasmic-by-sadness woman walking into an institution of embalmment. I'd learned to live by the "we probably won't see these people again" dictum long before. I said, "Let's go see if they got a landline."

Funeral homes in the South, for the most part, do not vary. This was a big antebellum structure with a foyer and four viewing areas that had one time been parlors of sorts. The family lived upstairs, I supposed, and the bodies first showed up downstairs, just like in the movies that caused my wife to cry. I said, "Anyone home?" like people do.

My wife and I held hands.

Listen, the stereotypical mortician didn't come out from behind some curtains there at the Glymph Funeral Home. I don't know where he'd been standing before, but he plain appeared. He said, "Are you here for the Munson services?" And like that, I jumped. And Mella began laughing. Laughing! What kind of weird dyslexia is that? Right away I thought back about to how she and I had never been to a funeral service together—both our parents seemed needful to crank onward to the age of 140 or thereabouts, something I'd never have predicted as an actuary, and was glad that they all had different supplemental health insurance policies than the one offered by my company.

I said, "No," after making a noise that might've sounded like "Muhhh!" according to Mella. "No, it seems that every belt under my hood popped at the same time and our cell phones aren't working for some reason."

The funeral home director said, in that quiet voice always used by funeral home directors—what did their college football team's cheerleaders sound like?—"You're early for the Munson viewing. His family's receiving friends at two o'clock."

Mella shook her head. She laughed again, but she said, "I was so sorry to hear about Mr. Munson. Tragic, really."

I said, "My name's Tenry," and stuck out my hand. I'd never shaken hands with a funeral home director, and I wanted to see if his hand felt dry and scaly from all the embalming fluid. It didn't. "No, we're not here for the Munson thing. I was wondering if we could use your phone." I looked at my wristwatch. We had an hour.

"Harold Glymph," he said. "I see. I'm sorry. I was preoccupied. There's some talk that there might be a little bit of a brouhaha at the viewing. Nelroy Munson's widow has reason to believe that…well, you know, seeing as where Nelroy had his heart attack."

Mella said, "Who could blame her?!" and I understood that she'd ventured into some kind of role-playing improv game. She said, "You know, I've always wanted to ask a funeral director one question, and that question is, 'Why?' I mean, I know most of the time a son takes over for his father. I wonder what percentage of morticians come from a family of morticians." She looked at me. I shrugged. "It's like sourdough bread starter."

I said, "I guess I don't really need to use your phone if you can just give me the name of a decent mechanic. Place this small, I can probably just walk over there." I looked past Mr. Glymph into the next room and saw a white-white man laid out in a casket, or at least his head. He parted his hair in the middle in such a way that made him look like he'd just broken a lake's surface.

"I think it's quite a percentage," Mr. Glymph said to my wife. He pointed to the left, toward Calloustown's couple blocks, I think to show me where a mechanic worked. "I don't know for sure." He started smiling and shook his head. He touched my wife's upper arm. "A lot of young men become lawyers in order to work in their daddy's law office. Dentists seem to have dentist sons. But it can't be anywhere near what it is in my line of work. I might be one of the exceptions. You know why I got interested in running a funeral home? I got picked on bad as a kid here. I wasn't one of the Munsons or Harrells. About ninety percent of the population here in Calloustown's made up of Munsons and Harrells, and they're all still ticked off that General Sherman swerved away from their ancestors' town because he didn't see it fit to waste fire on. I don't know when exactly I realized that my best bet for retribution came in seeing my classmates naked. I'd be the only one in town to say I've seen everyone who ever made fun of me naked. Harold Glymph," he said, and stuck out his hand to shake again.

Well of course Mella started crying when he finished the story. She said, "That's the saddest thing I've ever heard," which was hyperbolic, seeing as the saddest thing she'd ever heard had to do with Tom Hanks walking away from Meg Ryan without knowing the truth of the situation.

"I might be the richest man in Calloustown," Harold Glymph said. "It ain't all that sad. Listen," he turned to me, "there's one real mechanic in town. I'd rather not send business to this old boy named Mink, if you know what I mean. He'll more than likely fix your fan belt and puncture your radiator. So you can borrow my car and drive out to an AutoZone about ten miles away. If you ain't comfortable driving my car, we can take the belts off mine—if they fit—put them on yours, and then you can drive back here and we'll swap everything back to normal."

Listen, understand that the first thing I thought went something like, what a great, generous man. How lucky were we to have car trouble right by the Glymph Funeral Home?

I said, "Oh, I don't want to bother you any. It would probably be faster and safer just to deal with that Mink fellow."

Mella walked right off from us. She started sniffling, and then she let out one of her loud blurts. She wandered into the viewing room of Mr. Munson, draped herself on the closed-up end of his casket, and started having orgasms. Harold Glymph said, "Is she all right?"

"No," I said. "She has some kind of weird thing about crying."

"I've seen it before," the mortician said. "Some women have a nerve that goes directly between their tear ducts and nookie. I've talked to doctors about it before, but they say it's a medical impossibility. Who would know better? I'll tell you who: the man who drains a woman and looks around, and a husband, that's who."

Before we could get back on track concerning my automotive predicament, the door opened and a middle-aged woman came inside wearing a lavender hat with four-inch black netting in the front. Harold Glymph said, "Ms. Harrell."

She looked like she used the same make-up as dead Mr. Munson. She said, "We know how everyone's talking. We thought I'd come early and get out of here so's they's no trouble."

"This is Mr. Tenry," the mortician said. I didn't correct him. What would it matter? It wasn't like I'd see these people again.

Mella let out a giant moan in the other room. One of those oh-god-oh-god-oh-god-oh-god-yes-yes-yes moans. "Mr. Tenry's wife,"

Harold Glymph said, jerking his head once to the back. "Let me go make that call about your car."

"We had car trouble," I said to Ms. Harrell. "We're not from around here."

The woman looked at me for about five beats too long, the same way I look at people with vertical wrinkles lined up like hatch marks between their noses and upper lips when they tell me they've never smoked. The woman stared at me, then moved her head toward Mella in the next room. "Well, welcome to Calloustown, Mr. Tenry," she said. "Is that a French name, Tenry?"

I couldn't help myself but to say, "Oui, madame," only because I realized that no other actuary in America, at that particular time, spoke French. Or at least the likelihood of it was miniscule.

Ms. Harrell curtsied, I swear to God. My wife blurted out from the viewing room, "Right there, right there!" like that.

"I better go check on Mella."

Ms. Harrell grabbed my arm. "Are you okay with this?"

I said, "She's got a problem. She has an undiagnosed problem."

She walked two steps forward and craned her neck into the other room. "Well I guess I can say that I have a problem with it. I thought I was Nelroy's only mistress."

I thought, the chances of Nelroy's parents being named Nelta and Roy were one hundred percent. Ms. Harrell started walking into the other room with some conviction. I said, "No, wait," but evidently she didn't hear me. Mr. Harold Glymph floated back into the room and said, "Mink will be at the viewing today. He said he'd be more than happy to work on your car after he pays his respects to the deceased."

Mella walked back in without Ms. Harrell and said, "Let's go sit in the car and wait." I knew what that meant— she'd been interrupted, and she needed to "complete" her little "chore."

I said to Harold Glymph, "Um."

Ms. Harrell started making noises there next to Nelroy's casket, noises that sounded like the blubbery sobs my wife had made earlier, but without the additional outcome. The last thing I heard was her yelling, "We were supposed to be together, Nelroy. You know that for a fact. You and I and God knew it. And the fellow who checked us into the room."

I wanted to be home, looking at meaningless paperwork.

We sat in our car with the ignition turned on, the windows cracked, the radio turned to the only station we could find in Calloustown, an AM selection that on this particular Saturday morning ran one of those doctor call-in shows. People called up this guy and asked questions about snake bites and numbness, about temporary blindness and bleeding pores. I couldn't tell if it was a local doctor or one of those syndicated shows. As an actuary I guess I'm supposed to love doctors who do call-in shows—I need people to live a long time so they keep paying off monthly premiums but don't get sick enough to go see a specialist—but nowadays I feel as though too many doctors won't let people plain die when they should. And it all goes back to the insurance companies, which makes me sad. It doesn't make me so sad that I cry and soil my underwear in half-zygote, but it makes me feel as though everything's doomed and hopeless.

"I'd like to have those wrought-iron wall sconces inside the funeral home," Mella said. "I could sell those things for some good money on eBay. There's a whole wrought-iron sconce-collecting community out there."

From where we sat in our car we would be able to see everyone who came in to look at dead Nelroy Munson. I could tell already that it was going to be similar to sitting at a drive-in B movie horror show, or like standing off to the side of a fair's freak tent. I said, "I just want to get the car fixed and get out of here."

A woman called in to the radio program and said, "Long time listener, first time caller, Dr. Ubinger," which made me realize that we listened to a syndicated show, seeing as there was no one named Ubinger within four hundred miles of where we, minute by minute, succumbed. "I have been passing out for no reason over the last year or so. My blood pressure's fine. I'm thirty-six years old. I'm five foot six and weigh 145 pounds. I work out four times a week at the gym and take yoga classes twice a week. I lift weights, do aerobics, swim, and I ran a marathon last year! I rode my bike in the P-to-P road race on Groundhog Day! But I'll be walking out to get the mail, and the next thing you know my neighbor's throwing water on my head trying to revive me."

Dr. Ubinger said, of course, "P-to-P?"

"Pittsburgh to Punxsutawney. It's a big thing around here—for cyclists, at least. Which means it's a big thing!"

I said, "She's passing out all the time because she doesn't have any oxygen going to her brain."

Mella said, "You remember that time?" which I knew she would say. If I'd've turned on the radio to a hard rock station and Lynyrd Skynyrd's "What's Your Name?" or "That Smell" came on, she'd find a reason to tell this story, too.

A carload of mourners drove up and parked. The women looked like Ms. Harrell and the men like dead Nelroy Munson. I said, "Go on."

"Man, you'd think none of those men had ever seen a prone woman."

We'd been at the mall. It wasn't my idea. I went off somewhere to buy Mella some overpriced Le Creuset cast-iron pots, because she thought she couldn't pour a can of Campbell's soup in anything less. She went wandering around, as far as I could piece together later, and saw a sad kid sitting on Santa's lap who asked for a bottle of hand sanitizer only so that when her daddy hit her momma on the face she no longer got infections from his germ-ridden fingernails. Mella cried, she got all orgasmic, and she crumpled to the floor. Someone yelled out, "Is there a doctor in the house?" just like on the TV shows.

I lugged my pots back to where I was supposed to meet my wife—right by a temporary special occasion holiday incense kiosk—to find her surrounded by a female allergist, a male dermatologist, a guy with a Ph.D. in history, a woman gynecologist, a chiropractor who seemed to be ambisexual, and two men wearing tweed coats with honorary doctorates for their contributions to the well-being of South Carolina. When Mella came to she said both "What's your name?" to the strangers who wanted to know what caused her to flail around orgasmic, and "What's that smell?" to the incense nearby.

There in the stalled and relentless car, I said to my wife, "Yeah, I remember."

I didn't hear what Dr. Ubinger said to the faintful woman. The next caller came on after a commercial concerning Gold

Bond foot powder to say he had a boil on his next-to-big toe. He seemed to be either in pain or ecstasy about the situation.

Mella said, "You should pop the hood. Maybe this mechanic has a good soul and will understand how he should come over and fix us up before he visits the dead. The dead can't do anything about it. Pop the hood."

It wasn't a bad idea. I reached down and pulled the latch, then got out of the car to lift the hood rightly. I thought about Thucydides as I performed this action, for I thought of Thucydides on an hourly basis—he might've been the godfather of actuaries. At least that's what an economics professor told me in college. I don't know if Thucydides had anything to do with insuring soldiers during the Peloponnesian War, but if he did I bet it was an easier time than my insuring that Mella didn't unconsciously act fool in public.

The time passed, as time does. People showed up. Dr. Ubinger talked to a man about his theory that lima beans might ward off skin cancer. Mella and I watched as people dressed in polyester suits and near-gingham dresses got out of Ford and Buick sedans, out of Dodge and Chevy trucks, in order to look down on a man who may or may not have owned a quirky ability to woo local women outside of his betrothed.

"There are people called Slopeheads up in Tennessee," I said. "They're not supposed to be insured, according to all the actuarial charts and tables. I might have to talk about people around here to my bosses. This could mean a big bonus for me, one way or the other."

"It's sad," Mella said.

"Please don't start."

"I mean it. People dying every day. Before their time. Look inside there." She pointed to Harold Glymph's establishment.

"You know for a fact that we just witnessed unrequited love involved in that tragedy. I've never known unrequited love to really happen in the real world. If Calloustown is the real world."

The parking lot filled up. Mella got out and slowly walked around, looking through people's car windows. Sometimes she wondered what people kept in their backseats, and she made a point to later acquire and sell these objects over the Internet. At least she didn't cry or howl. I tried to imagine what went on inside the funeral home. Did Ms. Harrell stand in the receiving line, right next to Nelroy Munson's widow? Did she consider the sconce as a likely weapon?

Mella wandered back, smiled at me, and closed our hood. When she got back in the car she hummed one of the more famous dirges, though off-key. She told me that everyone in Calloustown took great care in keeping their car interiors free from collectibles, child safety seats, or fast-food wrappers, though she did spy more than a few empty liquor bottles. Something happened to the radio station, and we barely heard the doctor talking about the importance of old-fashioned hardback books, for a reason that I couldn't tell. I think the topic dealt with either depression or carpal tunnel syndrome.

I said, "Why'd you close the hood? The mechanic might not find us."

Mella scooted over. She said she wanted to look at the sky in front of us, seeing as there were clouds that looked like the ones she remembered from childhood.

Ray Charles Shoots Wife Quenching Earth

Until my wife discovered the unending tunnel in our back-yard, we'd approached our record for ignoring each other, which is to say she'd not spoken to me for four days. The record was six. There'd been innumerable bouts that lasted between twelve and forty hours. Those so-called therapists, counselors, and magazine writers who're all about communi-cation for a healthy, survivable marriage have never bothered to study up on us and discard their ancient and impenetrable findings. I had gotten up early—she discovered the unending tunnel on a Saturday—and driven away from our house. I didn't leave a note. There was no cell phone for me to take along. I headed out.

When I returned, a few hours after normal lunchtime, my wife said, "Hey, come out in the backyard. You need to see this."

Every window in the house was open. It didn't take ab-normal auditory skills to hear her voice. When she opened every window it seemed as though we resided, quiet and baleful, inside a screen room. I looked in a number of direc-tions, thinking that she spoke to another outdoor person, a person lounging in our backyard. We didn't have neighbors back then. The adjacent land hadn't sold, and the developers hadn't horseshoed a subdivision around us.

I reminded myself to fetch the ledger and mark down that she spoke first.

"You want a beer or anything?" I said. "While I'm in here, do you want something?"

She shook her head. My wife held one hand up. In the other she kept our garden hose shoved straight into the ground. Our soil, for what it's worth, makes red clay seem like heated petroleum jelly. One time I planted sweet potatoes back there and when I pulled the tubers up 110 days later they looked like I'd harvested flat, flat lip plates. "I don't want to lose my focus. I need to concentrate. And I need your assistance," my wife said.

I picked one of my Nikons up off an end table.

Unfortunately I had never fully documented the causes of our silence. It went both ways, of course. Sometimes Didi said I drank too much and got verbally abusive. There were matters of finance, especially after I "retired early," at the age of thirty-nine, from my position as photography instructor at Graywood County Community College, in order to "specialize" in wedding portraits, graduation photos, and annual arts and crafts show entries that offered prize money. We argued as to who bought the dog food last, who fed the dogs last, who paid for vet bills, who cleaned up after the dogs last. I couldn't count how many times I closed my mouth, intending muteness until one of the dogs chewed on a lens cap, because Didi "made a decision" about our telephone service provider, the arrangement of furniture, laundry detergent choices, how much money to send her nephews and nieces on birthdays even though they never sent thank-you notes, how come the car's engine threw a rod when Didi'd lied about taking the thing over to our mechanic for an oil change.

She didn't like it when I holed up in the darkroom, listening to Ray Charles. "I hate Ray Charles," she said about daily—or at least when we were on speaking terms.

My name happens to be Ray Charles.

It's a gift to have such a moniker, to be able to own Ray Charles Photography. I'll admit that I didn't love third-rate community college students saying, "How hard could it be to make a A from Ray Charles?" or "How would Ray Charles know if he was in a darkroom or somewhere else?" or "What kind of crazy zoom lens does Ray Charles need?"

Ray Charles, photographer. One time the local paper wrote a human interest piece about me. I'd just received a first-place prize at the Mule Days festival for a photo I'd taken of a Civil War reenactor sitting beneath a cypress tree, holding a Happy Meal box. The newspaper guy titled his piece "Ray Charles Shoots and Scores."

Didi said he made fun of me. And then she went silent.

"I've had our garden hose shoved down here since eleven o'clock," Didi said. "It's on full blast, and it's not coming back up. There's no end." She wore her gardening attire: Bermuda shorts and a gray sweatshirt advertising Ortho.

I said, "Water's not free," because it's the first thing that came into my head. "There's also a train of thought that goes something like, 'Hey, let's be environmentally correct and not waste water. Let's conserve it.'"

Didi didn't ask about my earlier pilgrimage. She didn't spit out, "So I take it you've been sitting down at Worm's bar wasting what could've been our vacation money," which only meant that Didi stood there focused, obsessed, and infatuated. My wife said, "If the snake's size has anything to do with the length of its lair, we might need to be concerned."

I stared at her. What was she saying? Did Didi break the unspoken truce? I looked down and said, "It's because of the drought, that's why we're supposed to conserve water."

"It has to be coming out somewhere. There's no way I could be filling up an underground cavern. Walk around in circles, Ray, and see if this is bubbling out somewhere I can't see from here. Do snakes have back doors? What about voles?"

"You better hope it's not a yellow jacket nest," I said. "Is this your way of telling me I'm too fat and need some exercise, walking around in circles?"

Didi remained half-hunched, steady with the nozzle below. "If I thought that, then I'd say it flat out, Ray. Now start circling me. You know, maybe a stride farther out each lap."

I did. And I took a photo of my wife from behind with each lap until I stood in the road. The best picture, near dusk, looked like she had a tail between her legs. I thought about telling her, but we seemed to get along so well with this, a mysterious chasm, in our midst.

If we had well water I'd've gone to the spigot and shut Didi's experiment down. Having a dry well, like a dry socket in one's jaw, is a painful situation with the inherent endless bad consequences of anticipation. Even way out here where Didi and I lived in Calloustown, we had "city" water provided by Lower Piedmont Sandhills Water. They say that if ten thousand more people move to within the town limits, maybe they'll make a sewer treatment plant, dig sewers, and get all of us Calloustowners connected. Only ninety-five hundred to go, or thereabouts.

Our water bill would go up, sure, but to be honest the mystery tunnel had me wanting an answer too. Was there a Chinese man on the other side of the planet cursing Mandarin because of an artesian well sprung up on his property? Or maybe he praised Buddha for filling up a rice paddy more so. Were there fishermen on the Congaree River wondering how come the current took their boats downstream without warning?

If my wife filled up the septic tank—or our neighbors' tanks down the road—how long a silence would I be able to muster after saying, "I told you"?

Didi said, "I don't expect you to keep walking circles at night, but I don't want to slack up what I've started."

"I can redirect the floodlights," I said. "Hell, with floodlights you can stand there waiting for water to bubble back up at you all night long." Because I didn't want to precipitate another communication malfunction I said, "That can't be all that great for your back. Let me take over for a while. You can go pee, get something to eat, do whatever you need."

My wife looked at me as if I'd disrespected her ancestors. Our longest "fight" occurred two weeks after she'd gotten on the computer and joined that Ancestry.com ruse. Didi emerged from our "study," opened up my darkroom door without knocking, and said, "I knew it! My great-great-great-great-great grandfather was an Indian. He married a woman who's listed as 'Unknown Indian,' and they had a son who married a white woman!" She went on and on. "And then my great-great grandfather had a wife whose father started up a silk mill, and they had a child who lived just two days and another son who was retarded somehow. Anyway, my great-great grandfather married a Jewish woman, and she had a brother—what kind of uncle does that make him to me?—who worked for a man whose father was born in Istanbul and later became a diplomat of one kind or another!"

There was more. I listened to it all. I didn't say anything about how she could've ruined some rolls of film I had of the Cosby-Coleman wedding if she'd barged in five minutes later. I said, "Who cares? Maybe you should worry about making a mark in history your own self, so that knobheads in the future can look on Ancestry.com and say, 'I had a great-great-great-great-great aunt who led the anti–Second Amendment movement in America,' instead of, 'My great-great-great-great-great aunt sat around hoping to find importance in herself because of what her ancestors supposedly achieved.' Do you see what I mean? If not the anti–Second Amendment, then at least something like 'I wrote a novel' or 'I won the lottery and gave half the money to an orphanage.' I mean, the whole reason I have Ray Charles Photography is so future generations can understand the importance of marriage and debutante balls, among other things."

Didi locked herself in the study for six days. I'm pretty sure that she peed in a jug the whole time and only ate and used the bathroom otherwise when I left to make women's trains and veils appear more spectacular than they really were, to keep a viewer's eye on the dress instead of the look of condemnation that plastered the bride's face.

———

There exist a number of inexplicable veins that traverse planet Earth. The best one I've found, in all my research, when Didi let me use the "study," occurs in Turkmenistan. It's a flaming pit of natural gas called the "Door to Hell" and measures almost a football field in diameter. No one knows how deep the pit distends, or where the gas begins.

There are strange holes in the bottom of oceans, with gasses and such leaking out. People believe in portals, like in the movie *Being John Malkovich*, a film that Didi abhorred. She wasn't president of the *Eraserhead* fan club, either. Willing suspension of disbelief didn't show up anywhere on her family tree, evidently. If you put a freakish baby or a workplace with four-foot ceilings in a movie, Didi didn't care about buying a movie ticket.

I took over atop the hole at nine P.M. on that first night. I thought about pulling out my Zippo to see if, perhaps, the "Door to Hell" had its back entrance in my yard, all the way underneath the Caspian Sea, the Mediterranean, the Atlantic Ocean, and so on. But I didn't. What if it shot up a flame and burned my eyeballs useless? How many times would Ray Charles Photography get mentioned on all those TV shows then?

I sniffed and listened and waited only ten minutes before Didi returned, a bag of pimiento sandwiches in hand. "I don't want to say I don't trust your being able to keep a nozzle in the hole, Ray, but I don't trust your being able to keep a nozzle in the hole. Go on back inside and take care of the dogs. I'll call if I need you."

I let go of the hose when she latched on. I said, "Hey, I got an idea. Maybe this endless vein holds gas. I'll leave my lighter with you in case you want to check it out."

That night I didn't sleep, same as I didn't when we lived together tongueless. The explosion never occurred. My wife didn't return inside, needful to relate the narrow tunnel's limit. Back to back to back to back I watched *Down by Law*, *Barton Fink*, *Harold and Maude*, and *Deliverance* on two of those indie film networks that Didi tried to talk our cable provider into dropping.

"Watching these kinds of movies helps me 'see' better portraits," I always told her.

"It helps you see freakish people in a relentless world," Didi shot back. And then, more often than not, we'd stare through one another before walking off to separate rooms in the house.

That stuff I said about furthering humanity instead of living off past do-gooder capitalistic ancestors? Didi studied studio art in college. Somewhere along the line she gave it up and took up framing. She spent her time in a frame shop, and five generations from now some kind of insecure relative-to-be will tell everyone how she's related to a misunderstood and unjustly sentenced woman who suffered a series of miscarriages quietly. I don't think it's fair. Somebody should at least notice how Didi can use a miter box.

I'm not the only photographer named Ray Charles. There's another one in Baton Rouge, Louisiana. Maybe there are others. The singer Ray Charles was born as Ray Charles Robinson back in 1930 or thereabouts. I've never typed "Ray Robinson photographer" into a search engine, but if there is one, then there's no way he gets the ribbing or double-takes that the Baton Rouge guy and I get, I doubt.

Here are some fun facts: There's a photographer in Georgia named Willie McTell, and two photographers who go by Doc Watson—one in Pittsburgh, the other in Riverside, California. Those last two men might be professors in an art department, thus the "Doc" title.

I'd be willing to bet that more than a few professional photographers have "Homer" for a name, but who in America remembers how that old poet couldn't see?

Do not doubt how much I loved my wife for the quirks she forgave of me. Back in the bad days, I went off a-drinking about daily, took a uniform along with me—some days I was a soldier, others a police officer—and changed my clothes before driving home even though it wasn't more than ten miles and the sheriff's deputies knew me anyway. I had this notion. I believed that a cop wouldn't think a man in uniform irresponsible enough to drink hard in a place like Worm's then get behind the wheel. Didi never said, "So you're a member of the Oxford, Mississippi, police force today," or "Where exactly is the Army-Navy store where you're spending good money on these uniforms?"

We had met at the frame shop, a place known by the odd, existentially challenging demand Hang Me Here. At the time, I'd been considering a series of photographs that involved an interesting-looking woman—somewhere between a woman with an ineffable port-wine stain birthmark that covered exactly half of her face and a supermodel with a desperate look in her eyes—half-clothed, standing amid vacant, rundown, out-of-business cotton mills throughout the southeast. Half-clothed leaning against idle, rusted spinning frames and looms! It would be symbolic!

Upon my job offer Didi said, "I don't like to have my picture taken." She said, "I've read up on how men say they're photographers, and then the next thing you know these girls are working escort services in Tokyo, Bangkok, and Dallas."

I said, "I understand your trepidation. If you should ever reconsider"—I pulled out one of my newly printed business cards—"give me a call. I promise I'm not some kind of pederast, or human trafficker, or Republican."

Didi wasn't supermodel or birthmark material, understand, but I couldn't not stare at her. Her green eyes hinted at thyroid problems. She stood six-one and weighted about 130, but didn't seem malnourished. Didi didn't bother waxing her eyebrows, which a less-sophisticated aesthetician might consider as looking like two fragile misplaced moustaches on perfectly porcelain skin. And that hair of hers—as soft and brown as a common field rat's.

"Your name is Ray Charles and you want me to pose semi-nude for you?" she said on that first meeting. Didi quit framing a paint-by-numbers clown than someone from the Junior League wanted to hang in her foyer. "Get the fuck out of here."

We married three months later before a justice of the peace. Didi agreed to move to a land where Witness Protection people might be moving soon. I made some promises. For one, should we have a child—and we wouldn't—I was never to make the kid eat newspaper after each meal. Didi's own father—I don't have a clue about psychology, but this seems relevant and causal—believed that the ingestion of paper products helped clean out one's GI tract, thus saving money and the environment, in regards to bathroom tissue.

"I'd like to take your father's photo," was my only re-sponse when Didi divulged her childhood, there on date number one.

"If a skilled archaeologist dug up my childhood septic tank he could piece together American history from Water-gate to the Iran-Contra affair," Didi said.

"What about your mother?" I asked. What could I say? We ate Mexican food, and I wanted about quatro or ocho margaritas.

"A skilled archeologist might find her in the septic tank, too, for all I know," Didi said.

At the end of the third day I had walked the perimeter of our house so far away, looking for odd springs, that I had to use a zoom lens to catch Didi stooped over, filling the hole in our yard. If this kept going on I'd have to set up a magnifying glass pointed toward my wife, and then zoom in on that. I walked in circles, unconcerned with work I needed to do. I thought, I can set up a magnifying glass, and then a survey-or's level, and finally my zoom lens.

And then I found water surging up in the middle of the Calloustown Natural Baptist Church's adjacent cemetery, among headstones that only read Munson or Harrell. If I had a cell phone I could've called Didi and said "Eureka!" like that, or, "Our hole is connected to the plot of little Er-nestette Munson, born December 26/died December 31, 1870. So basically we've had a wormhole between her coffin and our backyard, so her soul can come visit on occasion, which might explain those cries we've thought to be feral cats coupled and stuck nighttime."

Out loud, there on a slight bluff overlooking my own house, I probably said, "Uh-oh." I looked around to make sure no one stood around in the church parking lot. I found a nice three-foot-long fallen limb and stuck it in the hole, then kicked some dirt, then scooted a small flat rock over that. Finally—and I would have nightmares about this for the rest of my life—I kicked over little baby Ernestette Munson's miniature headstone to cover what may or may not have been a portal of sorts to our backyard.

The coroner, later, would pinpoint Didi's death to right about the time I covered the unnatural spring. To this pronouncement I would say, "Okay," and not explain where I stood, or what I did, at four o'clock that afternoon.

I have photographed every Munson and Harrell in Calloustown, whether they liked it or not. I've placed my camera on the counter of Worm's Bar and Grill and tapped the shutter release button with my elbow. I've done the same at the Tiers of Joy bakery and Southern Exotic Pet Store. After my "Interesting Woman in the Middle of a Failed Cotton Mill" project never developed, so to say, I thought it necessary to encapture the blank, dull visages of a relentless people committed to proving General Sherman pointless and myopic and downright cruel for choosing to leave Calloustown unsigned, unscathed, still bloomful.

There are the "natural" and "unsuspected" photographs, and there have also been the normal family Christmas portraits, the near-coming-out pictures of eighteen-year-old girls walking down a staircase, the "Fifty Year Anniversary" photographs intended for newspapers, engagement and wedding photos. I shot Biggest Watermelon! photos, and the odd fa-vorite dog/cat/mynah bird portraits with said animal stand-ing in front of a Rocky Mountain or Niagara Falls backdrop.

Good God I wish I had more photographs of my wife.

Why did I find it necessary to chide her when she bought expensive dresses from catalogs, had them delivered, put them on, then sent them back for a refund, only so she could say, "I've worn Marc Jacob, Valentino, and Sue Wong"?

Why didn't I say, "Fuck you," and click my camera in her direction even though she made such demands against it? Why, over these years, did I not show up at Didi's job and snap some seemingly inconsequential and inconspicuous photographs of her, face close to a miter box, checking forty-five-degree angles?

"She had a massive heart attack," a man told me at the hospital. I had requested an autopsy in order to make sure—call me selfish—she hadn't taken an overdose of pills, finally tired of our long silences.

"Women have heart disease and heart attacks more than people think," someone else told me, a man who taught Bi-ology 50 to students who needed to be able to identify arms from legs on their remedial tests at the community college. "Dead men on the golf course get all the headlines, but wom-en have just as many heart attacks, if not more. They call it 'the silent killer.' Wait. That might be wrong. The brown recluse might be the silent killer. Or coral snake. Now that I think about it, just about everything's a silent killer."

This monologue took place at Didi's visitation inside Glymph Funeral Home. I didn't know what to say, shook the biology professor's hand, and tried to remember his name. I thought, are you making fun of me? I thought, I'm about to be your silent killer. I thought, if only I'd made the decision to cut off that water on the first day.

I could've walked back home and said, "Hey, pour some food dye down the hole and let me run back over to the grave-yard to see if it comes out." I could've said, "Food dye would get diluted beyond recognition. Let's put a marble down that hole and see if it comes out in the cemetery." I could've said, "You remember that time we got in a fight, Didi, a day before we flew to New York for a vacation? I have a confession to make. When I went to the e-ticket kiosk, I requested that my seat be changed so we wouldn't have to sit next to each other all that time." I could've said, "I wonder if we can send a piece of kite string down the hole, then knot both ends to empty lima bean cans and talk to one another, you know, like people did back before everything got so goddamned complicated."

Luckily there were available plots at the Calloustown Nat-ural Baptist Church's graveyard. Didi would've never agreed to such an eternal resting place. I bought the plot right next to hers, too, even though I had no love of Christians in gen-eral and Baptists in particular. Fuck it, I thought. Would I be able to see anything in the so-called afterlife? Does anything matter? If, by chance, things turned out differently than I believed, couldn't Didi and I take the mysterious tunnel back home nightly?

Oh Didi, Didi, Didi—how I wish you never roamed the earth out back. How I wish I'd've either shot you more, or never.

Muddling

A guy on the local news said most gas stations lowered their prices at nine in the morning and raised them at four, something about fucking over people who'd already driven to work and then again for drivers who didn't leave their cubicles until dusk. He didn't exactly use those words, but any rational cynic knew what he meant. I don't think the guy was an economist or soothsayer, but he evidently worked honestly at something in between or no one would've interviewed him on Channel 4. I didn't catch his name or occupation, but he wore a blue shirt and striped tie. He combed his hair. The guy seemed to know more about oil corporations than the rest of my friends, relatives, or instrument-needy prospective customers.

So on Friday morning I drove from where I live on the outskirts of Calloustown and began circling a block that held a Citgo, a Sunoco, an Exxon, and a locally owned Rajer Dodger's that had two self-serve pumps out front. I circled and circled, starting about 8:30. Each establishment sold regular unleaded for $3.65 a gallon, plus that 9/10ths—twenty cents less than the national average, but like my friends, relatives, and instrument-needy prospective customers always say, "So what? It's still fucking Calloustown." Though, again, not in those exact words.

Three-sixty-five, three-sixty-five, three-sixty-five, three-sixty-five. I rounded the block—this is the Columbia Road, over onto Old Calloustown Road, onto the Charleston Road, onto Old Old Calloustown Road. What I'm saying is, I circled the heart of town where supply and demand mattered. In between I noticed six or eight church signs, the funeral home, Southern Exotic Pets, Worm's Bar, and so on. Worm had a new piece of plywood leaned next to his door that advertised TOPLESS, which meant he'd be in there behind the bar not wearing a shirt. He'd done it before, during lean times, like the last time gasoline prices reached $3.65 and people rarely left their houses. One of the churches had a magnetic letter sign out front that read SIN COOKS FRY LATER, which took me about sixteen right-hand turns to figure out, what with "cooks" being both a verb and noun, and wondering if someone forgot a comma. At least the preacher or signage person wasn't asking me to go to the library forty miles away, find a Bible, and look up what's spelled out in a particular chapter and verse.

At nine o'clock, just as I was about to run out of gas, sure enough, assistant managers started coming out of the four stations and/or convenience stores. They took their poles and exchanged a 5 for a 3, bringing the price per gallon down to $3.63 plus that 9/10ths. Maybe I said aloud, "They need to hire that dude on a permanent basis on the TV, the guy who figured out this raise-and-lower-prices ruse. Fuck the weatherman, who's never close to being right."

I circled around two more times, then pulled into Rajer Dodger's only because I liked to hear the Indian guy in there yell things to his wife in whatever dialect they employed. It didn't matter to me much that they offered gas that came from one of the major oil companies, or that they charged an extra dime per gallon if you used a credit card, just like every other station on the block.

I pulled up to the pump. I got out and unscrewed the cap. I read PLEASE MUST PAY FIRST PLEASE on a handwritten sign taped to the pump's torso, and although I wanted to say, "Oh fuck me give me a break, what kind of gas station doesn't have one of those fancy credit/debit acceptors plus a place to slide in cash a la any of the video poker machines up at Harrah's Casino up in Cherokee?" I locked the door to my pickup and started inside.

This is when I noticed a white man, of the normal indeterminate age of these parts—which means between fifty and eighty—sitting in front of a fifty-five-gallon plastic barrel, his legs splayed out with ten or twelve pints of blackberries in between. He said, "You need you some berries, Chief. Keep away the cancer. Eat them on ice cream or whole under milk. Or by they selves. Keep away the cancer. You don't want the cancer for you and yours, right?"

Remember that I said "dusk" earlier—about people leaving work—which means I'm talking winter. Blackberries emerge in July. No one has local fresh blackberries in November. They have spinach—which fights cancer, too, according to spinach farmers—but not blackberries. Hell, I've been around long enough to hear how everything fights cancer—radishes, peaches, cord wood, getting your driveway sealed.

I said, "You up early selling," because I couldn't think of anything else.

"I ain't no worse than you," the blackberry man said. He scrambled up without corrupting one of the cardboard containers. "You ain't better than me, Chief."

I would like to say that the price of fuel caused people in my town to act all bowed-up and cocksure, but even if Rajer inside decided to sell his gasoline at pre-1979 prices and hand out wedges of free garlic naan, everyone around would still pick fights and scowl.

I said, "Just came in to fill up my tank, man. That's it. If I come across anyone today looking for vine-ripened berries, I'll send them your way."

I walked into the store trying to figure out what $3.63 times twenty gallons would end up, because I didn't want to tell Rajer I wanted seventy-five bucks' worth and then have to go back in and get change if I filled the tank prematurely. Rajer yelled out, "Hello, Mr. Finley. How are you today, fine sir?"

I had told him not to call me Mr. Finley. Hell, he'd started off greeting me as Finley sahib, so I guess we'd made some progress over the last few years I'd known him. He'd gone from Finley sahib to Mr. Kay, to Mr. Finley Kay, to Mr. Finley. In a decade he might plain say, "Hey, Finley, what up, bro?" like any other American.

I said, "Hey, Raj, I need to fill up. Or at least I need to get about seventy dollars."

"Do not blame me for the price of gas! I make two cents only for every gallon. Two cents! Everyone think that we are setting the high prices, but it is the oil companies. And the Arabs. Mr. Finley, please—as you go about your daily duties—tell people that I am not from Arabia."

I can't say for sure if Raj Patel suffered from one of the more common forms of short-term memory loss—Korsakoff syndrome, for example—but he found it necessary to explain the nuances of oil company/distributor/individual operator every time I walked in, fuel-needy or not. If I wasn't busy and didn't have an order to complete back home, I'd hang out with good Raj, look over his various Ganesh pictures and figurines, listen to his weird music, ask about the incense he burned. In time he'd explain what pathetic profits he received for beer, Little Debbie oatmeal pies, charcoal lighter fluid, white bread, daily newspapers, cigarettes, pickle relish, and hot sauce. He must've been some kind of champion oratory/forensics/debate contestant back in his Mumbai, Delhi, or Bangalore school days.

I said, "I'm not blaming you on the price of gas, buddy. I know." I didn't tell him how I'd become aware of every goddamn gas station in America dropping prices when fewer people pulled into stations, when the "average price per gallon" people went around and concluded that things weren't as bad as they seemed.

"You are my favorite customer, Mr. Finley," Raj said. I'd heard him say it to people named Mr. Bubba and Mr. Larry, to Ms. Darlene and Ms. Tiffany, when I stood nearly out of earshot at the twelve-packs.

I started to say, "Yeah, yeah, yeah but I never see you giving me some lamb saag or whatever it's called." I started to say, "I sure could use a little of that good goat vindaloo that we can't get around Calloustown."

But I couldn't, because the blackberry dude charged in and yelled out, "I can get y'all a deal on telephone poles! Who needs some beet sugar? I can get y'all sugar, beans, gourd birdhouses, snow peas, book matches, and rebuilt carburetors. Y'all need of those things? I got a line on Royal brand typewriters. I got fescue, putters, fog lights, boogie boards, aluminum siding, fire ant killer, and plastic lifelike nativity scenes. Did I mention telephone poles? And blackberries."

I stood there staring at him. He came across much taller inside the store. I'm talking this guy might've been six-four or six-six, tall enough to've played some basketball in his day. He should've been selling peaches, apples, or oranges, what with that height. I said, "I only need the gas."

Raj Patel said, "Hello, Mr. Ruben Orr. How are you today, fine sir?"

"I got everything cheap and legal, as usual," Ruben Orr said. "Chief."

"You got any ukuleles?" I asked him. If he did, then I knew he'd stolen them from me. Me, I had gone from being a normal luthier to specializing in ukuleles—an instrument that had become more sought after that most people believed, probably because of ADD.

"Little guitars? Ukuleles, like tiny guitars?" Ruben said. "I had me some sitars while back but Rajer here bought all them things up."

"My nephews back home are very good sitar players. They are professionals!" Raj said. He nodded and didn't blink. "One of them is now the number-one steel sitar player in all of India."

I said, "Huh," handed Raj over three twenties and two fives, and walked out to pump my gas before it went back up in price.

I didn't have my camper top attached. I'd only had to put the thing on one time in order to transport sixty custom-made Finley Kay ukuleles to a group of Hawaiian music enthusi-

asts who wanted to break some kind of world record in regards to number of people standing waist-deep over in Lake
Calloustown while strumming and singing "Tiny Bubbles."
So it wasn't difficult to see, in my rearview mirror, Mr. Ruben Orr tailing me on his moped. Six-four or six-six on a
moped, is what I'm saying. I took some turns—there weren't
many options—onto Old Savannah Road, then Old Charlotte Road, then Old Myrtle Beach—and the guy stayed behind me. I thought, fuck, do I want to waste all this cheap
two-pennies-off-normal-price gas trying to keep a black-
berry-to-telephone-pole-selling, moped-riding lunatic from
perhaps following me back home? Maybe he actually lives on
the route I'm taking, I thought.

I looked down at my gas gauge and noticed how I'd already spent a good eighth of a tank trying to lose the guy.
I turned left, then right, then right again until I got on
the road where I lived—where my ex-wife and I lived
until she said out loud how she didn't believe in a ukulele-
making husband and took off for Raleigh, North Carolina, where, evidently, men have jobs that're more secure
and less suspect.

I checked my rearview mightily, and sure enough Mr. Ruben Orr continued behind me, scrunched down as if to be
more aerodynamic.

I don't know that this has much to do with my story, but
I don't believe in the NRA. I mean, I believe the NRA exists, just like I believe that the Bible exists, for I've seen it,
but I don't believe in those virgin birth, parting of the Red
Sea, burning bush, dead guy Lazarus returning, water to
wine kinds of stories. Anyway, I don't believe that the Second Amendment allows all of us to carry little pistols around

whenever we want, for the only purpose to shoot people we fear. No, I believe in taking care of things otherwise.

I got out of my truck, reached beneath my seat, and pulled out half a Louisville Slugger. I pulled out nunchucks I didn't know how to use. Farther back I found an old length of a telephone line, maybe eighteen inches in length, notch marks at one end for a better grip. In my pocket I knew there was a razor-sharp folding Buck knife, but that would be my last option.

Mr. Ruben Orr puttered up behind my truck. He smiled and said, "Hey, you remember me from Rajer Dodger's?"

"What're you doing following me, man?"

He set his kickstand and turned the ignition. "You never let me finish my sentence. I thought you'd be coming back in the station. Anyway, sure enough I do have a couple ukuleles back at the trailer. Well, back in one of the filled-up trailers I got to the side of my doublewide. I got kerosene lanterns, pup tents, crockery, model cars and airplanes in the box, alligator heads, a stuffed bobcat. All kinds of shit. And two ukuleles, but I imagine the catgut's somewhere between compromised and useless."

I said, of course, "Well I sure would like to take a look at the things."

Ruben Orr said, "I tell you what, Finley. Do you mind if I call you Finley, or Fin? Raj told me your name. I tell you what. I'll go home, get the ukuleles, and bring them back over to Rajer Dodger's. I shouldn't've left all my blackberries there in the first place. You drop on by later and I'll have them there waiting for your inspection."

I closed my truck door so that Ruben couldn't see my nunchucks, sawed-off bat, or copper-wire-and-rubber billy club. I said, "I got some work to do around here, but I'll come back on by about after lunch."

"Sounds good," Ruben said. He stretched his back. "You got a nice little setup here," he said. "Damn, son, you look like you done good for yourself."

"In a previous life," I said, which was true, seeing as I'd married up. "Used to have a rich wife and a regular job."

Ruben Orr straddled his moped and turned the ignition. "I hear that," he said. He turned the ignition off and on again. "Same story as me, except for the rich wife and regular job." He shook his moped, then opened the gas tank lid and peered down close.

I said, "Let me guess."

"Goddamn it. This wouldn't've happened if you'd've pulled over when I kept buzzing my horn and flashing my lights. Man, I took off following you before I could even fill up at Rajer's. You know, they all drop their prices from about nine in the morning until when people get off work. I seen a thing on the news about it."

I had zero cans of gas in my possession, seeing as I feared my ex-father-in-law showing up, spreading it around, and burning me clear out of the state. Or of dousing the place myself and sitting in the middle of it all, surrounded by custom-made ukuleles that weren't selling like a year earlier. I said, "Let's get that thing in the back of my truck and I'll drive you over to Rajer's. I don't have gas here, and I fear siphoning out of my own tank."

"Goddamn it," Ruben Orr said. "I hate to put you out."

He picked the moped up by himself and laid it down on its side. Ruben strode over to the passenger side of the truck while I closed the tailgate. I said, "I'm not in a giant hurry today."

"Hey, what are all those weapons of questionable destruction doing on your bench seat?"

I couldn't lie. It's a fault. Not being able to lie ruined my marriage. Making and selling ukuleles doesn't require lying, since they are what they are. I dropped out of college first semester junior year because I enrolled in an acting class, and as it ended up I couldn't conjure up a dialect outside the one I owned, or memorize lines I'd've never said in a social situation.

I said, "Well. I don't own a gun. I don't own rifles or pistols."

Ruben Orr laughed. He banged his giant hand on my dashboard. "I had an old boy hit me upside the head with a two-by-four one time and I didn't even swerve off the road."

I tried to visualize a man getting whacked thusly while straddling a moped. I said, "I don't even know how to use nunchucks, to be honest," and backed out onto the road.

"I got this idea," Ruben said. "I don't live far from Rajer Dodger's, and I got gas at my own home."

A fireplace poker would fit nicely beneath my truck seat, I thought, and made a mental note to ask if he's got fireplace pokers for sale when we get there.

"Mahogany's good for a ukulele, isn't it?" Ruben said as we pulled up to his mobile home, which appeared to be surrounded by four single-wides, two Airstreams, and two yellow school buses plugged without wheels into the clay yard. When viewed from above, I imagined that his arrangement of aluminum abodes looked similar to ancient hieroglyphics, or one of Carl Gustav Jung's mandala examples, or a carton character's slit eyeball with crow's feet. "Over the years I think I had a couple oak wood ukuleles. One time I had one built out of balsa wood but I had it outside on a windy day and never seen the thing again."

I said, "If you have a mahogany uke—like a Gretsch, or a Harmony Company Vita-Uke signed Roy Smeck—I'd be interested. I'd be surprised, and I'd be interested."

Ruben pulled his moped out of the truck bed, straddled it, turned the ignition, and rode it forward when it started. He steered it thirty feet to a four-foot-high, tin-topped, three-sided enclosure of sorts and pulled the kickstand back down. "I'll be damned," he said. "I guess I had enough gas in it after all. Must be a jiggle-needy starter that's the problem."

I can't lie, like I said. I said, "I think you brought me out here on a ruse. I'm thinking that my ex-father-in-law hired you out to kill me."

He smiled. "You got you some kind of paranoia going for you, son. Look. I will confess to a thing or two, Finley Kay. First off, I know who you are. Two, I'm about broke. I just thought that if I could get you over here, you'd be the kind of fellow who'd appreciate my collections and possibly want to buy something. Everybody knows how much money you getting for custom-made Finley Kay two-tone soprano ukuleles, plus that monetary award you got from the arts commission for Craftsperson of the Year, beating out all the basket weavers down in the low country. That's it, I promise."

I believed him, I suppose. A mixed-breed dog came out from beneath the livable trailer, stretched, then slunk back in. "How come you didn't just show up at my house and ask me, then? Have you been hanging out at Rajer Dodger's waiting for me? Did someone say I could be lured by thorny-vined fruits?"

Ruben Orr pulled a ring of keys from his blue jeans and opened the door to the closest storage trailer. He propped the door open, then walked counterclockwise to open the other ones on the property.

I closed my truck door, finally, after feeling for my knife. "You start rummaging in that first one. Yell if you got any questions. I'mo go inside and make us some special Old Fashioneds. I hear you got a thing for the bourbon."

Fuck, I thought. I thought, Who drinks Old Fashioneds these days, outside of ninety-year-old Kentucky women and twenty-six-year-old hipsters obsessed and nostalgic for Brylcreem, money clips, cuff links, Vitalis, manual typewriters, turntables, cat-eye eyeglasses, and vintage paneled station wagons? I thought, my wife somehow got ahold of Ruben and told him how I never understood the notion of moderation, except in matters of love and mother-of-pearl inlay.

"I hope you don't have any raccoons holed up in here," I said, but Ruben had already entered his abode. I said to myself, "Go in, pick out a couple things, pay for them, and get the hell out of here." I walked up three concrete steps to what had once been a classic, off-silver and aqua single-wide, probably one of the remaining few manufactured circa 1960 that hadn't uprooted and flown away via tornadoes. Pick two things, pay what he asks, go home, and call somebody to install a home security system. Call up Rachel and tell her I'm not planning any surprise trips to Raleigh, should she worry, unless a knot of ukulele troubadours request some specialized instruments worthy of viable amplification.

I looked back at my truck to make sure there wasn't a visible bomb strapped to the undercarriage. And then I turned my head to inside the trailer: stuffed bobcats, coyotes, wild turkeys, hawks, owls, coons, skunks, a river otter, maybe a badger, groundhogs, one small pony, a nutria, foxes, two armadillos, and coiled venomous rattlers roamed the floor. I'm talking, again, that this was a sixteen-by-eighty-foot trailer.

Mounted heads of deer, wild boars, one moose, and a two-headed calf adorned the upper parts of the walls. I looked in between and saw no ukuleles, for one, or anything else I might be interested in transferring to my own living conditions. I should say that in between there were stacks of popsicle-stick baskets, tools, single- and doubletree yokes, a history of the boom box, and enough vacant wasp nest stucco apartments hanging from the ceiling to satisfy a homeopathy-leaning Chinese woman masterful in ancient reliable tonics and salves.

So I ventured over to the next trailer—a perfect Airstream—and looked in to find plastic bins of ashtrays, bottle caps, rocks, peach pits, and car cigarette lighters, among other things. Hubcaps covered the walls.

I thought, you need to call up that TV show where pickers come in and relieve people of their relentless habits before they end up on that other TV show that delves into people who won't ever discard anything, including trash.

"You found anything yet?" Ruben Orr yelled from the doorway.

I jumped in a way that didn't make me proud. I might've blurted out, "Not now!" or "This isn't how I'm supposed to die!" like that. I said, "Man, I've never seen anything like this. Do you have a website? You need to have some of your stuff listed on eBay, or Craigslist, or something like that."

Ruben Orr handed me a delicate glass with a slice of orange hanging on top. He said, "What?" He held out his own glass to clink. "Now, this isn't your run-of-the-mill Old Fashioned."

I waited for him to drink first, of course. I even thought to ask that we switch glasses, seeing as mine might be poisoned, but then I remembered a psychology course I took one time. Evidently people can smell paranoia, and they hold poisoned drinks in their own hands knowing that they'll be requested to switch.

My own ex-wife Rachel said that I let off distinguishable pheromones right before I admitted how I never wished to move out of Calloustown, work a regular job, have children, vote Republican, join a gym that offered spin classes, and promise that we'd one day own a timeshare in Myrtle Beach. That "vote Republican" part seemed to be what ended our marriage. Listen, I could've gone into the booth, come out, and lied, but it didn't occur to me until she'd already settled down doing whatever she found necessary.

"Cheers," I said, and we drank simultaneously. I took one gulp, and Ruben drank his. I didn't care that I might be poisoned, understand. Indeed this drink wasn't the traditional Old Fashioned I'd ever read about. I said, "Goddamn, Mr. Ruben Orr, what is this?" for I'd never tasted anything such.

"I normally don't tell people my secrets," he said. "Hell, I've had Worm offer me thirty-three dollars for this recipe, but I wouldn't give it to him. I might have to in time, what with my financial state, but not so far."

We stepped out from the Airstream and moseyed over to one of the gutted buses. From the opened door I could view what looked like an entire room of wooden finials. I said, "How come you and I have never run into each other? Calloustown ain't exactly a metropolis. How long have you lived here? I've been here my whole life, except for a couple years."

"The ukuleles ain't in this bus, I know. Let's go on to the next one." He said, "Hold on right here," and ran back to his trailer, opened the door, reached in, and retrieved an entire pitcher of his Old Fashioneds. "Here you go," he said on return, filling my glass. He pulled out an orange slice from the pitcher and floated it atop my drink.

"I might be interested in a finial or two. I don't have a staircase in my house, but I got a thing for finials. Maybe I could make a ukulele with a finial at neck's end."

"Most people insist on a couple dashes of bitters per glass. Me, I use muddled unripe raspberries. Most people insist on a maraschino cherry. I use a blackberry. See, I muddle blackberries, a lemon rind, a cube of brown sugar, the unripe raspberries, and I use rye whiskey instead of regular bourbon. I use a half and half mix of spring water and club soda. And then I put a taste of good moonshine in there—it's not more than a thimbleful per glass, you know. That's all I can tell you. There are two other secret ingredients I won't tell."

I finished my second glass. Ruben and I passed the fourth outbuilding, and then five through eight. We went by the first again and kept circling. I kind of forgot that we meant to find a vintage stringed instrument formed of pure mahogany.

"We've seen each other," Ruben said. "I guess you weren't paying attention."

He and I rounded his place another half dozen times, high-stepping over broken glass, weeds, pottery shards, old vaccination tags, deteriorating tennis balls, broken bottles, doll limbs, and what appeared to be the sun-bleached skulls of songbirds. I tried to pace myself. I tried to convince myself that it was okay for one of America's premiere ukulele luthiers to partake of something other than straight bourbon or rum or vodka. As a matter of fact, I rationalized, a premiere ukulele maker might want to drink nothing but cocktails that required an intense, precise, and specific muddling process, garnished with paper umbrellas. I said, "I'm not the first person to say that I'm self-absorbed. I'm the second. Rachel used to say it all the time. I think that's what she kept saying. Maybe I wasn't paying attention to her, either."

"I knew Rachel. She bought some Fire-King from me. As a matter of fact, I believe Rachel met my father one time. My one daughter. I believe you met her one time, too, son. At least one time."

I picked up on all the repetitive words. It didn't take a master's degree in psychology to understand that he wanted to make some kind of point. I looked into Ruben Orr's face and, sure enough, recognized the resemblance in his eyes of a woman named Mayley I'd once known. Fuck, I thought. The one local ukulele-lesson-needy woman who required private lessons that I'd ever fallen for and—in my inability to lie—told Rachel, "Um, I met a woman I'm attracted to." She wasn't even local, officially—just someone taking care of a sick relative for the summer months, as I recalled. Mayley'd signed up for the ukulele class over at the Calloustown Community Center, where I taught a six-class course. To Ruben I said, "Mayley Orr's your daughter?"

I guessed at the last name—our affair didn't last long enough for us to know family names. Well, I guess she knew mine, seeing as she strummed a Finley Kay ukulele.

"So, what do you think about buying a little something I got taxidermied now? Mayley's little boy ain't interested in animals at the time, but I bet he will be one day."

———

I had read somewhere along the way that owning a pick-up truck between the ages of twenty-two and thirty created a number of inescapable furniture-handling weekends for friends and strangers alike, and that ownership past the age of thirty brought about requests from friends and strangers to borrow the truck in order to haul firewood, mulch, and potting soil. Whoever came up with this little truism needs to update his or her adage to include a menagerie of rabies-worthy stuffed animals. Well, not quite true. I felt obligated to buy every available bobcat, fox, raccoon, and beaver that Ruben Orr needed to evict from his storage unit.

"I'm going to use this money to start my grandboy up a college fund so he can be like you," Ruben said as I tried to drive off. He said, "You know what his name is?" I didn't say "No," for I felt pretty certain it was Finley. I stared at Ruben Orr. He said, "That's right, you know."

I said, "I'll get you the rest of the money when I can," for, even though he offered me a deal—we went inside and looked on his Mac at various stuffed mid-sized mammals for sale on eBay, Craigslist, and some kind of Mountain and Lake Cabin Interior Decorator's site—we wanted to make sure that neither of us over- or underpriced the value of a beaver.

I began driving home, careful not to veer across lines that weren't even painted on our back roads, my eyes in the rear-view mirror. I didn't want my animals to topple roadside, for one, and I feared that Ruben Orr might follow me. What would I do if, as I pulled into my own driveway, he puttered up to tell me how his grandson kept asking who his father was? Would I reach beneath my seat and pull out one of my so-called weapons? Would I cry? What kind of explanation could I summon up honestly should he bring along a lawyer, social worker, or Mayley Orr herself?

I looked down at my fuel gauge and noticed how I no longer owned a seven-eighths-full tank. My truck missed twice, and I said to no one, "That fucker siphoned gas when I wasn't paying attention."

Rajer changed the price back up to $3.65 as I coasted into his convenience store. I looked at my wristwatch to read that, just like the smart man on TV pointed out, it would be between four and five in the afternoon. I looked over to check on Ruben's blackberry cartons, which seemed to be undisturbed. Rajer yelled out, "Hello, Mr. Finley, good to see you again! Are you going to construct a humorous diorama so that those weasels hold your special ukuleles? Very good! Very funny, when animals look like they possess musical abilities. I have seen many, many animals playing music on the Internet. Always good. Bullfrog with banjo!"

I said nothing to Rajer for two reasons. Later on I would fret endlessly that he considered it a snub. I didn't respond to him because I pictured all those stuffed animals actually holding ukuleles for some kind of promotional advertising, maybe in the back of *Taxidermy Today* or *Yuke and Yours*. Secondly, beyond the sparse afternoon Calloustown traffic I detected the faint sputtering—at first not unlike a brave gnat entering the ear canal—that turned to distant chainsaw, then unmistakable poor cousin of a Honda 150, or Yamaha 175, or Japanese electric turkey knife.

I said, "I know the trick y'all are playing on people, Raj. The noon news can do some kind of survey saying gas prices are low, but then y'all jack it up crazy when most people need to fill up."

Ruben Orr neared. I imagined him riding that moped with sawed-off shotguns swathed around his back. Rajer got off his ladder. He didn't smile. "You shouldn't drive all day long. You filled up this morning! In my city back in India, gasoline costs $5.03 all the time, no $5.01 between nine and four."

I started to say something about how my previous purchase must've gotten siphoned off, but Ruben Orr veered right up beside me and skidded to a stop. He cleared his throat hard twice, unstraddled the moped, cleared his throat twice again, bent over, banged his right knee with his right palm, straightened up, walked two steps toward my truck's bed, and petted the bobcat. He said, "I can't leave you, Robert. I'm sorry."

I held the gas nozzle in my right hand. I'd already clicked down that little metal arm, so I was ready to look like One, I could pump either in my tank, or Two be a probable villain. I said, "You stole gas from me."

Raj said, "Hello, Mr. Ruben Orr."

"I made a mistake," Ruben said. He touched every stuffed animal and called their names: Ringo for the raccoon, for example, and Slappy for the beaver. "Oh, God, I made some mistakes." He looked like he might cry. "This would be a good time for you to say how you, too, have made some mistakes in your life, both personal and professional."

He didn't look six-four or six-six anymore. As a matter of fact, he looked like the kind of man who could be a good grandfather to a ukulele-making man's bastard child. I said, "I have sure enough made some errors." I said, "I know this won't make anyone involved feel better, but my own father thinks I'm screwed up, too."

Raj went inside. I looked at what I carried in the back of my truck. Ruben Orr said he didn't want to go through with our original plan and gave me back the cash I'd handed over for starters. "These are like children to me. You can't just sell off or abandon children, right?"

I got it. I understood Mayley's father's less-than-subtle allusion.

I said, "I might want to rent out some of the animals in the future. I could use them for promotion, you know. We can talk about it after the blood tests."

What else could I say? I foresaw our odd future connection. He asked me if I wanted Mayley's phone number right before I asked for it. I said, "I swear to God I was just about to ask for it."

He said, "We should all get together some time, before and after, no matter the results."

I believed him, and put the nozzle in my tank. I looked into the store to see Raj giving me the go-ahead to pump. I pulled the trigger and thought about what I rightly owed a lot of people. What a bad person I ended up truly, I thought—I needed to call Mayley, my ex-wife, and anyone I had deceived into thinking he or she could achieve peace when strumming four strings on a miniature instrument.

Invasion of Grenada

Maybe we weren't meant to be possible pre-foster-parents-to-be. It's important to learn these kinds of things early on, I would bet. My wife had signed up for the entire project, and some Department of Social Services people showed up to make sure we didn't have firearms scattered around the house or booze bottles within reach. That we didn't keep Pine-Sol bottles on the floor, or rat traps. I'm sure they looked into our backgrounds to conclude we weren't child pornographers, dope smokers, domestic batterers, gunrunners, arsonists, that sort of thing. I had some questionable decisions in my past, but nothing worse than anyone else. Vandalism, mostly. Trespassing. I'd been married before, too young, and the vandalism and trespassing involved her. But I wasn't violent, or a repeat offender. I walked onto my ex-wife's property once, spray-painted CHEATER on the side of her house, then left. I spray-painted that, plus BITCH and TWO-TIMER and WHORE and EDUARDO—REALLY? on the side of what used to be my van. I don't want to think that I'm a racist, but it hurt my ego that she'd fall in love with a Venezuelan over me.

"It's kind of like being on-call 24/6," our personal social worker came to tell Bonita and me. I'll be the first to admit, psychologically-wise, that maybe I married Bonita just because she sounded like she might be Venezuelan, too. She's not. She's from West Virginia, insert joke here. When I met Bonita—at the Mid-Atlantic Independent Driving Range Owners of America trade show up in North Wilkesboro, North Carolina, inside the old racetrack—that's how she introduced herself: "I'm from West Virginia, insert joke here." When I told her I lived 127 miles from Myrtle Beach you'd've thought I asked her to move in with me to a five-bedroom mansion in some place like Orlando, or Knoxville.

For what it's worth, her West Virginia daddy owned a driving range outside Buckhannon, but he couldn't make it to Mid-Atlantic Independent Driving Ranger Owners of America because of a bout of black lung he contracted from just breathing in the vicinity of coal mines, so he sent Bonita.

She and I had no other choice but to fall in love, what with all the complimentary range balls, hand towels, ball markers, and divot repair tools handed out, not to mention the free symposiums that involved everything from fescue to front wheel pickers to tee-line turf. By the time she and I wandered toward a man about to speak about the importance of ball washers we couldn't take it anymore and retired to my motel room where I had a good bottle of Smirnoff's.

I'll jump ahead and say that I visited Bonita a few times up in West Virginia, her daddy died, she sold the land to one of those mining companies. She moved down to Calloustown soon thereafter and helped me watch my hometown disintegrate into near–ghost town status once the younger kids moved away and the older ones died, once the mill closed, and so on. I'm not complaining or whining.

"It's like 24/6 instead of 24/7 because we won't take children away from their biological parents on a Sunday. We don't want any child growing up and thinking anything bad about Sundays. You know how maybe your momma dies on Arbor Day, and from then on for the rest of your life you hate trees? That's how we feel about taking a kid away from abusive parents on a Sunday. Most parents get caught abusing on Saturdays anyway, and Tuesdays. I don't know why those two days. Someone did a study and concluded, you know," the social worker said. Her name was Alberta. Bonita had met the woman at one of those kitchen appliance parties. They noticed how they both had names that ended in -ta, and started meeting up at an Applebee's out by the closest interstate on Thursdays and calling each other plain old "Ta," so that when they encountered one another sometimes you'd hear "Ta-ta," like that, kind of racy.

"We're ready," Bonita had said.

Here's the situation: Sometimes children had to be taken away from their parents and sent to a safe place for anywhere from one day to a month. It's called "temporary protective custody," just like when somebody in prison tattletales on a gang member and the next thing you know the tattletale's got about six thousand death threats in and outside prison. So it should be called something else, if you ask me, but I don't know what. It should be called something else just so children don't feel as though they have something in common with prison tattletales for the rest of their lives.

"You need to have diapers handy at all time, and Gerber's. These kids coming in might be six months old, they might be fifteen. Boys and girls. So you might need to have some tampons in your medicine cabinet, too," Alberta said.

This conversation took place in our den, in our wooden-framed house, which sat on two acres of land with another twelve across the road where the driving range stood. My father had started Calloustown Driving Range back in the 1960s after he realized that nothing—not corn, soybeans, tomatoes, tobacco—grew in his soil. When Bonita came into my life she said, "Why don't we call it the Calloustown Practice Range? That way it comes out CPR. Get it? That would be cool. People could always say, 'I need me some CPR,' and then when everyone's sitting around, you know, Worm's Bar and Grill wondering who's going to give mouth-to-mouth, the first guy can say, 'No, not that kind of CPR—I need to hit me some dimpled balls.'"

It's not like we had a bunch of advertising in the Yellow Pages or weekly coupons in the newspaper. We didn't have either of those things in Calloustown. I went out and repainted the sign that day to CPR and kind of liked it.

Bonita was behind the idea, too, that I let the grass grow higher October through February and allow quail and dove hunters to partake of the landscape. She said they used to kill bears on their driving range in West Virginia, insert joke here.

So the first boy showed up and he was nine years old, named Pine. Alberta drove him over herself, and we showed him to the spare bedroom that we'd painted half pink and half blue. I said, "Pine? Are you sure about that?" I thought maybe Alberta had some kind of odd dialect, that she meant "Payne," and that the kid was named after the great golfer Payne Stewart, who died a tragic airplane death. What would be the chances of a kid being named Payne coming to live temporarily, under protective custody, with the owners of a driving range?

"Pine," she said. "Daddy got hooked on oxycodone, and mother got hooked on Lortab. You might've seen it on the news. They went into that Rite-Aid up thirty miles from here and tried to rob the place. Both of them are in jail, and Pine doesn't have any aunts or uncles we can find yet to take care of him."

Bonita and I hadn't seen it on the news, because we didn't have cable TV or one of those satellite dishes. We got one good channel some days, but mostly watched static and pretended like it snowed on the Weather Channel.

"Well, we'll take good care of Pine," Bonita said. "This is exciting! You know, we always wanted to have a child, but maybe we met too late in life to have one. We were both thirty."

It made me happy that we didn't have good television reception or newspaper delivery, because Bonita might hear about how women now had kids halfway into their forties. Sometimes I listened to an NPR station while sitting around CPR's "clubhouse," which was a metal storage shed filled with buckets of balls, a card table, four chairs, and an ice chest.

Alberta gave us a sheet of paper with some emergency numbers and said she'd be checking in daily to see how Pine fared. She said, "His parents homeschooled him, so you don't need to deal with getting him back and forth to Calloustown Elementary."

I should mention that this entire conversation took place in a whisper. I thought, I bet a nine-year-old kid is smart enough to realize that some things have changed in his life, and we don't have to be all hush-hush about it. But I didn't want to come off as a bad pre-foster parent.

Bonita said, "Edwin here's good in English, and I'm good in math. We can help out."

I didn't like for Bonita to say my name ever, because it always reminded me that my ex-wife left an Ed for an Ed, and that if the Venezuelan and I ever became friends we could go Ed-Ed to each other like that, even though it wouldn't be as spectacular and funny as Ta-Ta. I said, "Well I don't know that I'm so great in English. I can read, you know. I read a lot! Sometimes I'll go over and sit around across the road and finish a Mickey Spillane book in a day, if we got customers who don't mind retrieving their own balls." I said, "Sometimes I give special deals on people who want to go pick up their own balls."

"Okay," Alberta and my wife said at the same time.

Alberta said, "So we have his clothes, and we have his books and assignments—though I don't think he really ever follows any kind of schedule, from what we've figured out. I'll call tomorrow."

She went to walk out the door. I said, "We look forward to hearing from you. Listen, is there any kind of special meal he likes? Like cheeseburgers or hot dogs? Shrimp? Vinegar-based barbecue? Macaroni and cheese? I used to love macaroni and cheese when I was that age. I still do!" I tried to come off as both concerned and gastronomical. To be honest, I was brought up by parents who put a plate in front of me and said, "Feel lucky there's anything, seeing as we can't grow corn, soybeans, tomatoes, or tobacco in the field."

Bonita said, "That's a good question, Edwin."

"Well, yes, there is a thing you should know," Alberta said. "He's a quiet boy. He might have a speech impediment."

I didn't say, "That tells me nothing about his eating habits." I didn't say, "We'll try to keep him asking for such things as succotash, cereal, spinach, and syrup, if it was that kind of speech impediment." I said, "Any kinds of hobbies I might need to know?"

"You take him across the road to play golf and you should be fine," Alberta said. "Listen, I hate to drop Pine off and run, but I have a kid I need to pick up in Orangeburg whose mother left him straddled to a moped for four hours while she went into a bingo parlor."

Bonita's friend left. My wife and I stood there and looked at each other. From back in the spare bedroom it sounded like termites ate our molding. It sounded like the kid clicked his tongue over and over. It sounded like an old LP skipping, or one of those bush people clicking and clacking when a pride of lions has surrounded the encampment, or when a pickup truck's not running on all its cylinders, or a pileated woodpecker's intent on making its mark on fiberglass.

I said, "Well, you're not in West Virginia anymore."

Bonita laughed. She said, "I'm glad our first one doesn't need to breastfeed," which I thought was kind of a strange first response, but maybe I'd been shielded growing up in Calloustown.

So I would ask the kid a question and he made only those noises—dit, dat, dah, dit, dat, dah. I brought him out to our den on that first night and asked him things like, "Are you scared?" and "Do you know that we're here to protect you from harm?" and "Do you know what the state capital of South Carolina is?" only to get "Dah-di-dah-dah dit di-di-dit" or something like that. Clickety-clack, clickety-clack. Pop-pop-pop-pop-pop. Ptooey, ptooey—those kinds of noises.

Pine looked like a normal nine-year-old kid. He didn't have head lice, which was good. His parents—drugstore robbers—made sure that his bangs weren't crooked, I'll give them that. He owned good posture, wasn't knock-kneed, didn't seem affected by rickets. His ear had healed nicely from where he had a piercing for a day. It looked like only two green freckles on his arm where his father'd gotten the idea that his son should have a tattoo, then reconsidered.

Pine didn't make much eye contact and kind of reminded me of these kids brought down on a field trip to CPR one time from the School for the Blind. That was a catastrophe. A few of them had fine eye-hand coordination—well, except for the "eye" part—but their inner compasses didn't work well and I lost two windows on the house when this one child in particular got turned around on the tee box and smacked a three wood straight across the road the wrong way. I tell you who ought to be placed in temporary protective custody, and it's those good blind kids. They need to be protected from sadist teachers who take them to a driving range, ruining what little self-esteem they possessed.

"We had a boy back home who had a similar speech impediment," Bonita said. "I did some research on it when I went to college. It was called 'echolalia,' and he would mimic things that he heard. In the real world, a child with echolalia might just take off singing the theme song to *Gilligan's Island* or *The Addams Family*, 'cause that's what he heard a week or more ago. Back in Buckhannon, this boy made the same noises as Pine because all he heard was the machinery from the coal mines. And his daddy's misfitted false teeth."

Pine didn't seem either happy or distraught. He sat down and did his homework—I'm not even sure why we did it, but it gave Bonita something to do besides wondering if she made a mistake by leaving West Virginia. She didn't seem obsessed with ordering shoes from catalogs, taking photographs of her feet, then sending the shoes back saying they didn't fit right. Bonita no longer drove fifty miles to the closest Hobby Town store in order to buy decoupage, fake stained glass, or tile mosaic kits in order to sell her wares at the flea market or at the craft shows inherent to local festivals that took place celebrating the importance of pecans, cotton, peaches, Christianity, pumpkins, and tripe.

Bonita brought him over to the Calloustown Practice Range and Pine hit balls, playing like most people do, hitting some solidly, whiffing every sixth shot, topping most of them. His reaction to every swing was about the same, either a series of dits or dots or dats. I concentrated on the kid and tried to figure out if he followed the melody of a song, and sure enough sometimes it sounded like he rocked out on the opening guitar licks of "Sweet Home Alabama," though Alberta told us over the phone one night that the kid had never left the confines of South Carolina's borders.

"You should take him down to the Invasion of Grenada festival," Bonita told me ten days into Pine's stay with us. "What the hell? You never have any business on that day 'cause all the locals are over there. Nobody even hunts on that day."

She spoke the truth. Every year since 1984, Calloustown had hosted the Invasion of Grenada festival—more of a reenactment than a festival, though Bonita hoped that one day there might be rides and craft shows—because one of Calloustown's own, a young Marine named Clarence Reddick, was one of nineteen fatalities. After Clarence's death, some of the more forward-thinking denizens of Calloustown thought it tribute-worthy to reenact the United States's dominance in the military conquest by dressing up people as either Grenadian and Cuban supporters of the New Jewel Movement, or as members of the Marine Amphibious Unit, the 82nd Airborne Division, the 75th Ranger Regiment, Navy SEALs, members of Delta Force, and those others.

There, on a small island in the middle of Lake Calloustown, a couple of skydivers came in to join the reenactors who arrived via pontoon boat. People fired shotguns into the air and shot off Roman candles in a lifelike rendition of the actual invasion. In the end, somebody planted an American flag on the island—though that's probably not what really happened—and then the "body" of Clarence Reddick got brought back to shore on the pontoon boat. It was supposed to be an honor to get picked as Clarence's body, and even women put their names in a bucket in hopes of being selected. Afterward, there was a community-wide covered-dish picnic, square dance, and regular carnival-type games to play.

I said, "I don't know, Bo. You might want to call up Alberta on this one. Do you think exposing an echolalia-ridden homeschooled child under temporary protective custody from his drugstore-robbing addicted parents to the horrors of what was also known as Operation Urgent Fury, fully supported by President Ronald Reagan in order to shift Americans' focus from the ten percent unemployment rate, is a wise decision?" I'd done some research. I'd been reading up on U.S. history in case I needed to help out Pine with homework in that area.

"It might make him feel better about his upbringing," she said. "My father took me one time to a John Brown thing down at Harpers Ferry, and I knew right away that I was better than okay."

I don't know how many Civil War reenactments take place yearly both north and south of the Mason-Dixon line, but it has to be over eighty-five. I know this because one day before I met Bonita I drove down to Charleston and met a guy in charge of the Fort Sumter Museum, but he kind of scared me all dressed up in regalia and I thought he lied, so I just drove to the closest library and looked things up to count eighty-six of the things, not counting the unsanctioned ones in Hawaii and Alaska and Puerto Rico. Civil War reenactments bring in droves of people, both participants and spectators, so you can imagine how many people drive from afar to witness Calloustown's Invasion of Grenada's reenactment, the only one in the country.

Pine and I got there a good hour before two paratroopers flew in from Fort Jackson outside of Columbia. I doubt that the Air Force used a Cessna in Grenada, but it was still quite exciting to see a skydiver in faux action. Pine looked up from where we sat at a wooden picnic table on the outskirts of the Lake Calloustown Public Swimming Area #2—that had been labeled BLACKS ONLY up until 1968—surrounded by locals, older veterans wearing their Garrison caps, half-stoned long-haired Vietnam vets, and a couple women who kept yelling, "USO! USO! USO!" as if they were sad, forgotten debutantes.

Pine let off a slew of his noises, and for a second I thought he imitated "Taps," or a slower version of "The Battle Hymn of the Republic."

"You damn right those boys are going to land right on their targets," this man next to us said. "You got that right, son."

Of course I looked over at the man. He wore a white curled navy gob on his head, and had his shirtsleeves up to show off two anchor tattoos. I turned my head from watching the pontoon take off and said to the man, "Hey."

Pine went off on a rant, in his clicky way.

The man next to me said, "Jesus Christ, boy, slow down." He said, "It's been a long time since I worked as a radioman." I learned this later, for what I heard went, "Di-di-dat di-dah-di-dit dah-dah-dah di-dah-dah dah-di-dit dah-dah-dah-di-dah-dah dah-dit," which came out "Slow down," and then he went into all the rest of that stuff about his days as a petty officer.

Pine fucking beamed. That's the only way I can explain it. He broke out into a smile that would've made Miss America look toothless.

I said to the man, "Hey, hey, what's going on?" and introduced myself and my near-foster child. I said, "Is he talking in a language that no one can understand?"

The skydivers came down. Shotguns sounded. People who came by my driving range to hit scarred and damaged range balls whooped and hollered a couple hundred yards offshore. "I'm retired Radioman Petty Officer Ronald Landry, and I haven't been able to keep up with my Morse code since retiring," the man said in English. I think he must've said the same thing in code to Pine right afterwards, for the radioman went off ditting and dotting until they saluted each other.

I looked at Pine, who nodded. Oh, he understood the English language just fine, but made a pledge not to speak it for some reason. I said to Pine, "Is this part of your homework?

Are you taking Morse code for a foreign language and need to practice? You can tell your answer to retired Radioman Petty Officer Ronald Landry, and he can translate to me."

Pine took off coding away, gesticulating with his hands. He looked like some kind of foreigner with a stutter. Landry nodded and laughed. I got bored after about ten minutes—it seems to me that the armed forces could come up with a quicker form of communication, like plain calling up people and speaking Pig Latin—and watched as the American flag went up on Lake Calloustown Island, then this year's Clarence Reddick got shoved onto a raft and pushed with the help of reenacting Navy SEALs toward the spectators on shore.

Presently there would be a celebratory three-legged race made up solely of Purple Heart–awarded veterans from Iraq and Afghanistan, all of whom teamed up to have left prosthetic and right prosthetic legs in the sack. Those vets could still run the hundred-yard dash in something like eleven seconds.

"It's a long story," Landry finally said to me. "It all boils down to Pine here having an imaginary friend. His name is Di-dah-dah-dah dah-dah-dah dit, which comes out to 'Joe.' Listen, I used to be an adjunct professor of Morse code over at Eminent Domain College on the edge of the Savannah River Nuclear Site before the place self-imploded. If you want, I'd be glad to come over and do some translating, plus give you a crash course in the code. I'll do it for minimum wage. And beer. Dah-di-di-dit dit dit di-dah-dit. That means 'beer.'"

Pine nodded and smiled, rubbed his stomach in circles like a 1950s kid overacting in a TV commercial for whole milk. Then he ran off to partake in the bobbing for grenades contest. I made a mental note to tell him not to mention this part of the day to Alberta or Bonita, seeing as it would mean the end of our pre-foster days. They weren't real grenades, but miniature finials. Still, social workers and wives frown upon toy guns, too.

A handful of women wailed, reenacting how one mourns the death of a Marine, when Clarence Reddick's body got transferred to a pine coffin, then placed up on a stage where, later, a John Philip Sousa tribute band would play two hours' worth of marches and people would try to do-si-do.

I don't know why I said, "That's a kind offer," and asked for retired Radioman Petty Officer Ronald Landry's phone number. I had no intention of calling him. My theory went thus: Let's say I became fluent in Morse code. By that time, Pine would be back living with relatives or bona fide foster parents. Even if Bonita and I took in another emergency child, what would be the chances that the child communicated only in dits and dahs? What would be the chances that I'd have a field trip of military personal at CPR who would find it amusing to speak in Morse code? Hell, I would be better off filling my head up learning Hindi, or Gullah.

I walked over to where Pine stood, his head dripping, a wooden pineapple in his jaws. I said, "Dah-dah-dah-dah-dah," just jabbering, not knowing that I had looked at him and said, "Zero."

We got home and I told Bonita everything that I learned. She said, "Is that true? Six hundred thirty-eight Cubans were captured in the real invasion? Where did they go?"

I said, "That's not what I want you to focus on. We met an old guy from the Navy. He communicated with Pine just fine, because that noise he's been making has actually been Morse code. There's an imaginary friend involved named Joe. Maybe it's G.I. Joe. And if it is, that would be even more worrisome. I think you need to call up Alberta and tell her this isn't working out."

Bonita shook her hair out. She laughed. "Are you serious? I had an imaginary friend in West Virginia named Charlie. As in Charles Manson. Who was brought up in foster homes in West Virginia, insert joke here, when his mom was off in prison and whatnot."

Pine had walked straight back to his room. I looked over my shoulder to make sure he didn't stand in the doorway. To Bonita I whispered, "I think Pine's parents damaged him in ways we're not capable of handling. I'm serious."

"Pine! Come on in here, Pine! I got to get to the bottom of something!" Bonita yelled out. He came running. She spoke in a voice I'd not heard before, with really hard long "I" sounds, and Ts that came out Ds. She said, "Why's your head wet? Back where you come from you walk around with a wet head all the time? You know who walks around with a wet head all the time? Fish. You just a fish, Pine? That what you consider yourself to be? A fish ain't come out of the water yet to join the rest of us humans on dry land?"

I looked at Pine and noticed how he teared up. I said, "Goddamn, Bonita. Ease up. It's my fault about letting him bob for apples."

"You can speak in English, and you're about to do it pronto, Pine. I don't care about your mom and dad sitting around in their trailer letting you say dit dot dit dot all the time with your head and shoulders wet. This is a whole new ballgame here, where you got to interact with us in a polite and honest procedure."

I'd never seen my wife get so wound up. In a way it made me wish we had had children of our own, but in another way I saw it as a blessing that she didn't go all mountain girl on our kid—yelling, speaking in a way not that much different than Morse code, not blinking, and looking like she could pull out her own teeth and use them in a mosaic portrait of her father in mid-hack, bent over a bucket of balls on the edge of a cliff.

I walked around my wife, opened the refrigerator, and pulled out two cans of ginger ale. I handed one to Pine. We pulled our tabs open within a half second of each other, to make a dit-dit sound. And then fucking Pine said, in a voice that came out as gravelly as the oldest cigarette-smoking, bourbon-swilling, black blues singer of all time, "I'll dry off in time. It wasn't apples. I bobbed hand grenades."

I said, "Hey, you talked," and Bonita said, "What?"

I said, "Okay, Pine, good job. Don't wear yourself out in one day. Go on back to your room and take a nap. Later on we can go across the road and hit some pitching wedges at doves flying up."

"They bob for hand grenades at the Invasion of Grenada reenactment? No goddamn wonder we got problems with the youth of today," Bonita said. "What else did y'all do, play ring toss on severed heads? Enter a hollering contest see who can yell 'Kill!' the loudest?"

"Dah-di-dah di-dit di-dah-di-dit di-dah-di-dit," Pine said, which Bonita and I knew spelled out K-I-L-L.

She said, "No. You are not going to be having any secret language with a secret invisible friend from this point on."

She pointed at the telephone on the wall and said, "You want me to call up the Department of Social Services and have them come pick you back up and take you to a family might try to exorcise you? That what you want, Pine?"

"Okay, let's just settle down. It's only been a couple weeks. Things will smooth out," I said. I drank my ginger ale and burped accidentally, which made Bonita glare at me.

Pine shook his head. He said in that ancient voice—just a grating rasp off of being that of an old-school tracheotomy victim—"I'd like to go visit that drugstore my parents tried to hold up. I got me some money. I'd like to go to that drug-store, maybe buy me a Timex watch."

Bonita held a self-satisfied smile I'd not seen since she found some kind of study that ranked West Virginia ahead of my home state in regards to education and quality of living. I felt pretty sure she wrote it herself, sent it to a friend some-where, and had that person post it on the Internet. I said, "Well, then let's go to that drugstore."

I loaded Pine into the car and off we went. We drove past the remnants of the Invasion of Grenada reenactment to see straggling "Cubans," "Grenadians," and "Americans" laugh and clink beer cans, gauze wrapped around their heads. We drove by Old Man Reddick's nursery, and the defunct bus station where men still met mornings in order to think up ways to resurrect Calloustown. Out on Old Charleston Road we passed children selling used golf balls—under normal circumstances I would've stopped to make sure they weren't stolen from me—and then another group of children selling sweet potatoes.

Pine made his noises off and on, I assumed spelling things out in Morse code. I didn't have it in me to tell him to stop, that he should speak English. Little steps, I thought, kind of like spreading democracy whether Third World nations wanted it or not. I said, "Is there a reason you have to go to this particular Rite-Aid?" I didn't say, "I understand how you might want to apologize for your parents, that it's a healing process," that sort of thing. I didn't even think about it until later that night, when Alberta came to pick Pine up and take him out of our home.

Pine shook his head. We got there. The saleswoman took a small key and opened the rotating Timex display case. Pine chose a regular, old man's silver wind-up wristwatch with a stretchy flexible band that caught arm hairs too much, in my opinion. He shoved it all the way up his arm past his elbow, stuck his ear to it, and said, "Tick tick tick tick tick."

The woman said, "I bet we can find you a watch with a band that'll fit better."

Pine shook his head. "I'm going to use it to make a bomb anyway," he rasped away. The woman stepped back a bit. "Y'all took my parents away from me after they came in here to get what they needed. I'm going to make a bomb."

Maybe there's a reason Bonita and I never had children of our own. I didn't know what to say or do. My father would've beaten me with a nine iron right there next to the perfume counter, but I knew that kind of behavior no longer found acceptance. Should I have laughed and said the boy was kidding? Should I have told the woman she should feel honored that he didn't say that entire monologue in Morse code? I guess, in retrospect, I should've waited thirty minutes in line for the pharmacist and asked him or her to explain to Pine how scared everyone gets when a robbery takes place, and how a nation cannot be considered civilized until its citizens stop attacking each other with little provocation. Evidently the wrong thing to say was, "You got that right, son. I don't blame you."

Sonny Boy Williamson for Dinner

Normally I don't answer the side door if a man's knocking outside while holding a shotgun in his crooked arm. I don't even have guns in the house. It's not like I tell everyone around here—that could only lead to break-ins, and talk that I was truly queer, capricious, unpatriotic, and/or nonresistant—but I don't keep guns, rope, safety razors, gas stoves, tall kitchen plastic garbage bags, garden hoses, or pills around. There's a chance that my DNA makeup isn't the same as my parents, aunts and uncles, grandparents on both sides, and some stray cousins, sure, but I don't want to take the chance. Because I might have what microbiologists, geneticists, psychiatrists, and palm readers haven't yet discovered—the suicide gene. I won't marry, I won't have children, I'll barely have a pet unless it's a shelter dog over the age of nine. I'll drive on occasion, but always attempt to take routes without bridges or thick roadside trees seeing as I might become manically depressed and veer. I've been thinking about moving to one of those southwest deserts—no rivers to cross, and most cacti are probably no match for my pickup—but the boredom there might, of course, send me outside to juggle vipers in a careless fashion.

It's not like I've always been aware of my family's sudden choices to exit a world made up of unemployment, broken hearts, IRS audits, early onset arthritis, hypertension, lackluster restaurant choices, terminal skin conditions, and alcoholism. I grew up with parents who understood their ancestors—thus why they would let me read everything except Hemingway, or why they blacked out Greco-Roman history tomes when Nero showed up, or told me I needed to swerve from any Rothko paintings should I ever take a field trip to a museum of modern art.

They brought me up as best they could, shielded me from how my uncle Carl asphyxiated himself, how my aunt June cut her wrists with a Bowie knife, how one of my grandfathers stepped in front of an Amtrak and the other went skydiving without a parachute. Then my mother and father—right after I graduated college—spent a Sunday night drinking bourbon while eating a special barbiturate pie. I took some jobs, I did some family research, and then I retreated for the most part. No matter, if I make it to forty-nine years old I'll hold the record for longest-living Gosnell on this particular sad branch.

I expected my "common-law wife" Harriet to be knocking on the door, locked out, and that's why I thought nothing of opening up without considering what dangers could be out there. Harriet doesn't have the possible gene. She's originally from North Dakota and has a great-aunt who's something like 114 years old. Sometimes I say things to Harriet like, "What does a woman who's 114 years old do?" and the answer's always, "She looks forward to making peanut brittle for the volunteer fire department's annual fundraiser." Makes fucking peanut brittle once a year! Sorry, but I side with my dead family members when it comes to this. I side with Socrates—who drank some god-damn hemlock—when it comes to how the unexamined life is not worth living. Harriet says, "Well, maybe she's examining whether or not she can make the perfect peanut brittle each year, just like you think you can design the perfect kitchen utensil."

I said to the shotgun guy, "Hey. Hey, hey, hey," and looked behind me for some kind of weapon while closing the door.

This was from my ex-garage, which I used for a work-shop. People who know of my possible genetic flaw say to me, "Duncan, why would you leave a job finally making such good money as an optometrist in order to move to the middle of nowhere and run hand tools that might backfire on you?" They say, "What's to say you won't get depressed one day and run the circular saw across your jugular?"

To them I say, "What's to say I wouldn't get depressed from women arguing with me about how they don't need bifocals, then one day self-dilating my eyes and run out into midday traffic?"

"I ain't here to hurt no one," the man said from the other side of my door. "I'm kind of your neighbor. Here. I've put my gun up leaned against your truck."

I cracked the door back open, armed with my DeWalt Variable Speed belt sander in one hand and a Black & Decker cordless twelve-volt lithium drill in the other. For some reason I thought it necessary to blurt out, "I know all about the goddamn Second Amendment."

The man didn't stick out his hand. He said, "Gosnell, right? Me and my wife's been meaning to come by here and welcome you to Calloustown. I'm Ransom Dunn, from up the road."

I said, "Good to meet you, Ransom. Duncan," and set down my tools to shake his hand. I didn't say, "We've lived here for four years." I thought, Ransom Dunn? What a cool name.

"I just wanted to tell you that I hit a deer down at the end of your driveway. It ain't dead, and I want to put it out of its misery. Way we do it around here, you get half and I get half, seeing as it's on your property."

I stepped outside and looked at his shotgun. It didn't look all that stable leaned against my bumper—what were the chances of it falling over and discharging? I said, "Damn. Your truck okay?"

I don't want to ever say anything about anyone else's vehicle, but Ransom's truck looked as if he'd hit a good fifty deer. He said, "It's running."

I looked down the gravel driveway. The deer—a doe— kept lifting her head in an attempt to get up. I said, "Listen, you go ahead and take her all. I appreciate the offer, but my wife and I are about venisoned out, if you know what I mean."

See how I did that? I made it sound like A) I hunted on a regular basis and had a freezer full of deer meat; and B) we weren't vegetarians for the most part, though Harriet was a vegetarian who wouldn't let me cook what with the chances I'd put Drano in the soup.

Ransom Dunn said, "That's mighty neighborly of you, my man," and "Y'all come on over some Saturday night we'll chew some venison jerky, drink beer. Your wife oughta meet my wife, Boo. Women 'round here need women. Does your wife like to paint by numbers like mine?"

Ransom and Boo Dunn. Boo Dunn sounded like that good sausage from down in Louisiana. I thought, if Harriet and I were named Ransom and Boo Dunn, we'd probably go out on the road and never question the apparent meaningless of life. I said, "Okay," and picked up my tools.

Back in my workshop I cranked up some Sonny Boy Williamson singing "Keep It to Yourself" and turned on my electric fan. I didn't want to think about that deer with a barrel to her temple. I wanted to drown it out, much like I used to drown out people screaming about how they didn't have glaucoma, or hypertension, or diabetes, or torn retinas. I had one man spit right in my own eyes one time when I told him that he had a cataract. They say dentists have a high suicide rate, but I would bet any dentist who says, "You have a cavity" doesn't equal the effect of his or her saying, "You're about to go blind" when it comes to the depression that follows for both health professional and patient.

Let me say that even Sonny Boy Williamson's good loud harmonica won't drown out a shotgun blast from a hundred yards away.

I put a cheap, handleless rolling pin in my vise, drilled out what needed to be drilled out, and shoved car cigarette lighters into both ends. Sometimes I make sure they match—two Buick Electra lighters, two Comets, two Dodge Dusters, two Fairlanes. But I understand that, in the real world, modern marriages suffer through mixed allegiances, that there are Chevy-only women married to Ford-only men, and that they won't purchase one of my one-of-a-kind rolling pins unless they're both represented. It's just like Yankees/Red Sox families, or Auburn/Alabama families, or Harvard/Yale families. It's like Wonderbread/Sunbeam families, or Duke's/Hellman's mayonnaise families.

People pay $66 dollars apiece for my one-of-a-kind rolling pins, even in the recession. My average rolling pin—it's twenty inches long and might best be called a "dowel" before I shove the lighters in both ends—costs me about nine bucks. I get the lighters for a dollar apiece, down at a number of auto salvage places in and around the Calloustown area, plus up in Columbia when I get Harriet to drive me past EyeCU Optical, where I worked for twenty years.

I sell my work in boutique kitchen appliance shops, through a website, on eBay, and on Amazon.com. I understand the notion of supply and demand, and go full force. One day there will be no more cigarette car lighters, seeing as the automotive industry now designs vehicles without even ashtrays. One day there will be no more flour, and carbohydrate-addicted people will commit suicide.

I heard a blast, and then I heard another. Did Ransom miss the first time? Was he some kind of sadist? Did the doe's eye stare back at him in a way that made Ransom Dunn take a second shot to eradicate the sad doe-eyed glance from his future dreams?

I worked on a second rolling pin: a specialty order made from a wooden Louisville Slugger baseball bat so that when the breadmaker rolled dough there'd be an indention that spelled out "Willie Mays" in script. Who has that kind of money to ruin a vintage ash bat? I looked on the Internet and saw where such bats went for $65 apiece in and of themselves. The signature was at the sweet spot, which meant I had to cut it down, then sand down the thicker end. I don't want to question anyone's motives or needs, but I wondered about this particular person's ego in regards to rolling out biscuits with "Willie Mays" on the top crust.

Sonny Boy Williamson—I should mention that this was Sonny Boy Williamson II, who was born Aleck Ford in Tallahatchie County, Mississippi in 1899, or 1908, or 1912—sang that song of his called "Nine Below Zero" that just about every other blues singer covered at one time or another, when Ransom Dunn knocked on the door again. I turned off my sander. I turned down the CD player. I opened up and said, of course, "Could you just plain come in at night and kill me while I sleep?"

Ransom Dunn said, "It's me again. I don't have my shotgun." He didn't have it leaned against my truck, either. "Listen, I got a couple favors ask you." He stood with his feet spread apart, as if he were from one of those Midwestern states. I noticed blood splatter on the thigh parts of his blue jeans. He blinked unnaturally, as if he had a foreign object in his eye.

"I'm not doing any more eye exams," I said. "I guess I can give you a deal on a rolling pin, seeing as I wouldn't have to add on postage."

Ransom Dunn shook his head. He said, "I got no idea what you talking about. People told me that I wouldn't have no idea what you talking about, but I don't always believe what other people say."

I looked to the left of Ransom. A car came up Old Old Calloustown Road and I prayed that it was Harriet returning from wherever she went to get away from me. I had met Harriet back when I looked into people's pupils. She had taught second-grade students. She was my patient and said we had something in common what with pupils, and the next thing you know we sat in a place called Sad and Moanin' drinking draft beer and talking about idiots we knew in college who now worked on their third Christian marriages. Locals called it the S&M. So did I.

The car passed onward. I said to Ransom, "What's up?"

"I just realized that I don't have any room in my freezer for this deer meat. You got any room in your freezer for this deer meat? I mean, do you mind if I chain her up on that tree out front and dress her out?"

We had a freezer we kept in my workshop, half filled with corn, beans, quartered tomatoes, and blackberries mostly, nothing else. I stepped out of my workshop again and looked down the driveway. The doe no longer lay there. Ransom'd already strung her up in the tree. I walked out ten steps and looked down the road in the direction Harriet would come. "Listen, go ahead and dress it out, but if my wife comes please tell her that you just assumed it would be okay. She won't be all that happy. It's a long story." I didn't mention how part of that long story might be about how Harriet wasn't my wife technically. Before we moved to Calloustown a real estate agent up in Columbia told us how someone spray-painted SODOM AND GOMORRAH on the tailgate of two organic farmers' truck one time, and BOOGERISTS—probably meant to be "buggerists"—across the back windshield of a Subaru wagon owned by two men who moved to Calloustown in order to start up some kind of artist retreat that didn't last.

Ransom Dunn said, "I appreciate it, Cuz. I had a chain in my truck, but I ain't got no hacksaw. You got a saw I could borrow? I got a hawkbill knife, but I ain't got a saw. And I need a Hefty bag of some sort, maybe some newspaper."

I let him in my workshop and pointed over to where I kept a variety of handsaws. I said, "Use whatever you need." I didn't say anything about how I couldn't keep Hefty bags in my household.

"Man, you got you a nice setup in here," Ransom said. He looked over at the rolling-pin-to-be I had in the vise, the Willie Mays Louisville Slugger. "Hey, someone stoleded my boy's baseball bat and I think that's it, my man. Did you god-damn steal my boy's bat?"

Fuck, I thought. Did I save the box that the baseball bat came in? I said, "It got sent to me because somebody wants a rolling pin made out of it. Listen, there had to be thousands of bats made way back when with Willie Mays's signature on them."

Peripherally I saw a Phillips-head screwdriver I could pick up and use for a weapon, right in this guy's left eyeball. One time I had a one-eyed man for a client who kept complaining with the bifocal monocle we got for him.

I considered a rasp, ball-peen hammer, and an X-Acto knife. I said, "Look, man, I didn't steal your boy's baseball bat, I promise. I got other things to do besides steal baseball bats," even though I thought about how easy it would be, in the old days, to lurk around Little League games before they started using aluminum.

Ransom Dunn pulled his head back somewhat and looked at me as if he wore a pair of reading glasses. He cleared his throat. "I guess it's fair, then, for you to stock my meat," he said.

"This isn't a question of fair or not, fucker," I said. "I didn't steal your boy's baseball bat. That's that. If you want to cut her up and stock her in my freezer, fine. I couldn't care less one way or another," I said, almost throwing in how we don't eat meat outside of wild salmon we had to drive sixty miles to buy, or farm-raised catfish from Mississippi they stock down at the Calloustown Superette.

Ransom started laughing. He said, "I wouldn't've believed you, except you said 'fucker.' That means you're telling the truth. If everyone said 'fucker' at the end of a sentence, it'd be more believable. 'I am not a crook, fucker,' like that. 'I did not have sexual relations with that woman, fucker.'"

I said, "You need any help out there with that deer?"

He said, "You know what? I bet I could use some help. Hell, I ain't field dressed a deer in a while."

I thought, damn. I thought, had to ask. I wondered if Sonny Boy Williamson ever sang a song about dead deer hanging from a tree, and said, "Let me go get some old paper bags and paper."

Ransom cut the tendons on the deer's back- and forelegs. He stripped the animal's hide down much like I had seen Amazonian tribesmen pull bark from a tree in order to make cloth. He stripped that doe's hide down much like I—as a child—had pulled a catfish's skin down using a pair of pliers while it still croaked. Ransom cut out meat from the animal's back, handed it over to me to bag, and then swiveled the body around to slice out roasts from its haunches.

The deer's inner organs—heart, liver, spleen, kidneys, bladder, colon—spilled out finally right there at the base of my best oak tree.

I said, "Man."

"Good meat," he said. "We're lucky to get this thing so fresh. One time I hit a deer up there," he pointed, "about five miles away, and by the time I could get back to it she already had turkey buzzards atop her."

I said, "That fast?"

He said, "Well, in between I got arrested for some things, and had to spend a few days in jail. You know how that goes."

I nodded. I had no clue what he meant, of course, but I nodded. I said, "I have a hawkbill knife. Don't think that I don't have a hawkbill knife. I got all kinds of knives! Hawkbill's my favorite, though."

I should mention that I often drink bourbon while making my specialized bread rollers. Hell, I did the same when checking people's vision, from time to time, though no one ever complained.

Ransom said he'd never heard of Sonny Boy Williamson. He said he listened mostly to George Jones, Merle Haggard, Buck Owens, and Loretta Lynn. Tammy Wynette, Johnny Cash, Patsy Cline, Hank Snow. He said, "If they was on Hee-Haw back in the day, then I listened. Me and Boo went to Nashville one time, and we seen a old boy named Elmer Fudpucker right there on the street where people hung out. Boo got his autograph. She keeps it in a box right where she keeps her momma's engagement ring."

We'd stuffed my freezer with the venison, which didn't take up more than a couple cubic feet, to be honest. I don't know if Ransom wasn't much of a butcher, or if a deer doesn't offer up all that much meat, but it didn't take up space, to speak of. I said, "How long you been living in Calloustown?"

"Life," he said. "I left one time for Vietnam, but I come back. That was my only time out of here."

I nodded. I said, "You don't look old enough to have fought in Vietnam."

"No, I'm not. I left for Vietnam just because I wanted to go over there to do some fishing, back in about 1998, but I never made it any farther than the airport. I got this cousin over in Forty-Five who lied to me. He said people didn't need a passport to go to Vietnam. Played a trick on me. He also said you can just walk into an airport with some cash and they'll put you on a plane. I don't hold that one against him, seeing as at one time it was probably true. But you can't just up and go to a foreign land without a passport, it ends up." I stared at Ransom for a while, wondering if he japed me. He kept eye contact, then said, "Fucker." He said, "I listen to Willie Nelson, David Allan Coe, Waylon Jennings, Hank Williams, and that other guy. Lefty Frizzell. And I like the way Crystal Gayle looks."

Sonny Boy Williamson kept singing about a funeral and a trial, that song about how he'd kill his wife and then undergo prosecution. I waited for Ransom to say something about how I might be an N-word lover. He didn't. He even seemed to nod his head at the right times, and then said, "I take it all back. I went to Jackson, Mississippi, one time, too. My mother had a first cousin who married a man down in Jackson, and then she died. We went to the funeral, for some reason. I was a kid. This was summer, and we were on our way down to Tybee Island anyway. Next thing you know, I was sitting in some place down in Jackson eating a pig ear sandwich," Ransom pointed at my speakers, "listening to music a lot like this here."

I said, "You want a beer or something? I got some cold beer inside."

"You know what, I believe if I listened to this kind of music for too long I might take that shotgun of mine and blow my brains out. Yeah, I'll have a beer," Ransom said.

I didn't get up immediately. I got stuck wondering if my parents listened to Sonny Boy Williamson, or if my other relatives did. "Wait, I forgot. I don't have any beer left," I said, seeing as I needed to get him out of my house for one, and go find one of Harriet's happy CDs—the Go-Gos, maybe, or the B-52s—and see if it would turn my mind around.

Ransom sucked at his teeth twice, something that irritated me in people. One time I had a receptionist named Donna who sucked her teeth, and I finally talked her into applying for a job I found in the want ads at a dental clinic. Ransom said, "They say you had a nervous breakdown, Duncan. You don't seem to be all that on edge, if you ask me. My wife Boo—now she's on edge. But you seem pretty normal to me."

How come Harriet shows up nonstop bothering me when I don't want her to, but she won't appear when I need her? I said, "That's what they say, huh? Well, I didn't have a mental breakdown. I just made a decision to stop what I was doing. End of story."

Ransom got up out of his chair. He patted the freezer and walked over to run his hand across the rolling pin I worked on. "They say a lot of things. They say I'm crazy! They say I joined the volunteer fire department because I like to light fires. They say I broke into Calloustown High back in the day and changed all my grades so I'd graduate top of the class. There's a lot of things they say. Fuckers."

I got up from where I sat, pulled out the drawer where I kept my collection of awls, and pulled out a half-filled pint of Old Grand-Dad. I took two hits, looked at my watch, and said, "Oh, man, I'm supposed to call up Harriet." I pulled out my cell phone, pretended to punch some numbers, and put the phone up to my head. I said, "Hey, I forgot to call you up," and then waited for what I thought was the proper time for a response. I said, "Oh, man, I completely forgot," and then a series of okays.

I hung up and said to Ransom, "If it's not one thing it's ten others."

"Wife's got you on a short leash, huh?" he said, smiling. "I know what you mean."

"She's on her way home, and we're supposed to meet some people for supper. She's at the store, buying store things for this supper we're going to."

Ransom said, "I get it. I've overstayed my welcome. I get it. Light wasn't on on your phone. Anyway. Okay." He walked to the door. "Listen, I appreciate your holding onto my venison. I'll come over and get half of it when we got room back at the house freezer."

"I was talking on the phone," I said. "Here!" I held the phone out. "Punch Redial," I said, praying that he didn't take me up on it.

He had his hand on the doorknob. My phone rang at the same time that a horn honked in the driveway. Ransom opened the door. I flipped open the phone. Harriet was screaming into the receiver, but it didn't matter, because we could hear her voice from outside. "What's this deer carcass doing hanging out on the tree?" and "I can't leave the house ever without something bad happening!" and "Goddamn you, Gosnell, are you trying to make our property value go down?" and so forth. Stuff like that.

I shrugged toward Ransom Dunn and said, "Wife's home."

Ransom said, "I didn't really hit that deer out in front of your place. I hit it, but I brought it back here and pretended, just so I could see you for myself. Around here they say that if you're ever feeling like life can't get any worse, come by your house and check you out."

I said to my wife, "Hey, honey."

She held her hands on her hips. "I can't take it anymore, Duncan." She pointed back to the deer hide hanging from Ransom's chain. "I know you have some issues, and I've tried to skirt away from them, but turning our front yard into an abattoir is about the last thing I can take."

Ransom said, "Ma'am," and got in his truck. He backed out of the driveway, then chugged out onto Old Calloustown Road. I think I could hear him laughing, and then he honked his horn.

I said to Harriet, "Where did you ever learn the word 'abattoir'?" Or I yelled it, as she followed Ransom out, then turned the other way, back toward Columbia, I figured. I thought, issues.

There's something about eating venison alone, probably. I didn't wait around like most people would—say, a month— to see if Ransom Dunn would return for his half of what I had in the freezer. I knew. I'm not saying that I'm a soothsay- er or anything, but it's the same way I could tell how people coming into my office wanted to argue with me concerning their vision. As soon as I saw a eighty-year-old woman show up, walking as forceful as a Parisian runway model, I knew for certain that I'd hear, "I need you to tell the DMV that I have a good breadth of vision field" within two minutes, like I did with Mrs. Esther Crawford that time, whom I felt sorry for, and for whom I filled out the information saying that I performed a vision screening, plus some other things.

And then she drove through a four-way stop sign two months later, and her two grown children showed up at my office blaming me for everything, which might've been true.

Thirty minutes after Ransom and my wife left separately I got out this cookbook put out by the Southern Foodways Alliance and figured out how to season my deer meat and cook it just like a regular roast in a pressure cooker. I went around the house and put different CDs in every available player I had—a regular stereo system, a boom box in the bedroom, another in our unused third bedroom. I played Little Walter, and Snooky Pryor, and James Cotton to go along with Sonny Boy Williamson playing in my workshop. I set the shoulder meat off on the counter and read through the recipe twice. I pulled out carrots, potatoes, and onions from the refrigerator, found a Ziploc of jalapenos I'd frozen from the summer, and listened to those harmonicas howling cheerless from every direction. I'd be willing to bet that, if asked, most old white country boys in this area would say that banjos provided the best background music to cooking deer, but they're wrong: it's a pure, clear blues harmonica that's necessary for serenading a recently killed ruminant.

I brought the venison to a boil twice, to get out any wild taste, then set it in the cooker.

And I listened for the door to open, which it finally did.

I expected Harriet to return on a rampage. Then I figured that Ransom might show up with some kind of story about how his own wife kicked him out—I kind of doubted that he even had a wife, for some reason—and that he wanted some bourbon. Out of all the scenarios that went through my head, as Snooky played a song called "Big Guns," I didn't expect Boo showing up, all apologetic for her husband's rudeness.

I yelled, "Hey, hey, hey!" like that, because I thought she had a pistol in her hand.

"Mr. Gosnell?" she said. "I thought I heard someone say come in. I'm sorry. I'm Boo Dunn, Ransom's wife."

I still held a wooden-handled Mr. Bar-B-Q stainless-steel two-prong meat fork in my right hand, wondering if anyone would buy something like it with a car cigarette lighter shoved into the end. I said, "You scared me. Hey. Jesus, you scared me. I didn't hear you come in."

"I knocked. I rang that doorbell, but I noticed the light wasn't on so I doubt if it works." Boo Dunn looked pretty normal, compared to her husband. She wore a pair of olive-green army pants and a gray T-shirt with Calloustown High Ostriches printed across the front. Her sandals didn't appear to be of a disreputable quality. Sometimes back when I worked with women's vision I caught myself fixated on their shoes more than I did their pupils, probably so as not to fall in love, have them plead for both marriage and children, then have to warn them that I came from a long line of Gosnells who lost the will to prosper. Someone should do a scientific study, by the way, comparing people with flat feet and their tendency toward astigmatism.

I said, "Calloustown High Ostriches," knowing that it might come out more like "Calloustown Hostages," which it did. I said, "Half of this venison is mine. I'm not stealing from you."

Boo Dunn shook her head sideways. "My husband said he was a little worried about you. He wanted me to come over here and teach you how to cook up that thing. He thought you looked like you maybe didn't have a clue."

I said, "Who's your husband?" just to mess with her. "I'm kidding. Hell, you might as well call up Ransom and tell him to come over. What's it take for this? Like, two hours? You want a beer or anything?" I said. I opened up the refrigerator and pulled out two cans of PBR. My classmates made fun of me back in the day for drinking PBR, until they all noticed that there was a P B R right in the middle of the standard Snellen eye exam chart, line eleven.

"He's right outside. You want me go get him?" She took the can of beer from me, and I thought about how I would have to tell Ransom Dunn that between the time he took off, I drove down to the Calloustown and Country Pick-Pay-Go.

I stared at the pressure cooker's top and imagined what it would be like to shove my face straight down into the meat. I wondered if it would be enough to kill me. I'd heard somewhere along the way that burning to death was the worst of all, and that drowning was the best. People always had these kinds of lists. Cancer worse than a massive heart attack, hanging worse than drug overdose, those kinds of things. My relatives had found a variety of ways to kill themselves, but none out of boredom, which was the means of dying I feared worse. Muddy Waters sang songs about wanting to be a catfish, or about being a diving duck. Those were animals that didn't consider the heaviness of existence, evidently.

With no warning I found myself enveloped in that miserable, relentless feeling that I needed to be elsewhere, as in living with my ancestors. I'd not felt this particular feeling since that last official day of working as an optician, a day that included six glaucoma and two diabetes patients one after another all blaming me for their conditions.

I looked at the two-pronged fork and thought about a story I read back in college—for the record, future opticians shouldn't be forced to take literature courses—wherein a

Japanese soldier disembowels himself. I imagined that, on the list of death pains, disembowelment would be right below self-immolation. I thought of the long-term forms of suicide—smoking and drinking, working out in the sun for years on end without sunscreen, tearing down asbestos-riddled attics, driving without a seatbelt. I thought of Hansen's disease and realized that I got off track in terms of self-inflicted downturns. Somewhere along the line I got stuck wondering if it would be worse jumping off a building head first onto the concrete below, or picking up a live electrical roadside line following a tornado or hurricane. I wondered if two black mamba strikes simultaneously would be worse than jumping out in front of a Greyhound bus driven by an impatient man with blues songs running through his head and a questionable wife at home.

When the Dunns and my wife walked into the kitchen, one after the other, I thought two things: "How long have I been out of focus?" and, "Is this one of those interventions everyone's talking about lately?" My wife laughed and enwrapped Boo Dunn's shoulder. I'm talking Harriet slung her head back in a way that showed off her back molar dental work. Ransom Dunn carried in two bottles of Merlot that appeared to be bought either online or from a real wine store sixty miles away. My wife said, "We've not had anyone over for dinner for a long time. Well, ever, now that I think about it."

Boo Dunn said, "Why don't y'all let me make some pizza dough, and we can put some of that other venison on it for a topping. I know it sounds weird, but there's nothing much better than deer pizza. Let me use one of your specialized rolling pins, there, Duncan."

"I'm not much of a wine man, myself," Ransom said. He stood close to me and stared down at the pressure cooker. "I saw where you had some bourbon back there in your spot," he said, pointing his thumb. His wife and Harriet seemed to be running off to look at a shower curtain, or throw rug, or curio cabinet, or stylish Venetian blinds, or baker's rack, or collection of swizzle sticks, stuff like that.

My nineteen-year-old ex-stray pound dog Sophocles dragged himself into the kitchen and looked up at me. He directed his nose toward the pressure cooker. I said to Ransom, "I've had this dog ten years. He won't die."

"Yeah," said Ransom. "I guess he don't want to."

I walked Ransom into the den. We turned on the television. What else could we do? Sophocles followed us, pulling his back legs the way he did. In the kitchen, something bad happened and the pressure cooker blew. Maybe I didn't crank the top on tight enough. I said, "Damn."

Boo and Harriet came out of the guest bedroom saying "What was that?"

I said, "We might have to call out for some food." I said, "Ha ha ha ha ha ha ha."

No one responded. The Dunns looked at me, though, as did Harriet. Did I see in their faces some kind of accusatory glance? Did they think I rigged the pressure cooker to blow? I looked down at Sophocles and thought about how I could've just as easily named him Homer or Ray Charles. Even my dog seemed to look at me as if I'd done something wrong and on purpose.

"The deer's on the ceiling," Boo Dunn said.

We all looked up that way. Harriet walked into the kitchen and opened the wine. She didn't say anything about how I was a loser with bad luck. She didn't look up at what dripped back down on our floor. Me, I looked at my wristwatch and thought about how many days I had to break my family's record. Barely—if anyone listened closely—we could hear Sonny Boy Williamson singing about bringing eyesight to the blind, I swear. Ransom said something about how he didn't think what plastered itself to the ceiling would eventually start a fire. Then he asked me if I had two harmonicas anywhere around.

Spastic

The Calloustown station remains open twenty-four hours a day, though no Greyhound or Trailways bus has pulled up for passengers to disembark in fifteen years. The building—plastered-over cement blocks that nearly look stucco, thus exotic among the mobile homes, wooden bungalows, shingle-sided shotgun shacks, and fieldstone salt boxes—holds, still, a linoleum-floored waiting room with chairs shoved in three rows along the walls. There are two restrooms, both with working sinks and toilets, and a glass-fronted booth where someone sold tickets, offered advice, and tagged luggage. A television's mounted in the southwest corner of the waiting room, six inches from touching the ceiling. There's a half-filled gumball machine, the proceeds of which aid small children with birth defects. No one has ever thought to crack open the globe and steal its pennies. An empty cigarette machine with a rust-splattered mirror and rusted silver knobs stands in the corner—$1.75 a pack for Lark, Camel, Lucky Strikes, Pall Mall, Viceroy, Kent, Winston, Marlboro. There's the smell of Juicy Fruit in the air, of plastic, of instant coffee.

The personnel's vanished, the bus line having chosen a different route between Columbia and Savannah, but the electricity's still on. Because there's no community center, YMCA, Lions Club, rec center, Moose Club, Jaycees, Kiwanis International, Rotary Club, or Shriners Club in Calloustown, the more community-minded men—the ones who've lived to retirement age, or given up altogether—meet daily at the depot. They have come to realize that their town needs a famous resident in order to attract tourists, which will revive the economy. They have realized that it's better to have a diverse population instead of nearly everyone named either Munson or Harrell. These free thinkers have concluded that annual festivals—such as their own Sherman Knew Nothing celebration to point out all that the general missed by swerving away between Savannah and Columbia during his march—don't bring in the recognition or revenue. How can, like the old days, a Calloustown child grasp enough knowledge and culture to understand the importance and benefits of fleeing?

Munny Munson says daily, "If our kids fear the outside world, or never comprehend its offerings—good and bad— then those kids will remain here. You think the gene pool's not wet enough to emit a mirage now, just wait another two generations. We got to do something."

On a particularly bleak day, there in the waiting room, one of the other Munsons, or one of a number of men named Harrell, might say, "Low IQs means less personal hygiene. Less hygiene means more contagious diseases. And then everyone dies and people elsewhere might never appreciate William Tecumseh Sherman's apparent myopia." Or one of the men might go off saying, "Lower IQs means less ambition. Less ambition means not taking care of the yard. High grass means field rats. Field rats attract snakes. Bite from a viper on an ambitionless slow-witted person with influenza would be fatal."

For eight hours a day these men nod, clear their throats, blurt out versions of slippery-slope possibilities, all the time while watching *The Price Is Right*, soap operas, reruns of *I Dream of Jeannie*, *Gilligan's Island*, and *Hogan's Heroes*. They veer from local, state, or national news—"I'm depressed enough, change the channel, I think that one station's doing an *Addams Family* marathon"—and no one ever questions how they could get cable television in a closed-down bus station where no one admits to paying the electric or water bills.

They don't brag about sexual conquests, or reminisce about first times, for each of them has a wife whose brother and cousins stand nearby.

Mack Sloan wipes his soles on the worn rubber Trailways mat out front, turns the knob, and walks into the waiting room. At first he thinks that the men congregated inside laugh at him—as if they judge a man by the overalls he wears and anyone who decides to go out in public wearing fluorescent warm-up pants and a matching windbreaker stands worthless. Then Mack Sloan realizes that the laughter emanates from the television program's laugh track, the volume cranked full. The men watch *The Honeymooners*.

Mack Sloan nods. Munny Munson stands up and turns the volume knob. He says, "Are you the man from the Guinness Book of Records we been waiting on?"

Mack shakes his head. He says, "I'm turned around a little. Any of you men know where I can find the local high school?"

Flint Harrell stands up and leans backward awkwardly so that this stranger—the first non-Calloustowner to enter the bus station in fifteen years—can admire Flint's gold-plated belt buckle embossed with SOUTHERN REGION DISTRICT 4 LEVEL 6 SENIOR DIVISION THIRD PLACE HORSESHOES. Flint says, "If you looking catch a ride there from here, you're late by 1996. Last bus come through ended up taking people down to those Atlanta Olympics."

Mack Sloan does not feel threatened. He almost laughs. This is perfect—he loves being the first scout in a backwards area, coming out of nowhere like some kind of savior to extract an unknown high school athlete from humble beginnings, promise questionable future monetary outcomes. "No, I got a car out front. Just looking for the high school."

Munny Munson says, "We been waiting on the World Record fellow. Me and Lloyd one time played dominoes for sixty-seven straight hours straight. That's got to be some kind of record."

And then, as if in a rural AA meeting when the floor opens up for personal testimonial one-upmanship, each man offers his declaration:

"I can lace a pair of logging boots in fourteen seconds."

"I ate four whole barbecued armadillos in twelve minutes."

"I've stared at thirty-two solar eclipses and ain't gone blind yet."

"I trained an ostrich to clean gutters."

Mack Sloan says, "Okay. This sounds like quite a town. Listen, I know it's pretty small here and everyone's probably related to one another. Do any of you know about Brunson Pettigru, the track star? I'm supposed to go clock this fellow and see if he can really do what they say." Sloan pulls a stopwatch from the pocket of his windbreaker, as if to prove his being an authority.

The waiting room regulars quit talking. What did this man mean by "related to one another"? Had word seeped out about the gene pool?

Munny Munson says, "Track star? No. Never heard of him."

"We don't even have a team anymore, not that I know of," says Flint Harrell.

"Let me see that fancy timepiece," Lloyd says. "I could use one these when I dismantle and reassemble my 1970 Allis Chalmers D270. I believe I got the record unofficially, you know." Then he went into how the world record take-apart-and-put-back-together-a-tractor man might pull in visitors to Calloustown, and then they'd buy hot dogs, and then everyone would gain financially, and then there would be no more threat of pestilence within the failing, bleak, doomed community.

Mack Sloan, indeed, had not heard of Brunson Pettigru via *Track and Field News*, *The Florida Relays*, *Runner's World*, or *Parade* magazine. No, a man named Coach Strainer—who taught PE over the Internet through the South Carolina Virtual School—boasted of his unknown students on his Facebook page wall: 57% of his students could figure out their BMI. One kid had taken online physical education so seriously that he'd dropped five pounds over the semester, and another could explain all the rules of two different darts games, plus badminton. And then there was Brunson Pettigru of Calloustown, a homeschooled white kid, a six-foot two-inch, 155-pound country boy who had—once he fully understood the cardiovascular system's nuances—dropped his quarter-mile time from fifty-five seconds to forty-six, his half mile from 2:08 to 1:50.

Sloan understands that, even at a regular high school with traditional teams, coaches exaggerate. He'd scouted, in the past, a boy who heaved a shot put eighty feet, only to find out the boy's father worked in a machine shop and had shaved weight from the iron sphere. So Mack contacted the S.C. Department of Education, which sent him to the Department of Charter Schools, which sent him to the Department of Online Schools, which eventually offered to have Coach Strainer—"one of our finest educators"—contact Mack in Oregon.

"I didn't believe the kid, either," Strainer had said from his office in Myrtle Beach, which doubled as his dining room. "But I seen it with my own two eye! I got me a friend retired down here from the CIA and he seen it, too, and says they's no way the tape's been sped-up doctored."

One of the waiting room men points out the door and says, "School's down there a piece. You won't miss it. They mascot's a ostrich, so they's a big bird right out front of the place. I mean, a sculpture one."

Another man says, "I know who you mean. He ain't no runner, though. He's a spastic."

"We don't want to be famous-known for spastics," says Munny Munson.

Brunson Pettigru's mother homeschooled her only son, for she viewed the public school system in general disdainfully, and the Calloustown school district in particular. Mrs. Pettigru did not fear that her child might receive secular teaching in regards to science, literature, and religion. To the contrary, she believed a public school filled with children of one denomination only—a school with a population made up almost exclusively of Harrells and Munsons—might corrupt her son into believing in virgin births, no dinosaurs, ribcage wives, and talking bushes. Unlike ninety-nine percent of homeschooling parents in South Carolina, she didn't choose to direct her son's studies so that they would include daily recitations or sing-alongs of the Pledge of Allegiance, the Lord's Prayer, the Star-Spangled Banner, America the Beautiful, and the Second Amendment of the Constitution. No, Betty Pettigru feared that touched-by-God born-again teachers might chance reprimands and recrimination for "doing what God believes to be right."

"If you want to see yearbook photos of people who did what they thought God wanted them to do, go check out any state's Department of Corrections file of mugshots," she told her son often, as she had told her husband, Finis, before he gave up and died of a heart attack in the middle of trying to break the world record for smoking cigarettes in a twenty-four-hour period.

Mack Sloan drives up to Calloustown High and sees Brunson wearing vintage gray drawstring sweatpants down at the cinder track that surrounds what might have been a football field. There isn't but one goalpost, for the Calloustown Ostriches won a game due to forfeit three years earlier—the team from Forty-Five had been forced to suspend all of its players at the last minute when its appeal was denied by the South Carolina High School Athletic League, in regards to having a number of thirty-year-old players who didn't go to college—and the fans in attendance stormed the vacant field and with the use of Harmon Harrell's tractor knocked over the goalpost and carried it into town. From that point on, when a visiting team scored a touchdown, or wanted to attempt a field goal, the teams had to turn around if indeed they had no goalpost in which to direct a kick.

"You're Brunson?" Mack says when he gets down to the field. "You're Brunson's mom?" he asks the woman who stands there, holding what appears to be wide rubber bands meant for strapping furniture to a flatbed's frame. "I'm Mack Sloan."

Mrs. Pettigru says, "I wouldn't be allowing this to happen if there was homecolleging."

Mack says, "What are those things?" and points at the rubber bands.

He hasn't looked closely at his prospect yet. Brunson wears eyeglasses that appear to be fake, the lenses are so thick. He has them tied to his head with what looks like a bra strap. And in a voice that Mack would later describe as something between a tracheotomist's and a kettle spewing steam, Brunson says, "Because of the cardiovascular limits of the heart vis-à-vis oxygen intake, I tie my forelimbs with these industrial bands before I run so that my most vital organ vis-à-vis the running process does not need to validate anything between my glenohumeral joint and my phalanges."

Mack looks at Brunson. He thinks, what if aliens come down to the planet and discover this guy? Wouldn't they wonder if they'd never left home? He says, "All right. You seem to be the kind of guy who might have pre-med in his future."

Mrs. Pettigru, wearing a cotton-print dress, says, "My Brunson has always been interested in animals. Does your college have a veterinary program?"

"I like cheetahs," Brunson says. "They're the fastest. If this school had been called the Calloustown Cheetahs, I might have had to fight my mother about allowing me to matriculate. What's your college's mascot?"

"It's a duck. They're not much on land, but they can fly. Some of them can fly." Mack looks down at Brunson's shoes. The boy wears a pair of regular, flat and slick-bottomed Keds-brand canvas boatshoes. One of the Pettigrus took a bottle of Wite-Out and marked a Nike swoosh on the sides. Mack says, "Duck."

Brunson twists and ties his upper biceps with the two rubber bands. He sits down cross-legged on the track. His mother says, "It's important for Brunson to achieve the correct amount of tingling in his arms before he runs a lap."

Mack Sloan thinks, there's no way I'll ever recommend offering this kid a scholarship. He thinks, people think members of our track team are freaks already?—get a load of this new guy! He thinks, hell, I'm here—I might as well see what happens. He thinks, cardiovascular vis-à-vis cheetah glenohumeral joint and my phalanges veterinary school vital organ homecolleging.

"A fun thing to do is have me run a quarter mile without the additional garments, and then compare and contrast what happens once my heart no longer has to pump blood to needless expanses," Brunson says.

"Okay," Mack says. He'd dealt with runners who insisted on smoking pot the night before a race, runners who drank six beers the night before a race, runners who had to fuck two different women the night before a race and then another one a couple hours before the starting gun. Mack had dealt with runners—world-class runners—who insisted on eating sushi, or Vienna sausages, or Fig Newtons. He'd had runners who had to watch *The Godfather: Part III* the night before a big race, and others who insisted that virgins recite the poems of Gerard Manley Hopkins.

But not this.

"You about ready?" Mack says.

Betty Pettigru says, "I'm going to take my spot in the stands. I always sit in the stands. When I'm in the stands, my son's never lost a race."

"Wait a minute," Mack says. "So you're on the track team here?"

"I've never been in an actual race," Brunson says. "Do you think that might make a difference? I mean, psychologically, it might make me run either faster or slower."

While I'm down this way, Mack Sloan thinks, I might as well go down to Myrtle Beach and kill that Coach Strainer dude.

"Uh-oh," Brunson says. He stands up, and half lifts one arm toward the parking lot. "Somebody's here."

Mack turns around to see every man whom he'd met at the bus depot. They walk down the embankment. One of them says, "We just thought we'd come on down here and see if we got us a savior."

Mack pulls the stopwatch out of his pocket. He says, "I didn't even think to ask—are you sure this is a quarter-mile track? It looks like a quarter mile, but are you sure?"

"It's 440 yards," Brunson says. "I've circled it ten times with the Lufkin MW18TP Measuring Wheel, and it came out to 13,200 feet. And then I divided that by three, which comes out to 4400 yards, and then divided that by ten, which comes out to 440 yards. I thought about doing a hundred laps, just to make sure, but it was getting dark and I still had to write a term paper for my mother comparing and contrasting the Suez Canal with the Panama Canal. A cheetah can swim across both of them, by the way. A cheetah's not the fastest swimmer, but it can swim."

"I'm ready!" Betty Pettigru yells from the wooden bleachers.

The bus depot men arrive trackside. One of them says, "I don't know."

Mack Sloan says to Brunson, "You don't need any blocks or anything? Don't you think you better stretch, or warm up a little? You might want to take off your sweats, too."

Munny Munson says, "I still believe we got a better shot at making Calloustown famous if we become home to a serial killer, as opposed to a spastic." He says, "Hell, Betty Pettigru's ex-husband had the right idea, up until he smoked himself to death."

"I'd like to fuck her," one of the Harrells says. "She ain't nobody's sister."

Brunson says, "I've heard about those block things. Do you think they'll really help?" He pulls off his sweatpants to reveal what may or may not be an old pair of his mother's hot pants from the 1970s. When he toes the line, his arms swing half useless.

———

"Go!" Mack Sloan says. He's performed this task so many times he can't remember. He has timed prospective athletes in thirty states. He's gone down to Central America and found sprinters, South America for middle-distance runners, and Africa for long-distance runners.

Brunson takes off. His mother bellows, "Catch that big cat, honey, catch that big cat!" and makes some odd noises in between, like long, extended Ummms that might point toward a nervous tic, or Tourette's. Mack Sloan keeps his eyes on his prospect, but the Munson and Harrell men stare up toward the stands. Betty Pettigru's mid-sentence, guttural noises—by the time Brunson hits the 220 mark—now sound as if they're caused by orgasm.

"Jesus Christ," Mack says. "Twenty-two seconds flat." He yells out to Brunson, "Keep it coming, my man. Push through it. Keep your form!"

Brunson takes the back straightaway and—there was no way for Mack Sloan to explain this later to his colleagues— his arms go haywire. He keeps running well, and stays in his lane, but his arms, out of blood flow, look similar to those twenty-five-foot ripstop nylon sky tubes normally used for advertising purposes in the parking lots of car dealerships, mattress warehouses, and buffet-style restaurants managed by the criminally insane.

Was the kid dancing? Mack thinks. Is he fighting demons that no one but his mother—still ululating in the stands— can see?

He clicks the stopwatch when Brunson hits the finish line, slows down to a jog, and continues forward, untying the rubber bands from his arms. Forty-six flat, sure enough, just like Virtual Coach Strainer declared. Mack Sloan looks up in the bleachers and notices how Betty Pettigru sits with her legs splayed open. He looks at the bus depot men and says, "I've never seen anything like this in all my years. I've been coaching since I was out of college. This is the damnedest place I've ever seen. Is this one of those trick TV shows? Is someone playing a trick on me, and I'm being filmed covertly?"

Munny Munson says, "I bet I know why old Finis's heart give out, and it didn't have nothing to do with smoking 144 cigarettes in a row the way he done. Hot damn that woman's a regular vixen."

"She appears to love her son, you got that right," says Mack Sloan. He calls Brunson back to him, but keeps looking up in the stands. Betty Pettigru has pulled her hair up in some kind of topknot. "Listen, don't you men have something to do with yourselves? I'm working here."

Mack jogs down the track. He says, "Good God, man, you can flat-out fly. But I don't know about those rubber bands around your arms. I'm not so sure they'd let you run like that in a race, what with the possibility of injuring other runners. Especially in the eight hundred."

Brunson says, "What about if I go ahead and cut off my arms? Is that what you want? I'm not going to cut off my arms just to please you."

Mrs. Pettigru comes down from the bleachers and says, "Brunson. Don't start, Brunson."

"I'm sorry."

"Brunson has some anger issues," Mrs. Pettigru says. "That might be an overstatement. He has some issues with patience."

"Can I see you run without those strange rubber bands?" Mack asks.

Betty Pettigru stands close to Mack. Is she flirting with me? he wonders. Is this her way of seeing her son get a scholarship?

"Do you have no imagination?" Brunson blurts out. "You saw me run once. Now imagine me running again, without the rubber bands that enhance my cardiovascular capabilities."

Mrs. Pettigru says, "Brunson," again, this time drawling out his name, in a higher pitch.

"Is there any place we can sit down and talk?" Mack asks. He wonders if the rubber bands affected the oxygen supply to Brunson's head, thus causing the sudden evident fury.

"I'm sorry," Brunson says. "I'm sorry, sorry, sorry," he says, and takes off running around the track, then over a fence and into the woods.

Betty Pettigru looks at her wristwatch. She says, "I'm about ready for a martini. What about you, Coach?"

There's no one inside Worm's Bar and Grill. There's no bartender, either. Betty Pettigru walks behind the counter, pulls a fifth of Absolut off the shelf, and pours four shots into a metal shaker, throws in some ice, swirls it around, and pours two glasses to the brim. "I like mine dry," she says. "You want an olive in yours? Worm doesn't believe in cocktail onions."

"Yeah, I'll take a couple olives," Mack says. He had followed Betty on the one-mile drive between the high school and downtown Calloustown, and noticed that she drank something from a Thermos along the way.

Betty Pettigru slides a jar of Thrifty Maid–brand green olives down the counter. She says, "This should answer any questions about why I didn't move away when Brunson's daddy died. Not many places around will let you walk in and drink on the honor system."

"Will he be all right?" Mack asks. "I'm worried about him."

"No, he's probably going to stay dead. We had him cremated, so even the most advanced advances in science won't bring him back." She walks around the counter and sits down on a stool beside Mack.

She puts her hand on his shoulder.

"I'm talking about your son. Is he going to be all right, that's what I meant."

"He's fine. He has a lot of things on his mind. He took the SAT and scored perfect on the math but only made a 740 on the verbal. He's taking the thing again."

Mack drinks and says, "This is like straight vodka."

"I don't know what I'm going to do when he leaves the nest. Listen. Do you think the university would want a student who scored a perfect SAT and can run that fast? I'm willing to bet that just about every college would want such a student."

Mack thinks, is that lipstick, or are her lips really that red? He thinks, I need to make some promises I can't keep. "I'm thinking Brunson wouldn't have a problem getting a full ride."

"And what about me?" Betty says. She scoots over closer. "I hear tell of some colleges hiring on parents, you know, to work at the college. Coach. Work as a secretary. Me, I could fit right in teaching in the education department, seeing as I'm batting nearly perfect with my past students."

Mack Sloan nods and laughs. He says, "I don't know of any bars that'll let you go in there and drink on the honor system, though."

She puts her hand on his left thigh. Mack thinks, no, no, no, no, no. He says, "It's only track and field, Ms. Pettigru. It's not like football or basketball."

"I like to do this in alphabetical order," she says, getting up from the barstool. "Absolut done, Grey Goose next." She looks at the bottles lined up. "Worm got some Ketel One! That'll be a good segue before I get on to that cheap shit Seagram's and Smirnoff, before heading out to the," she picks up a bottle and raises her eyebrows to Mack, "Three Olives."

"You're going to have to go that route alone, I'm afraid," Mack says. "I got to get down the road and check out a two-miler from somewhere," he lies, though in fact he's scheduled to talk to a distance runner from Georgia tomorrow.

The phone rings. Betty shrugs and picks it up. She says, "Hello?" instead of "Worm's Bar and Grill." Mack stands up and thinks about going to his car and driving away. Betty says into the receiver, "I'm not doing anything wrong. You can come on over here and see for yourself," and then the door opens, Brunson walks in with a cell phone to his head, and both he and his mother hang up.

Brunson says, "I told you I could rig this cell phone to get good reception, even here where we don't get reception." He says to Mack Sloan, "I've been reconsidering."

His mother walks back carrying the bottles of Grey Goose and Ketel One. She says, "I'm about to get you a football scholarship, too, boy."

Brunson says, "Can I have a beer, Mom?" He says, "After I drink some olive juice to replace the salt I lost running, can I have a beer?"

Betty reaches over the bar and slides back the cooler top. She reaches in and gets a can of PBR. To Mack Sloan she says, "I'm not a bad mother. Or a whore."

Worm walks in through the back door. He says, "Well, well, well, I heard we had us a bigshot stranger in town. Hey, Betty Pettigru." He keeps his eyes locked on Mack. "Hey, Brunson. You got your ID for that beer?"

Brunson says, "I forgot it again."

"Bring it on in next time," Worm says. He wears a sleeveless white dress shirt, blue jeans with holes in the knees. He sports a tattoo on each arm—a speed bag on his left, and a heavy bag on the right. To Mack he says, "Just come back from the depot. You're the talk of Calloustown." Worm sticks out his hand to shake, which Mack does. "Next to some old boy from the Guinness World Record book showing up, I guess you're about all that and a roll of duct tape, ain't you?"

Mack doesn't know what he means. He says, "Are you a boxer, or ex-boxer?" and points to the tattoos. Betty Pettigru leads her son over to the jukebox. They stare at its buttons and choices as if it were a time machine.

"That's the way we are here in Calloustown," Worm says. "We try to make things easier for everything. Back in the day, my great-great-grandmother went out to what's now I-95 and tried to lead General Sherman back to Calloustown so he could burn it. Least that's the story. Anyway, back when I was in junior high school I got bullied a bunch seeing as I'm so skinny and got called Worm, so later on—maybe in the tenth grade—I went over the state line and got these tattoos so my enemies would have a target to punch, you know."

Betty and Brunson return to the stools. Worm goes around the other side, to work as the bartender. Brunson says, "I guess I could try out as something like a kick returner. If you confess that my mom's not a whore, then I'll be willing to try out as a kick returner."

Mack tries to think if he actually called Betty a whore. Worm slides another double shot of cold vodka his way. He says, "Because all that reading you do, Brunson, I'm sure you've come across how constant—heck, even infrequent—constriction of limbs can result in nerve damage. Next thing you know you got gangrene and have to have the limb amputated."

Brunson drinks his beer like a professional. He says, "I don't care. What would it matter? If getting my arms cut off in the future is the only way I can get out of Calloustown, so be it."

"You don't mean that," his mother says.

"Come over here and hit me in the arm," says Worm. He tenses his muscles. "What you need, boy, is a tattoo like mine. That's what's made it worthwhile for me to stay."

"When's the last time the cigarette man came by here, Worm? I want me a pack of cigarettes, but I don't want any of those you got in there stale. As I recall, Finis bought his last cigarettes from that machine," Betty says. She pulls the hem of her dress right on up to her eyes and wipes them, showing off a pair of panties that weren't bought anywhere in South Carolina, Mack thinks—SHAKE, RATTLE, AND ROLL printed in red lettering across the front. She says, "I'm sorry.

I don't even think Brunson knows this, but it's our anniversary." To Mack she says, "How about you giving me an anniversary present?"

Brunson hits the floor. He either wants attention or undergoes a full-scale seizure. Mack says, "I have a carton of cigarettes out in the car. Let me go get you a couple packs."

"Menthol?" Betty says.

"Yeah. Let me go get them right now for you. Is Brunson okay?" he asks as he opens the door.

Mack Sloan starts up the car and takes off. He needs to U-turn at some point, but he wants out of there. There's something bad in the water here, he thinks. He thinks, I will go back home and say that the virtual high school P.E. teacher didn't know what he's talking about. He turns on the radio and hits Search, only to find nothing, then switches over to A.M. stations, hits Search, and still finds nothing. He thinks, a forty-six second quarter-miler with a near-perfect SAT. When will I ever come across another one of those? Mack flips open his cell phone and gets no signal.

When he approaches the bus depot he notices that a number of handwritten signs now dot the roadside: Told You So. Don't Come Back Unless You Mean It. Sherman Sucked, Too.

What can he do but turn around? What can he do but try not to think ahead to the future, when he's sitting around his house at night, awaiting a knock at the door, knowing that someone wants to come in and talk about his or her problems in regards to homesickness, or nerves? The radio catches a station. A man gives the weather report and says that the drought has been modified from extreme to exceptional. He reminds listeners to put water out for animals, and notes that not all foaming-mouthed dogs have contracted rabies.

These Deep Barbs Irremovable

After Louise took off, and seeing as I didn't fully believe my doctor's prediction in regards to what would happen inside my liver should I ever attempt to dry out the states of Kentucky and Tennessee again, I found myself wanting to enter Calloustown proper and find a bar. I'd gone beyond thinking rationally and mentally side-stepped loading up on sweets or downing six pork chops—everything I'd read up on in regards to ways to quench a sudden urgent bourbon twinge. This was at my dead mother's house, which had been my parents' house where I grew up before Dad got sent to prison. I returned to settle affairs, as they say. I had to go through personal effects, pile things up for auction, retain what I found necessary to keep for sentimental reasons. I had at this point only set aside my father's .22 rifle, an item that indirectly offered me the notoriety I'd received from the age of thirteen on. Maybe I wandered around the house talking to myself. Maybe I felt certain that Louise had waited for the right time to leave our marriage and used my mother's death and my new entrepreneurial mishap as her excuse.

To be fair, "took off" isn't exactly what Louise did. "After Louise changed all the locks on our doors back when I returned to Calloustown, the place of my upbringing, in order to bury my mother and work as the executor of the will," might be a more appropriate way to put it. This was sixty miles from where Louise and I had lived together for fifteen years. Louise called to say I could return for clothes, but that her lawyer advised her not to let me take anything else. "My lawyer says you should probably stay in Calloustown. You can come get your clothes. And your goddamn pets, which are driving me insane." I doubted she even had a lawyer at this point but found no reason to argue.

I could've easily told my wife to turn off the heat and lights, but thought this: if she couldn't withstand an entrepreneurial mishap—especially after everything else I'd endured in regards to jobs and the Guinness World Records anthology—then I wasn't going to give her any pointers. I never found out, but I might've been roaming aimlessly in my mother's house actually saying aloud, "Turn off the heat and lights if you want to quiet my so-called pets," when I realized that a woman stood on the porch, cupping her hands into the screen door.

She wore a nametag with ADAZEE printed out in block letters. She said in a quiet voice, "I know you. You're that guy in the famous book."

My first words to Adazee, as she stood there wearing an apron, holding one of those cheap, unhealthy, overly frosted rectangular sheet cakes, were, "No. No, I'm not in the Bible." It's a response like that that got me fired from my last job, something I said drunk to strangers wanting to pay good money for a sub-par education.

Listen, not everyone knew my story. People already knew that Louise left me, probably, but not everyone in the county knew how my father gathered bald-faced hornets' paper nests and then sold them to the Chinese for medicinal purposes, how he would shoot nests the size of medicine balls off of oak tree limbs with a .22 and I would stand below to catch them so they wouldn't get damaged. My father used high-powered binoculars and watched the prospective nests for activity. It's not like he was an idle, irresponsible father. Before I helped him he had learned the nuances of paper nest–collecting through trial and error; then—after I became his thirteen-year-old assistant and the accident happened—he never re-lied on first frosts killing off all members of the hive.

I said, "I'm kidding. I know what you're talking about. Yeah, I'm still in that book, from what I understand," though to be honest I bought the latest edition each September and looked for my name. "It's plain called the Guinness World Records book, by the way. Most people call it the Guinness Book of World Records, but they're wrong. It's the Guinness World Records book, and then a year after it." I didn't go into how a few of the new editions had special features, like how the 2008 anthology had glow-in-the-dark sections, and 2009 featured "all new 3-D photography." Personally, I thought the Guinness people should go back to a plain old black-and-white format, but that's just me.

"Tell me how many times you got stung," Adazee said. I thought, oh, I get it: A to Z. Her parents were idiots.

I said, "Do you want to come in?"

Adazee didn't move. "I work over at Tiers of Joy bakery, and we've been remiss in sending you a cake. No one's ever made it official, but we're like Calloustown's Welcome Wag-on, especially now that we don't have a florist anymore."

"I forget how many stings," I said, and hoped she didn't bring up how some guy named Johannes Relleke got stung

2,443 times by bees back in 1962. First off, that was in Rhodesia, which isn't still around. Two, a bee's stinger is probably one-third the size of a bald-faced hornet's. I said, "I still carry some stingers beneath my skin, they say, so the official count's not exactly official."

Beneath her apron spilled out on her chest an A and a Z, left to right. I wouldn't know until later that she wore one of those tourist shirts from Alcatraz, with a number beneath it, as if the old famous convicts wore such garb. Adazee said, "Buzz something. Your name is Buzz something or other."

I shook my head. "I was just thinking about cake, I swear to God," I said, but didn't go into details about how I'd been shaking and wanting booze.

No, I thought about how I got called Buzz, all right, from the moment I returned from the burn clinic in Augusta—I still have no clue as to who thought that would be the proper setting for a boy with a thousand-plus hornet stingers in his body—to my desk at Calloustown Junior High, then right up until I understood that I needed to vacate my hometown's limits, go to college, get married, attempt to change the world, lose my job due to "unprofessional behavior and insubordination," then return half-heartedly without my wife to settle my mother's affairs.

My father, still alive, couldn't work as the executor seeing as he lived in prison for selling bald-faced hornet nests to the Chinese without fully understanding antitrust laws plus forgetting to pay taxes over twenty years, among other questionable practices in the realm of business ethics.

"Buzz Munson? Buzz Harrell?" Adazee said, hopeful, smart enough to know that since ninety percent of Calloustown's population ended in a "Munson" or "Harrell" she would likely hit the mark.

Man, by this point there with lovely Adazee—I had already experienced my near-daily flashback of standing beneath a paper hornet nest that hadn't gone inactive, mid-November, my father aiming for the slight branch that sagged from the gray orb's weight, the shot's crack, my perfected soft catch, and the hornets streaming for neck, face, hands, and bare arms—I jonesed for booze worse than a stung boy yearns for a slather of saliva-enhanced cigarette tobacco atop his wounds. I looked at my wristwatch and said, "If you ain't coming inside, how about you show me the closest bar in town? I need a drink. I'll buy."

Adazee smiled. "Here you go," she said, handing over the cake. "It's the freshest we had. Well, it's tied for freshest with six others that no one came to pick up. Ever since they changed the requirements for high school graduation, not everyone quite made it, I guess. Or their parents forgot what they ordered, but I doubt it."

She handed over a cake that read MISTY! CLASS OF 2010! CONGRATULATIONS! in gray and black frosting, the school colors for the Calloustown High School Fighting Ostriches.

I said, "I don't get it," because I wondered if she meant to bring the cake to someone else. "I'm not Misty. My real name's Luther Steadman."

Adazee said, "Seeing as we're not officially the Welcome Wagon, we just give out cakes that we either messed up or that the people didn't come get."

I flipped back the cellophane-windowed cover, scooped out about two thousand calories, and shoved it in my mouth right there on my parents' old front porch. I'm talking I scooped up MISTY with my bare hands and funneled her in. My teeth hurt from what refined sugar scraped against my enamel. I tried to say, "I am Luther Steadman" again, but blew crumbs out of my mouth.

"So, they're saying that you might be moving back for good, and that you're wife isn't coming with you," Adazee said. "And do you really think you should go back to drinking? I always heard that you had a slight problem, and that it started right after you got stung over a thousand times."

I don't know if any psychologists have delved into this, but if you ask me there's nothing but trouble that can happen to a person who comes from a small town, gains notoriety that's deserved or not—which causes locals to either hate said person or treat him like a celebrity—then have that person move away, return begrudgingly, and try to fit in. I don't know if there's something called You-Think-You-Too-Good-for-Us-Now-Son? syndrome, but there should be. I left Calloustown for college, found out that most guys on my hall didn't care about how many times I'd been stung, didn't care that I was the only person at the college with his name in about one-point font inside the Guinness World Records book, sulked for a few years, graduated, and immediately got a job at the college in the admissions office as a "recruitment specialist." Someone there figured out that I might be valuable as a recruiter of prospective students in the Carolinas, say things like, "If someone like me can graduate, then you can, too!" all giddy. It should've been "like I can graduate," I know, but the higher-ups didn't want me coming off like I had an IQ over 96.

On top of this great job, which kept me on the road meeting some of my state's more low-bar scholars, I made money on the side as a pitchman for various exterminator companies doing well enough to buy radio and/or TV ads. "You don't want to end up in the Guinness World Records book like me, so call up Perry Connor's Pest Control and have him come snoop around your eaves for wasp nests. Annual check-ups might keep you from getting stung!" Stuff like that, which, too, should've been "in the Guinness World Records book like I," but most people who hired out Perry probably went to my alma mater. Hell, my work even bled into areas having nothing to do with hornets. It's my voice saying, "I got stung by so many hornets that it didn't look like I had a future. Remember, people, that you can't spell 'furniture' without 'f-u-t-u-r-e.' So go on down to Crazy Mike's and tell him, 'Who needs IKEA!'" which I'm surprised they didn't make me call "Me-KEA."

Then my father got thrown in prison. Then my mother died. Then some people starting talking about things I said to prospective students about how perhaps they should move out of state, or work at McDonald's. Then a lot of overblown stories went around about drinking I'd committed in prospective students' hometowns—I'm pretty sure these rumors emanated from Calloustown—and the next thing you know I got released from my college job and the radio spots evaporated. Sometimes, when I'm trying to dig out a long-standing stinger from my inner bicep, I wonder about all the cause-and-effect types of features in everyday life and wonder if maybe the answer showed up in a course I once took in existentialism. It's not like I could fully pay attention in that class. The professor was one of those nature guys who made us sit in a circle outside most warm days, and with bees buzzing by, or Weed Eaters going off in the distance, I pretty much sat around cross-legged expecting another swarm of hornets while trying to keep my sphincter from shaking hands with my uvula.

Adazee told me I could follow her a couple miles down the road to a place called Worm's. I picked up the cake from my mother's dining-room table and left the house without even locking up. If it matters, Adazee drove the bakery's van, which had bumper stickers that read PASTRY CHEFS DO IT UNTIL THEY'RE GLAZED and REAL MEN EAT MUFFINS.

Listen, I loved Louise before she took off, and I love her now. She was and is a beautiful, smart woman. I met her in college. She studied pre-veterinary, didn't get into vet school—man, that's harder than getting into med school—and got a job at AfriCall of the Wild, a fancy over-bloated petting zoo that catered to school groups and drew the ire of PETA, the regular zoo in Columbia, and the NAACP, according to Louise. She fed old ex-circus lions and elephants. She mucked stalls. I don't think her father ever said anything about how his investment in her college education didn't exactly pay off, but I can't be sure. He didn't talk much to me.

After we parked side by side and got on the sidewalk near the bar, I said to Adazee, "You seem to be a beautiful, smart woman." Looking back, it was all the goddamn sugar from the Misty cake. I doubt I would've been so bold without a diabetic onslaught on the horizon. "I don't need to have a drink anymore. If you don't want to go to the bar, that's fine by me."

"Well, I believe I might have carpal tunnel from the whisk. I need a drink every day. And just so you know"—she took off her apron as we walked in—"you're old enough to be my father, so don't get any ideas. I mean, I'm all excited to hang out with you and everything, but not in a romantic way."

I said, of course, "I'm not but forty. How old are you?"

This is where I saw that Alcatraz shirt, and her—again, I still loved Louise, so it's not like I started limping across the street—gigantic, ungainly breasts. Between dealing with a whisk, hunching over a mixer, and standing on her feet all day as a chef of one sort or another, Adazee had nothing but a scoliosistic future teeming with greedy chiropractors and hyperbolic support-brassiere manufacturers.

She said, "I'm twenty-nine. According to that book you're in, there has been an eleven-year-old daddy, so there. Or maybe someone around here was eleven, I forget." She opened the door for me so I didn't drop the cake. To the man behind the bar she said, "Hey, Worm. You remember Buzz Steadman, don't you?"

I knew Worm from the old days growing up in Calloustown. Back then he went by plain Stuart, as far as I could remember. He was one of the Harrell clan. Worm said, "No. Never heard of him," like that, which is what everyone had always said to me, even when I came back home for Christmas during college.

We were the only patrons. Stuart Harrell stood behind the counter, half of his gray short-sleeved shirt untucked. He wore work boots and blue jeans and could've been mistaken for most meter readers in the area. One of his eyes seemed to go off in a funny direction at times, and he might've cut his own hair. The place looked like every neighborhood bar I'd come across during all my years traveling the Carolinas after meeting in a high school counselor's conference room with students who planned to take the SAT again in order to make a 420 on both parts so they could say "Four-twenty!" as often as possible and light a joint. Dark walls and black barstools with foam rubber hemorrhaging out of mid-cushion rips. Lampshades that advertised Pabst and Budweiser. Burn marks trenching the wooden counter. Last year's calendar up on the wall from an auto parts company. I said, "Hey, Stuart. Or Worm." Instead of music, a man spoke over the bar's speakers. I said, "What's that?" and pointed to the wall.

Worm said, "Some kind of made-up ordinance. Before they'd let me open up this bar—we're within a hundred yards of a church—I had to agree to let Reverend Mixon make me play some cassette tapes he made of sermons he's said. Sometimes he sends in members of his congregation to check me out, see if I'm actually playing them. They drink and drink and drink, and all the time say they're making sure I'm playing his goddamn sermons. I don't know what's worse—having to play his sermons, or when the off-key Calloustown Second Baptist Church choir starts singing."

Adazee said, "I'll have a screwdriver."

Worm said to me, "I'm not supposed to serve you anything stronger than mixer. Your ex-wife called up and said she figured you might be coming by here soon."

I didn't go, "I thought you didn't know me." I said, "I don't want anything to drink anymore. It passed. You got a Dr. Pepper back there?"

He reached in the cold box and pulled out a can. "Four dollars. We're having a hard time getting these in. Supply and demand." Now, understand, in the old days I wouldn't have put up with a man who enjoyed being called Worm and who prided himself on getting one over on a man who'd remained in the Guinness World Record book for over twenty-five years. But I'd been reading up on some breathing techniques, and along with the muscle relaxers I took quadra-daily, I could handle just about every situation outside of the minor pangs of remembrance.

I said, "Can I run a tab?"

He handed Adazee her drink. Worm said, "I'da thought you'd want a tequila, what with all those Mexican jumping beans you got in your house."

I said, "A-HA!" like that, and stood up. "If you don't remember my living in Calloustown back in the day and even going to school with you, how do you know about those jumping beans?" Adazee didn't seem affected whatsoever. She looked at herself in the mirror and brushed flour out of her hair.

Here's the story: While driving around from high school to high school over the years, I noticed that no convenience stores sold those little plastic boxes—two by two by one inch deep—that held Mexican jumping beans. I thought, man, as a little kid I loved having those things around, and listening to them clack when I turned my desk lamp on. I thought, America has fallen into a deep chasm in regards to national pride, and perhaps it all goes back to small children not being able to understand the inherent hopeless qualities of the Mexican jumping bean. Sometimes while talking to prospective students I asked them about Mexican jumping beans, and they had no clue what I was talking about, or the smarter kids would accuse me of being politically incorrect.

So in a moment of weakness, between losing my job, my mother dying, and my father sending me a letter from prison asking me to come visit him some time and bring a cake with a sharp knife inside so he could cut off his cellmate's dick, I took out my savings, cashed in my retirement, and contacted a man named Guillermo down in the state of Chihuahua, who got me in contact with an ex-drug smuggler named Jorge. Meanwhile, I talked to some people at PlastiConCo and ordered little clear jumping bean containers that snapped open and shut. I typed up little instructions to be placed inside the boxes that pointed out that the Mexican jumping bean was really a moth larva living inside a pod produced by a shrub, and that the beans needed to be watered at times, and that the larva responded to heat.

I went all out. The beans showed up at my house in six boxes with COFFEE stamped on the outsides because, as it ended up, it was illegal to mail the things across a border without proper documentation and whatnot. I tried not to think about how some guy in Mexico was my father's doppelganger. Inside the boxes—which could've held large microwaves, or medium-sized television sets—were burlap bags with COFFEE stamped on them. In retrospect, I should be surprised that they even showed up. It would've been easy for my sending money down to Guillermo, who would take a cut before sending money to Jorge, and then those two hombres plain disappearing.

A box that size can hold a lot of Mexican jumping beans, by the way.

I got to work shoving the beans inside their containers. Louise came home and said, "I hope this works," but she was skeptical.

I wrote the main people at 7-Eleven, The Pantry, E-Z Mart, Stuckeys, Kum 'n Go, and all of the convenience stores attached to BP, Texaco, Citgo, Shell, Sunoco, Hess, and Exxon. I wrote to everyone. And talk about being politically incorrect and xenophobic: Every response I got back, somewhere between the lines, pointed out how Mexican jumping beans would either A) cause white people to think that the convenience store didn't care about border patrols, immigration laws, and so on, and then they'd boycott the store, or B) cause Hispanics to think that the convenience store made fun of them, and then they'd boycott the store. One vice president wrote to me personally and said his company learned a lesson when they chose to sell "rattlesnake eggs," some idiot kid choked on the paperclip and rubber band housed inside the envelope, and the company lost a lawsuit that made any too-hot-coffee-from-McDonald's settlement look like a parking ticket violation.

I should've written the stores first, as it ends up, before ordering the jumping beans.

So. I had stacks and stacks of jumping beans in the house. Every time I turned on the heat, or opened up the blinds, or turned on the lights, those things went off clicking and clacking. Louise couldn't take it, she left the marriage, and I moved my belongings.

Worm said, "Maybe I do remember you, then. I can't remember everyone who comes into the bar who thinks they should be remembered for being famous."

Adazee started laughing. "My brother Bernard could've dropped you down to second place." She looked up at Worm. "You remember? Tell Buzz here about my brother."

Worm stared hard at Adazee. From the speakers, Reverend Mixon's voice came out saying, "'Oh, that I were as in months past, as in the days when God preserved me...'" which was straight out of Job. My old college depended on mediocre students brought up in the church, so I needed to be able to recognize and quote scriptural passages on a whim. Worm said, "I don't know your brother. I have never heard you had a brother."

Adazee said, "Yes you have. Anyway, Bernard might have been the best trumpet player to have ever lived. He won first place in the state competition, and then got invited to play down in New Orleans for the national competition."

Worm walked away, and when Adazee didn't comment on his rudeness I understood that he already knew the story and that Adazee knew she'd told him the trumpet story at some point. I said, "How old is Bernard? Back when I went to Calloustown High we didn't even have a trumpet section in the marching band. Two of those Munson boys played bugle, which kind of limited the band's repertoire."

"Larry and Terry Munson," Adazee said. "They're probably third and fourth on the list of famous-from-here, seeing they got that award at a big Civil War reenactment competition up in Franklin, Tennessee. Don't quote me on that. There's Barry Harrell, who published his own book called *What I've Thought about Duct Tape.* He might be third."

Reverend Mixon said, "'Behold, I am vile; what shall I answer thee? I will lay my hand upon my mouth,'" which, too, was straight out of Job.

"Bernard's between you and me, age-wise. He's my big brother. Anyway, he got down to compete in New Orleans, and this band director from somewhere up north had the second-best trumpet player for a student. Bernard didn't even have a formal teacher, unless you include Herb Albert and the Tijuana Brass albums he used to listen to nonstop." Adazee got up off her stool, walked around the bar, seemed to be aware that her boobs might brush up against things, and made another drink. To me she whispered, "You want anything while I'm back here?"

I wanted everything, and maybe a little cocaine. I said, "I better be on my way soon," though I knew I wouldn't be able to go and hear that clack-clack-clacking. I pretty much believed that those jumping beans spelled out "This is why your wife left" in Morse code.

Adazee came back and shifted her stool closer to mine. "My brother's main competition, the number-two guy? He somehow got Bernard to play a drinking game. He told my brother it was a game called Instinct, and real musicians were best at it. In the game, a guy closes his eyes and puts his hands on a table palms down. I'm not sure what is supposed to happen next."

I said, "I know that game, except you keep your eyes open. We used to call it Slaps." Adazee's tits belonged in the Guinness World Records, I thought. I needed to find a way to bring that up, how I—as a regular contributor in the annual anthology—could be some kind of witness if she took off her Alcatraz shirt and brassiere, and let me band a measuring tape around her torso.

"I'm not talking rock-paper-scissors, or rock-paper-scissors-dynamite," Adazee said. She drank from her glass and grimaced. "I'm not talking rock-paper-scissors-dynamite-stapler-pee."

I think it was at this point where I said to myself, "You have made a mistake, Luther."

"Anyway, Bernard closed his eyes to play the game—he was the best brother in the world and didn't want anyone to feel uncomfortable—and the next thing he remembered was regaining consciousness with his right hand nailed to the table.

And I mean it wasn't attached to the rest of his arm. That fellow nailed his hand to the table, then took out an ax and chopped it right off. My brother couldn't play the trumpet in the competition, or ever again, really. So that's why you're still number one in Calloustown."

I looked across to the bottles of good bourbon—there's only good bourbon, even the ones that end in "Gentleman." I don't know if I opened my mouth and stuck my tongue out, over and over. I thought of Louise, and wondered what she thought, dealing with sick, damaged, and forlorn animals that once lived on a different continent. Did she talk to them? Did she try to convince these brutes I was a fool for working a decade and a half trying to recruit bootless scholars to an "institution of higher learning," then falling for entrepreneurial scams that I invented myself?

Adazee said, "Maybe it's for the best. You're probably the kind of man who understands 'maybe for the best,' right? I mean, Jesus, you'd have to, Buzz. Bernard quit playing the trumpet, and he took up singing, and the next thing you know he's appeared on Broadway in a couple musicals. He's been a pirate, seeing as he can wear a hook easier than anyone else! Bernard says he's planning to come back here someday to re-open the florist shop, seeing as it's been closed for a while and people shouldn't have to drive out of town to buy a bouquet. And he says that if someone beats him to it, he wants to come back and open an ice skating rink and teach the youth how to perform triple Axels."

I hate to admit, and I am not proud, that the first two things I thought were A) a florist shop might be the perfect place to sell Mexican jumping beans, and B) your ex-trumpet-playing, Broadway-singing, florist-aspiring, ice-skating brother who might've one day been in the Guinness World Record anthology as the trumpeter who can play "Flight of the Bumblebees" faster than anyone, is perhaps a gay man who would be ostracized more than I, and perhaps killed, in Calloustown.

I said, "Huh."

Adazee kept talking and talking for maybe twenty minutes. She named off everyone she knew in Calloustown who could've been a world record holder of one type or another, had they owned either luck or tenacity. She continued her monologue until Worm came back through the back door. They looked at each other for a second too long, I noticed, and then she excused herself for the restroom which, I learned later, had a hand-painted sign that read UNSEX on it.

I said to Worm, "Goddamn she's got the biggest boobs I've ever seen."

"You remember that time when we were at that 'spend the night' party over at Ms. Whalen's house the night before the Sherman Knew Nothing festival?"

It's not something anyone would forget. Every year Ms. Whalen—the sixth-grade teacher—had a sleepover party so that her husband could tell the boys about sex. The sixth-grade girls spent the night elsewhere and received sex ed from a woman. This was a Calloustown tradition, and the next day the boys and girls met up in order to watch men burn down a courthouse that never existed. According to legend, General Sherman thought our town worthless and swerved between Savannah and Columbia. Seven or eight generations later, descendants of the original Calloustowners still felt slighted, and it showed in their everyday goings-on, thus why Stuart "Worm" Harrell shunned me at first.

I said, "Yeah. Somebody pulled out his pecker to show off pubic hair, and you and I went back home. As a matter of fact, I remember our promising one another we'd never tell anyone about that night."

Worm said, "Exactly. I'm glad you remember. I'm about to tell you something, and I want you to make that same promise with me, at least for a day. Promise?"

I nodded. I said, "What's up?"

"Listen. You might be the man I been looking for. Listen. And don't think I don't know that a man like you gets good money for advice. Ever since you come back because your daddy's in prison for mass murder, I've been thinking about how I could get in that book of famous records. We need us another celebrity in Calloustown so we don't plain dry up. Economy's bad enough. Bad economy without even a Virgin Mary sighting on a tree trunk or pothole spells out disaster, if you ask me."

I said, "I'll trade free advice for one shot of Old Crow." I said, "My father's not in prison for mass murder, by the way. If he was, he'd be the most famous person from Calloustown ever."

Worm unscrewed the cap and handed over the entire quart bottle. He said, "You do what you need to do. I ain't a part of this. I ain't pushing you."

I thought, fuck. I thought, if I drink, I'm not going to stop until I get brave enough to find Louise, drive to where she and I once lived, and get pulled over by police for driving under the influence. Then I'll have the worst lawyer ever and get thrown in prison with my father. In between the court case and incarceration I'll drive out to AfriCall of the Wild, ask for Louise's forgiveness, and end up volunteering to muck the elephants' stalls. An elephant will step on my foot, I'll get gangrene, and then I'll die. Somebody will have to not only clear out my mother's belongings, but all of my Mexican jumping beans, and that person will do nothing but curse my existence, which will negate any notoriety I'd gained for the hornet stings.

The preacher on the cassette tape got all animated and said, "Everybody's talking about the importance of bonding. We ain't here to bond! If God wanted us to bond, He'd've given us a special glue gun instead of an index finger," which wasn't from the Book of Job.

"I got a few ideas. In that book of yours they got people down for eating hot dogs, Krystal hamburgers, pie, pancakes, deviled eggs, pickled eggs." He went on and on.

I screwed the cap back on the Old Crow without drinking from it and pushed the bottle toward Worm. Adazee came back smiling and said, "So I guess Buzz thought it was a great idea, huh? Y'all don't appear mad about anything."

Worm took the Old Crow and drank straight out of the bottle just as Reverend Mixon got back on track and said, "'Gird up your loins now like a man: I will demand of thee, and declare thou unto me. Will thou also disannul my judgment?'"

They looked at one another again, for too long, and I realized that something had been planned, something I wasn't in on.

Worm said, "I just broke into your momma's house—actually the door wasn't locked—and I ate exactly a hundred and thirteen of your Mexican jumping beans. I've looked everywhere and I can't find a Mexican jumping bean-eating world record, so I guess I'm it. Thirteen's my lucky number."

I took the bottle back from him. "What the fuck are you talking about?"

"We got us another celebrity!" Adazee said. "Callous-town's back on the map!"

Worm said, "I feel real bad about what I said earlier. What I made up earlier. Truth be told, your ex-wife didn't call up. Why would I say such a thing?" He hit himself in the leg. "I got to learn some things about business."

I said, "You can't just say you ate a bunch of something, or performed some kind of act, or had something happen to you like with me. There has to be witnesses. You have to have certified verifiers in a controlled environment." I'm not sure how that last sentence developed in my head, or why.

"That story about Adazee's brother's not true either, by the way. In a way it's all your fault, Buzz. He could play a trumpet real good, that much is right. But from what I understand, he nailed his own hand to the table and then cut it off with a ax. He wanted to get known as the best one-handed brass player in the world. At least that's what people finally figured out, once Bernard made it all the way up to New York."

Adazee jumped up and down quickly. It was obvious she'd taken off her brassiere when she was in the unisex restroom, probably because of discomfort, nothing else. She said, "That's not true about Bernard."

"It doesn't matter. Do you know how much those jumping beans cost me? You owe me some money, my man." I still didn't drink from that bottle of Old Crow.

Worm said, "I don't feel so good." He said, "I don't know if I can eat those things again, with witnesses or not."

Adazee said, "That's what you get."

Reverend Mixon said, "'They were children of fools, yea, children of base men.'"

I didn't make eye contact with either of them. I thought of my childhood, and how I, too—before and after the hornets' nest—wanted to be remembered. I wondered what my father did in his cell, at that very moment. I hoped that there was no afterlife, for I didn't want my mother witnessing anything I would partake of, ever, in the future. I said, "Well, I guess there's still hope." I said, "Those beans you ate will have moths emerge. It's got a big old Latin name that I have written down somewhere. I guess if you pull down your pants we can count the moths flying out of your ass and be official certified witnessing verifiers to that."

Adazee said to Worm, "I did my job. I got him here and I kept him occupied. Pay up."

They may have had an argument. I started daydreaming. Maybe I heard Adazee say something, again, about how I was old enough to be her father, and how she didn't have time to be making up fake Welcome Wagons just so people could make my acquaintance. I wondered what my wife did at that moment. Was she helping an ex-circus zebra foal? Did she study a blister on her palm from raking and shoveling too often? And then, unfortunately, I thought of the moths—*Cydia deshaisiana*—that might indeed emerge from the end of Stuart Harrell's alimentary canal. What kind of life-beginning is that for an insect that will live less than a week? It won't even have time to make its way into a bakery, attracted by bags of flour, in order to foul grain meant to be used in congratulatory and festive dessert, for people who completed an education or bested someone else's long-standing record or knew that their wedding vows were impenetrable and relentless. I thought, I am back in my hometown. I thought, it might be good to throw away my father's rifle, plus every book with my name listed inside.

Pitching Pennies

I expected a different downfall for my wife's brother, something akin to murder or forgery. Long ago—and you can ask my groomsmen, because I told them all about Lee Wayne at the bachelor party when he disappeared for a couple hours—I predicted kidnapping, grand larceny, felony DUI, drug and gun trafficking, bigamy, and any number of paternity suits. I thought Lee Wayne might finally get caught scamming people out of their retirement savings, or selling stolen goods, or hooking up with chop shop men working a tri-state area. That's how it is for men who insist on being called two first names, one of which is "Wayne." There's scientific and sociological proof. I predicted that Lee Wayne would eventually make his way to Nigeria to teach those Internet people how to siphon money from one account to another without repercussions.

The maximum penalty for the mutilation, diminution, or falsification of usable currency, according to United States Code title 18, part I, chapter 17, is about the same as the maximum penalty for littering. If I ever get married again—it's logically possible that it could happen—I'm going to mention this to my new set of groomsmen, who'll all be different than the first team I employed, seeing as those friends, for the most part, advised me against marrying Monica. In my defense, I found out only later that my wife went by Monica Marie up until the time she went to college. I don't know if there's ever been a scientific and sociological study about two-named women yet, but there should be. Kate "Ma" Barker. Mary Lou Retton.

"Lee Wayne's coming by to stay with us for a couple weeks, until he can straighten out his life," Monica said to me one day, seven years into our marriage, nine months after the last time we'd heard from her brother. "I don't want to hear any crap from you about this."

A minute earlier we had been getting along fine, talking about how it would never be socially acceptable for women to chew Red Man or Beechnut tobacco in public until they learned how to spit cleanly. We'd gotten on the subject because neither of us was doing very well when it came to nicotine gum, prescription Zyban, nicotine patches, prescription Chantix, hypnosis, and cold turkey. Monica and I stood out in the middle of our backyard smoking one-hundred-percent additive-free natural tobacco, because at least we'd gotten away from the more popular name brands. We had agreed that A) we should not smoke in the house because maybe the cleaner smell would make us eventually stop; and B) once we ran out of money from buying the one-hundred-percent additive-free natural tobacco cigarettes that cost twice as much as, say, Camels, Marlboros, and Winstons, we would have no other choice but to quit, or start robbing banks in a way more suited to her brother Lee Wayne. I'm not all that proud to admit that when I smoked cigarettes outside I found myself

looking at the tomato/Brussels sprouts/habanero/broccoli/
rosemary/basil garden and wondered how difficult it might
be to grow actual tobacco plants there, and learn how to roll
handmade cigars.

The neighbors next door had a cookout. It was a little more
than obvious that they pretended they didn't see us standing
there, a half acre away, puffing like special lizards. These were
new people who'd only moved in a couple months earlier. The
old neighbors evidently didn't pay their mortgage. I think
their last name began with either an L or a T, but I can't remember. I said to Monica, "Two weeks?" I said, "There's no
way that he can straighten out his life in two weeks. Did you
mean years? Did I mishear you? Did you say two decades?"

"Not funny, Clewis."

It's my last name. People always call me by my last name,
always—even when I was a child. Look at the other people in history known better only by their last name: Caesar,
Einstein, Plato, Shakespeare. There are a lot of them. Maybe Geronimo and Crazy Horse. Hemingway and Faulkner.
Castro. In the world of high finance: Rockefeller, Carnegie,
Hearst, Astor, and Buffett. In regards to art: Picasso, Pol-
lock, Dali, Renoir, Monet, Matisse, Toulouse-Lautrec, and
Warhol. Washington, Jefferson, Lincoln, Nixon, and Reagan, when it comes to politics. Churchill. Gandhi.

I don't count Hitler.

I didn't know Lee Wayne would show up by the time
Monica and I went inside, cooked supper, then came outside to smoke before going in to eat. I kind of wondered
how come she made a big point out of fixing a special

meal of fish tacos, asparagus, coleslaw, fresh-cut potatoes fried in olive oil, and a black bean soup concoction
we'd never had in the past. She had already baked bread
with forty-seven different grains and whipped up hummus
from chickpeas. Monica made a regular tossed salad and
cooked a pie made from canned peaches and pizza dough.
I thought maybe I'd forgotten our anniversary, or my own
birthday. I thought maybe it was Lee Wayne's birthday, or
perhaps he was coming over to ask us to be in a wedding
he had forthcoming.

"Are we cooking for the rest of the week or something?" I
said. Most nights we didn't even eat together—I ate a bolo-
gna sandwich, and she ate unsalted, unbuttered popcorn with
a side of eighteen-cheese quiche. I said, "When's your brother
showing up?"

She looked at her watch. She said, "If possible, try not to
mention the word 'penny.' Don't mention currency, copper,
recycling centers, or that thing up in Chicago that's not the
stock exchange, really. I can't remember what it's called."

I said, "Wrigley Field? Second City Comedy Troupe? The
Sears Tower? Oprah? That German submarine inside the
Museum of Science and Industry?"

"The Chicago Board of Trade. I think that's where it is.
Anyway, don't mention pennies."

I was about to ask why, there in the backyard, with the
neighbors still grilling what smelled like nice rib eyes and
our own tacos growing cold on the kitchen counter, when
Lee Wayne drove up palming an oogah-oogah-oogah horn
attached to the steering wheel of a late model Toyota hybrid.

"Pennies, or jail. Don't mention either one," Monica said.
"He just got out of prison."

My first thought, of course—maybe during my predict-able and likely second bachelor party I would say to those gathered, "Prison?! When and why did Lee Wayne go to prison?!" but it would be an exaggeration—my first thought was, "Who leaves prison and shows up at a sister's house driving a late model Toyota hybrid?"

Then I thought that stuff about when and why did Lee Wayne get incarcerated, and then the third thing I thought was, "Why would anyone put an oogah-oogah-oogah horn on a nice car?" There might've been some other considerations in between. I'm that way. I've been coming up with other con-siderations ever since I decided that I wanted to make more of myself than being a plain guy with a horticulture degree in charge of making sure city workers pick up branches, weed beds, and cut the grass in public areas.

Not to get sidetracked, but one time I made a movie of a man who cut the grass at his house, took a shower, then went to bed with his wife. They had sex for about two min-utes. All of this was done in silence—even when he was on the Troy-Bilt 17.4 horsepower manual 42" riding mower in the front yard—until he got into bed. Then he said, audi-bly, "I'll do the backyard tomorrow." And she said, "You ain't done the front yard yet, son," like that, all symbolic and ironic. Then the credits came up saying how my friend Fred Bingham played the part of the Grass Cutter, and his then-fiancée Kay Sue Platt played the part of Disgruntled and Unsatisfied Wife. I sent the film off to one of those movie contests but never heard anything. It might've been too short. It ran right at two hours, because I slo-moed the grass-cutting scene.

I slo-moed the mow, see.

The movie's called *Chores and Maintenance*, in case it ever comes out for real and people want to know.

Everyone called Kay Sue "Kazoo" behind her back until she took off from Fred. I'm hoping that *Chores and Maintenance* never gets picked up by a major distributor, just so she doesn't gain fame and royalties.

Lee Wayne got out of the car and skipped our way. He said, "All right! I smell something good!" When I say "skipped," I mean that he actually skipped, like a schoolgirl. He still possessed long sinewy arms, the face of a hatchet, the legs of a man who'd never used a ladder. He looked like my beautiful wife, minus the boobs.

I dropped my cigarette butt and stomped on it twice, then reached down to pick it up. As I stood erect, Monica dropped hers so that I'd have to stomp on it, and bend back over. At least that's what I thought about a year later. I said, "Hey, Lee Wayne."

He held his arms out wide and said, "Not bad, huh? That was certainly worth it." He hugged his sister, then nodded up and down toward me. We didn't shake hands or anything. The last time we shook hands that I could remember was at the bachelor party when he returned from a place I never learned. He came back, and shook my hand, and said, "I got to thank you, my man." My groomsmen had taken me out to one of those Hooters places. I think he might've hooked up with a barmaid out in the parking lot in the van he used to drive.

I said, "What've you been up to?" pretending I hadn't heard.

Monica said, "What you smell is those steaks over there," and pointed toward our neighbors, who had evidently made a pact to keep their backs pointed our way, like synchronized swimmers. Kind of too loud she blurted out, "We're eating fish, asparagus, coleslaw, potatoes, peach pie, soup, and hummus, because it's more nutritional than red meat!"

They were either Mormons, Jehovah's Witnesses, or one of those other denominations whose members prided themselves on clean living and pure spleens. I didn't know for sure, because I hadn't found the right time to take them some flowers or brownies.

While I spent my day telling men named Fred and DaQuawn to spread pine nugget mulch around the pansies, Monica taught kindergarten and, I imagined, had to raise her voice often.

"I need a beer," Lee Wayne said to me. "Let's go inside and get a beer. Y'all still smoking? I quit. They don't let anyone smoke inside prisons these days anymore, so I had to quit. What a good way to quit!" He put his arm around my shoulder as we walked inside and said, "Say, you got any pennies I could buy off you? I'm going straight back to my old ways, seeing it's worth it."

Monica shot me a mean look. I wasn't supposed to say "penny" and those other things. I said, "I think we might have some one-cent currency units, Lee Wayne. Why do you ask?"

We went inside. We ate the hell out of some fish tacos. If it matters, Monica chose catfish. Tilapia would've been fine, but she chose farm-raised catfish from down in Mississippi. We had catfish juices dribbling down our faces, and we drank beer, and we turned up the stereo so we couldn't hear the neighbors sizzling next door. We listened to Johnny Cash, because Lee Wayne said they wouldn't ever let anyone listen to Johnny Cash for the month he spent in lockup. We listened to Merle Haggard, and Social Distortion, and about anyone else we figured had a lead singer who'd done time. Robert Johnson. Steve Earle. The Monkees. Monica and I didn't have the most complete CD collection, but we made do. I said some things. I said, "Here are some people who will be in jail," and played one of those sad Italian operas.

We never even got to the peach pizza pie. We ate, and sang along, and then finally Monica said, "Tell me what happened exactly."

Here's Lee Wayne's—and then my, eventually—story: a copper penny gets a person one cent's worth of merchandise. Let's say that there's an item out there that costs a penny these days, like maybe one-tenth of a gumball. But a full copper penny—it takes 146 pre-1983 pennies to make a pound—was worth about $3.40 a pound when Lee Wayne envisioned his brilliant, prison-worthy idea. I've never been good at explaining things mathematically, and I had to listen to Lee Wayne twice. One hundred forty-six pennies minted before 1983 equals $1.46. In weight, 146 pennies equaled $3.40, what with the price of copper.

Again, it's against the law to mutilate or diminute. I doubt that "diminute" is even a word, but before Lee Wayne I'd never heard of "diminution," either. It's not a word used widely when telling employees to spread fertilizer or cull vines.

"What else did I have to do?" he said to us. "Y'all know how I was spinning my reel and not pulling anything in. Look, it only took time, and I had that going for me. I'd go to the bank, buy, say, a few hundred dollars in pennies, sort out the pre-1983 ones, put them aside, and rewrap the post-1982 pennies. Then I'd go down to the railroad track— you can't just take regular pennies to the recycling center and hand them in—and set the pennies down on the rail. Presto change-o! The pennies got flattened, I scooped them up and took them to a place where they knew, deep down, what I did but didn't care, and then I took that money—it would be quite a bit, and then I'd turn in the newer pennies for a penny apiece, you know—back to another bank and bought more. Over and over."

I wasn't accustomed to drinking anymore. Monica said I could only drink on days when she came home from kindergarten happy. I said, "Let me get this straight. You had the pennies smashed by trains, and then you took those smashed pennies to the metal recycling center and turned them in. Like I might do with cans I pick up on the side of the road."

"That's what I did," Lee Wayne said. "I hung out in a hobo jungle-like setting, and I put pennies down on the rails. There's a place I know where freight trains come by on the hour. I set down all these pennies, and then I picked them off after they rattled off the rail all flattened and unrecognizable. Meanwhile, I set down more and waited for the next train to come by. Then I took bags of flattened pennies down to this iron and metal place. They knew what I did, but somehow they didn't get charged. Let me tell you, a guy named Mike Wayne something or another who worked down there should've spent time in jail too. But I ain't sad or blameful about it."

I thought about a railroad track that ran straight through town, right in the middle of where I sent my workers to weed-eat cockleburs. I said, "How come not everyone's doing this?"

Lee Wayne craned his neck around and smiled. "The maximum fee is something like a hundred bucks and six months in prison. Or at least it used to be. I got charged a hundred bucks and thirty days in the county lockup. I wasn't really in a prison, technically. So what? You know how much I made, Cuz?"

Monica said, "Wait a minute. So you traded in dollars for rolls of pennies, and then went through the pennies and pulled out all the ones minted before 1983, when there was a bunch of zinc added or whatever. Am I getting this right? Is this what you did? And then you took the old pennies and laid them out on railroad tracks so they'd get smashed into unrecognizable, flat pieces of copper. Then you took the smashed pennies to some guy who paid you whatever copper costs by the pound, and walked out of there, and bought more. Is this right or is this wrong?"

I said, "You might be the smartest man I've ever met." I said, "Hey, whatever happened to you at my bachelor party?"

Monica looked at me for about one second and picked up her fork as if she were to scoop up some hummus. She said, "Why the hell can't you think up something like this so we can move into a nice subdivision and cook steaks out when we want? Goddamn. This isn't working. This here?" She waggled the fork between us, back and forth. She held her eyebrows high. "It isn't working, Clewis."

Monica wasn't accustomed to drinking either.

I went outside to smoke, and Lee Wayne followed me. Listen, I don't think they had any of this planned. You'd think Monica called up her brother, said, "I'm going to leave Clewis, and I want you over here in case he gets violent," and had her bags all packed to take off. As far as I could tell—I went back and looked at phone records and never saw a number that was Lee Wayne's, or the county jail down where he lived—Monica's epiphany and actions were spontaneous. "Epiphany" is a word we do use down at the city shop, seeing as there's a guy working for me named LeCrank who has a girlfriend named Epiphany who's always causing him to show up late for work.

I took my beer outside. The neighbors sat at two picnic tables, all of them sitting on the same side, staring at their own vinyl siding, their backs to my yard. I said to Lee Wayne, "What the hell just happened in there?"

He stretched backward, which caused his T-shirt to rise, which exposed a tattoo that surrounded his navel. It was that famous "Born to Lose" statement, and his belly button doubled as the "O" in "Born." He said to me, "I thought maybe this was one of those Candid Camera deals. One of those 'You've been punked' things, you know. They let us watch TV in prison, pretty much anytime we wanted. We could watch TV, but we couldn't smoke. If you ask me, it's healthier to smoke than to watch what they got on TV these days."

One of the neighbors stood from the picnic table, walked to a boom box, and turned up the volume. They listened to Lynyrd Skynyrd. Imagine that. They listened to that song that goes, "Ooh that smell/Can't you smell that smell." I guess it was all a joke to them, how we'd been yelling shit over there about their grilling earlier.

"We couldn't listen to that band in prison either. They got a song about a Saturday night special, you know, and I guess the higher-ups thought it would get all of us to thinking."

I looked toward the sliding-glass door and saw Monica pulling a suitcase behind her. "What could y'all listen to?"

"I know every lyric to Johnny Mathis," Lee Wayne said. He began singing "Chances Are," but in a rockabilly kind of way. He stopped after the "I'm in love with you" part and said, "Monica Marie's always been a little bit of a hothead. I haven't been the best brother when it comes to staying in touch, so I don't know all the ins and outs of y'all's matrimony. Has she been threatening to leave?"

I shook my head. I said, "I guess I better go back inside and talk to her about this." I stomped on my cigarette and didn't pick it up. I said, "Give me a couple minutes. Hey, if you want, you can go over there and pick some of those habaneros." I pointed. "If they're mostly orange, and about the size of a modern human testicle, then they're ready to be picked."

Monica had filled six boxes and that one suitcase that rolled on wheels. She didn't pack up things that we'd gotten for our wedding—I'll give her that—like the lava lamp, the matching set of Atlanta Braves shot glasses, the George Foreman grill, a great painting of Young Elvis on velvet, the microwave cookbooks. No, she only packed up her clothes, some school supplies, scrapbooks, the ashtrays she'd bought herself, and a set of knives she'd received for being Teacher of the Year at Calloustown Elementary.

Monica said, "I'm sorry, Clewis. I know this probably seems like a shock to you. And I didn't mean it to happen like this. Maybe I'm just embarrassed that you're embarrassed to have a brother-in-law like Lee Wayne."

"I like Lee Wayne," I said. "I've always liked Lee Wayne. Who doesn't like Lee Wayne? He's one of those people you can't hate, no matter what he does."

"I can't have him living with us," she said. "It won't be good for me, and it won't be good for you. What I'm saying is, it'll be bad."

Here's that thing I do all the time that isn't particularly beneficial: I began considering what Monica's kindergartners would be like twelve years hence, when they could only come up with monosyllabic arguments. I thought of a documentary film I could make that involved showing Monica saying "Good" and "Bad" to her students over and over, then following their lives, maybe splicing some Frankenstein in between.

I said, "Who invited him to stay with us until he got his life straightened out? I didn't. Give me a break, Monica. Come on."

She said, "Well it must have been for a reason. That's all I can say. It must've been the way things were meant to work out. I'm betting that things will change. I'll call you up."

And then she left, driving away in her Ford Taurus that she had use of for twelve months, what with the Teacher of the Year award.

I am not too proud to say that I sat down at the dining-room table, in front of three half-empty plates of fish taco remains, and nearly openly wept. Nearly wept. Nearly caught myself thinking about how I'd been a bad husband, et cetera. But I got all sidetracked thinking of how I should aim my handheld toward the neighbors for a few hours each night and call the documentary something like *They Turn Their Backs*, or *Someone Go Get the Paper Towels*.

"Everyone's always talking about hiding their money down in one of those Bermuda or Switzerland bank accounts," Lee Wayne came in the sliding-glass door saying. "Big waste of time when it comes to doing small time incarcerated, you know what I mean?"

I said, "Give me a minute, man." It wasn't, again, like I was crying. I needed to write down some ideas on the closest thing I could find, which meant one of the paper plates in front of me.

He dropped a dozen habaneros down on the table. "Man, I thought about hiding my money with my sister. Glad I didn't do that. No telling where it would be now. You kind of owe me, now that I think about it. If I'd've hid my money with Monica, she'd've left here a long time ago."

I thought about punching Lee Wayne, but he was bigger than me and there's no telling what kinds of mixed martial arts maneuvers he learned in the county jail. I said, "There's another twelve-pack in the refrigerator. She didn't take the refrigerator."

Lee Wayne didn't walk into the kitchen. He stood upright, with his chest poked out. "I need to go get my bags out of the car," he said.

I didn't respond.

"Am I staying in the guest room?"

I didn't say anything.

"You want to pitch some pennies up against the fireplace, just for fun?"

My crew needed to finish planting day lilies the next day, near what would become a walking path that went straight through the middle of town. According to city council, we would be paving over a set of railroad tracks presently—as soon as CSX freight trains quit coming through—for that "Rails to Trails" program that all the renovating towns had done already, after talking high and mighty about revitalization and quality of living so that *Time* and *Newsweek* and *U.S. News & World Report* could tell retirees where to retire and the health-conscious young where to relocate if they sub-scribed to a cardiovascular lifestyle.

What else could I say but, "You want a job, Lee Wayne? Listen, you come work for me. We'll get you all the pennies you want, and you do what you know what to do, and we'll split the profits. I don't have it all worked out in my mind yet, but I will. Can you pretend to run a leaf blower, or an edger?"

He said, "Well, I don't know."

I said, "Listen, you can bring all the pennies you want, and I'll set you out where there's that track, while there's that track."

"I don't know. Well," he said.

Like I said, I normally didn't drink that much. Maybe I wasn't thinking correctly. It seemed like a good idea—nor-mally I told half-hearted workers what to do, and then I sat around waiting for everyday citizens to call up complaining about something. My day went like this, mostly: "Hey, guys, today you need to go cut the grass around the fountain, corner of McDaniel and Lanneau." Ring-ring-ring: "Your men are cutting the grass on the corner of McDaniel and Lanneau, and they're not wearing shirts," or "One of them's cutting the grass while sitting down," or "My tax dollars shouldn't be spent on two men eating hot dogs out in the open." Stuff like that, which didn't get addressed in nine semesters of college horticulture classes.

I said to Lee Wayne, "How is this a bad thing? You'll have a regular income, and you'll have time to conduct your copper recycling business."

Lee Wayne drank from his beer. He shook his head side to side. "I don't know. I've been thinking hard about some other options I have." What options could my evidently new-ex-wife's brother have? What was on the horizon for a man driving a half-electric car with an oogah-oogah-oogah horn? He said, "I was supposed to show up earlier. I was supposed to show up a couple weeks ago. I've been out of prison for a month, and Monica Marie wanted me to show up a lot earlier to beat you up or something."

I said, "Why? Why in the world?"

"That's exactly what I said. I said, 'Has he hit you?' I said, 'Is he cheating on you?' I said, 'Has he taken y'all's nest egg and turned it into pennies just so he could take them down to a railroad track and flatten them, then turn the things in to the nearest copper recycling center?' Well, she didn't have an answer. I know that I'm supposed to be on my blood kin's side, Clewis, but I'd be willing to bet she's seeing somebody else, I hate to say. When I was in prison, which was really just the county jail, people were always asking me to go beat up somebody just because they had a new boyfriend. And just because I had fighting arms, what with lugging pounds of pennies for so long. Weird place, prison."

We sat there at the dining-room table. When Lee Wayne had come back in the house with two duffel bags he hadn't closed the sliding-glass door all the way, so through the crack came strains of the neighbors talking, and yelling at one another in a friendly manner. They had traded playing music for a game of charades, it appeared. I went outside to smoke what ended up being my last five cigarettes ever—who knew this was all it would take to quit?—and my brother-in-law followed me out. We took chairs to the backyard, sat down facing the neighbors, and watched. I hadn't played the game in years, but remembered quickly the signs for "movie," "book," and "song" title. Like I said, they weren't a half acre away, panto-miming out prompts they'd pulled from an empty char-coal briquette bag. This was a mother and father, their son and daughter, and some other man and woman with a son and daughter. The more they reached in and played, the more they got charcoal on their arms and faces, what with the bag's residual soot. I found myself in love with these people, I'll admit.

"I don't want to impose on you none, Clewis, but I kind of do really need a place to stay. I mean, I got out, I got my money, and I bought that car. I wasn't thinking! I got that car, not considering that I needed to rent an apartment or trailer or something."

I yelled out at my neighbors, "*Gone with the Wind*!" I yelled out, "Wait—'Blowin' in the Wind' by Bob Dylan." One of the young daughters looked like she tried to portray "wind." She kept waving her arms from left to right, floating-like. I thought, maybe she's doing one of those hula dances. I yelled out, "'Tiny Bubbles' by Don Ho."

My neighbor smiled at me and waved. The husband waved, that is. I realized it might take time to win his wife over, es-pecially if she'd somehow met Monica and they'd had a con-versation that went something like, "I'm your new neighbor," and Monica said, "I'm planning to leave my husband."

Lee Wayne said, "This is what it should be all about. Mi-nus my sister taking off. And having tacos that didn't include real meat. This is what it should all be about. Hey, Clewis, give me a cigarette."

I said, "No." I watched the neighbors. I stood up and yelled, "Air! The Clean Air Act! 'You are the wind beneath my wings'!" How come I wasn't more distressed about Monica leaving? I thought. How come I didn't get all upset and try to track her down? "'Pennies from Heaven'!"

I turned to Lee Wayne and said, "What about wheat pennies? You didn't put wheat pennies down on the railroad tracks, did you?"

"There aren't that many wheat pennies. Most of them are worth two cents, though, if you wanted to sell them at the flea market. Maybe a nickel. It's not right."

I stood up and, as if on automatic pilot, walked over to my neighbors' house. The smell of steak still hung in our humid air. They didn't seem fearful of my approach. The young girl said, "It was *Grapes of Wrath*. It's a book."

I got it. She tried to portray the Dust Bowl. I nodded and laughed. I pulled my arm for Lee Wayne to follow me over and said to the neighbors, "Hey, my name's Clewis. That's either my brother-in-law or my ex-brother-in-law."

The man said, "That's an unusual name."

I told him how my wife couldn't take it either. I asked if Lee Wayne and I could join in. They said okay, and I took their turning their backs on us earlier as coincidence. As it ended up, these people weren't members of an offshoot religion. They were normal. They explained how they believed in the extended family, and how playing games kept them closer, and how it's what they did back in Michigan before it became apparent that they'd never work there again.

I stuck my arm in the charcoal bag and pulled out a song I'd never known. Or maybe I couldn't concentrate, thinking about how I needed to drop by the bank the next day.

Fresh Meat on Wheels

Before ceremonially burning down a life-sized replica of the Calloustown Courthouse—which never existed in the first place—built over the previous year in a field adjacent to Mr. Morse's tree farm and nursery, it was tradition to take every sixth grader to the various attractions nearby. This included the Finger Museum, where a man had severed digits floating in formaldehyde from all the pulpwood men who had chainsaw accidents over the years. Then we would all go, via minibus, to a taxidermist's place where he'd set up The Safest Petting Zoo Ever. Our sixth-grade teacher, Ms. Whalen, said we were to understand what there is to appreciate about our hometown before viewing what General Sherman could've done if he'd understood Calloustown's meaningfulness, and not veered away on his march between Savannah and Columbia. My heart wasn't into this bastardized field trip because—and it's not like I had ESP back then—I foresaw the possible arguments, fistfights, and one-upmanship that would occur. If I had extrasensory perception back then I would've found my mother in the organic berry field she and my father operated and said something like, "Please tell me the sexual intercourse y'all have told me about is not like sticking your penis in an armpit filled with deep-cleansing moisturizer."

Since the invention of the minibus, sixth-grade boys at Calloustown Elementary spent the night at Ms. Whalen's house, for early in the morning her husband, whom up until this point I'd always thought an otherwise good man named Ben who somehow broke away from local DNA and closed-mindedness, would get us together and drive us around the countryside in order to point out what General Sherman missed by swerving away from Calloustown. The sixth-grade girls, I learned, all stayed at the other sixth-grade teacher's house, a woman named Ms. Harrell, in order to learn about what was going to happen to their bodies soon. I don't know if it's true or not, but before the minibus the Calloustown kids stayed at other ex-teachers' households for the night before embarking on mule-led wagons. And before the mules, those poor Calloustown kids had to plain walk to, say, the Finger Museum, which probably only held one finger on display.

"Do not bring up how we're Democrats, Luke," my mother reminded me as she pulled up to Ms. Whalen's house. "If anyone asks you if you're a Christian, it's best to go ahead and lie. What's it going to matter, seeing as we don't go to church anyway? If your teacher offers you a baloney sandwich for breakfast, just go ahead and eat it seeing as it's not going to kill you much."

I said, "Why am I here again? What's going on?"

My mother put the car in neutral, and then seemed to experiment with reverse and one of the lower gears. She said, "Are they not teaching you any existentialism at Calloustown Elementary?"

I didn't get it. I said, "Tell me again who Sherman was?" It's not like I wasn't from the South—it's just that my parents watched the news at night, and read books written by people who won awards, and they didn't sit around moaning about how things could've been, like my classmates' parents seemed to do. "And go through Jesus again, just in case."

My mother laughed. She leaned over and kissed my forehead and said, "You'll be fine. I got you some special gray flannel pajamas packed up for you to wear so you'll fit in. I tried to draw a stars and bars on your sleeping bag but it just came out a giant X. If anyone asks, say it faded and ran in the washing machine."

I didn't get those remarks, either. I said, "It's Valentine's Day. Do they do this everywhere on Valentine's Day?"

General Sherman burned Columbia, South Carolina, on February 17, 1865. According to the denizens of Calloustown, he should've burned their town on the fifteenth, if he had any sense of the right thing to do, on his way back north.

My mother said, "More or less."

General Sherman didn't consider our ancestors' town worthy of torching, and the consequences, over the next seven or eight generations, weren't unpredictable: a miniscule region of high-voiced men and women whose families intermarried endlessly, producing higher-voiced offspring, ad infinitum, all Yankee-hating, distrustful stumpgrinders and third-shift health professionals at what still got called the Calloustown Home for the Feeble and Discouraged. I exaggerate, but not much. Beginning in sixth-grade civics class a variety of students would blurt out, "Sherman didn't think Fairview Plantation was good enough to burn! Shows you what he knew! They got them four bedrooms there, and two roomses!" et cetera, their larynxes squealing in such incredulous-filled manners that at times—say later in South Carolina history class, or eleventh-grade American history when the Civil War section took up two nine-week grading periods—it sounded like one of those trick crystal glass band members wet-fingering a rim ceaselessly. It sounded like the emergency broadcast system's television test most days when the prodigy of Munsons and Harrells wailed out their disgust in regards to William Tecumseh Sherman's notions of aesthetics: "What's so good about Atlanta, Savannah, or Columbia? Sherman was stupid! He said he wanted to march to the sea, and Calloustown starts with a C."

I hate to think that I've always considered myself of a higher ilk than the typical Calloustowner hell bent on grasping worthful arson, but it's true to a degree. My parents arrived at my place of training only after surrendering law practices right before offers of partnership. They cashed in some savings, did some research, bought the cheapest arable land available in Zone 8 in regards to that Hardiness Scale, began an organic farm long before it became commonplace and chic, and then had their only child—me—in their late thirties. By "long before" I might really mean 1981, right after the Iranian hostages got released. Because of the hostages and a certain doomful outlook regarding economic growth and détente, and without doing research on how vengeful their new neighbors had become, my parents settled on a crossroads neither known to blues songs nor sulfurous flame.

I grew up with Munsons and Harrells alike pissed off that someone considered our cows, sheep, hogs, and chickens inedible, our women unattractive, our spring houses tainted. Maybe that's why my mother never allowed me to read the Bible in general, and Job's story in particular. It's a wonder that more than a few of us non-Munsons and -Harrells escaped with self-esteem higher than a collard stalk.

"If they ask you if you hunt, say yes. Fish, yes. Hate everyone north of Virginia, yes. If stupid Bobby Harrell asks you again about your pets, say you own a cottonmouth and a fire ant farm." My mother had a whole list that she went over daily as I shoved books in my backpack. My father started every morning reciting Latin terms he knew by heart before entering his torporous berry patches. "If one of the Munson boys keeps asking you if you've been with a girl, here," my mother would say, pouring Chicken of the Sea tuna water on my palm. "Tell him to sniff your finger."

That was another little action or saying that I didn't get, of course. But the half-feral cats that lived inside the school liked me, which, of course, got me called Pussy.

Mr. Whalen sat in his living room with a fishing pole. There were bags of store-bought ice all around the hole he'd fashioned into the floor, and the hook on the end of his line descended down into a crawlspace. Bobby, Donnie, Larry, and Gary Munson held poles, too, as did Lonnie, Ronnie, Billy, and Stonewall Harrell. These were my classmates. These were my sleepover comrades the night before the "What Does Sherman Know?" annual festival.

"Get you a pole, there, Luke," Mr. Whalen said. "We're playing a little game called Ice Fishing in Minnesota. We don't got no need to ice fish around these parts ever, so I thought I'd teach you boys a little bit about it."

I said hello to all of the two-syllable-named classmates. None of them said anything back. I said, "Do you have fish in the basement?"

"We're fishing for rats and mice," Ben Whalen said. He patted the lid to a plastic cooler next to him, as if there were caught vermin inside. "Put you a chunk of cheese on your hook and drop it on down."

These were bamboo poles, probably macheted over on the edge of Mr. Morse's tree farm. I threw my line into the hole and squeezed in between Gary and Lonnie. I tried to peer down into the hole, but couldn't tell how deep it was. I said, "Did you cut this hole in the floor by yourself?" because I couldn't think of anything else to say.

Bobby Munson yelled out, "Luke ain't a Christian!"

I said, because I'd been taught to do so, "I'm the only one here named after somebody in the Bible. There isn't a Book of Bobby."

"Boys," Mr. Whalen said. "This is all of y'all, right?" He drank from a plastic cup, and I could smell the booze in it. "Boys, while I got you all here I might as well use this opportunity to tell you about the birds and the bees, it being Valentine's Day and all."

Later on I figured out that because we had no male teachers in the sixth grade, one of the teachers' husbands would have to take over. Over at the girls' sleepover, it probably wasn't so uncomfortable for a woman to explain sex.

I think it was Lonnie Harrell who said, "My grandmother has a beehive in her backyard."

"I got pictures of my grandmother with a beehive hairdo," one of the Munsons said.

"I ain't talking about real birds and bees," Mr. Whalen said. "Let's pretend that I'm talking about mice and, and…I don't know. Let's just say I'm talking about mice, seeing as they reproduce like all get-out." He took a big swig from his cup.

My sixth-grade teacher came in the room carrying a tray. She wore blue jeans, which kind of freaked everyone out, and said, "Who wants some Pepsi?"

You'd think none of the Munson or Harrell kids had ever had Pepsi, which might've been true. Half of them dropped their poles down into the hole and rushed our teacher. They grabbed and kicked each other out of the way. Me, I sat there thinking about something else my parents had told me: "Pepsi Cola" rearranged came out "Episcopal." So I said, loudly, "We drink Pepsi Cola all the time at our house because it's 'Episcopal.' That's what we drink. At my house. Because it's a Christian drink."

Everything seemed to stop. It wasn't my imagination that all of my male classmates shut up and turned to me as if I'd spoken in tongues. Ms. Whalen—I should mention that her maiden name was Munson—said, "What did you say, Luke?"

I said, "I mean, we drink Gatorade."

I didn't think I had said anything blasphemous—in retrospect, I think all these children of Pentecostals had never heard of another denomination, except for maybe Baptist. I was glad that Mr. Whalen broke the tension by yelling, "I got one, I got one, I got one," and then pulling up a fake mouse that, like a blue crab breaking the surface and experiencing air, he somehow got to let go of the cheese and drop back down into the crawlspace.

My sixth-grade teacher screamed and took off running for the kitchen. My classmates brought their Pepsis back, and one of them said, "Hey, Luke, go under the house and get our poles we dropped."

I said, "You dropped them down there. You go get them."

"You scared to go under the house, son?" Ben Whalen said. Yeah, Mr. Whalen. You'd think that Lonnie, Donnie, or Ronnie would've dared me, not my sixth-grade teacher's husband, a man I'd up to that point thought to have escaped inbreeding disasters.

"Luke rhymes with puke," Bobby said.

I don't know why I thought it necessary to prove myself, to say, "Somebody at least give me a flashlight."

I walked outside the Whalens' house and didn't look back to see if anyone stared at me through the window. I could've walked home—it wasn't but a mile—but I knew my parents would've been disappointed. Somewhere between my father mumbling, "*A fronte praecipitium a tergo lupi*" and "*Ubi fumus, ibi ignis*," he always said to me that enduring frost only made one stronger. I walked up to Mr. Whalen's six-wheeled truck—this is why I thought he had escaped the normal Munson/Harrell mindset—a silver refrigeration vehicle that he drove around a few-county area with FRESH MEAT ON WHEELS written on the panels. He offered people rib eyes and filets and hamburger patties, chicken and fish and pork chops, for prices much lower than Winn-Dixie, Bi-Lo, or the A&P—grocery stores that might be thirty miles from Calloustown.

I went around the side of the house and paid attention not to get snagged by briars or the Whalens' neighbor's pit bull on a long chain, and then the back of the house where a short door led to the crawlspace. I turned on the flashlight and thought, somehow this is going to keep me being made fun of. In a normal world kids would say, "That Luke—he's brave." But in the land of Calloustown, a day before the "What Does Sherman Know?" celebration, it would probably come out that I was one with Satan, what with my non-fear of all things rabid that live beneath our abodes.

I got in and waved my light around. As it ended up, the Whalens' crawlspace was nearly high enough to count as a basement—six feet high, at least, where the hole stood—with a hand-troweled cement floor. I found the dropped bamboo poles right away, and saw light streaming in from above. I took a few steps and heard Stonewall say, "That's not how I learned how it works," then took a few more steps. Mr. Whalen yelled down, "Are you there, Luke?" but I didn't respond.

I walked right to the edge of the bastardized ice hole and heard my sixth-grade teacher's husband say, "That is how it works. It's just like this here hole. The sperm's the cheese, and the hole's the hole, and once the cheese hits the hole it don't take long for a baby to come out of the hole. The rat."

I was twelve. We were all twelve. Mr. and Ms. Whalen didn't have children at this point, and perhaps this was why. I yelled up at the hole, "Here," and started shoving poles upward. Somebody, one of my classmates, yelled back down at me, "Don't step on any of the babies down there."

Somebody else said something about a stork, and then Mr. Whalen said loudly, "I give up," and "Monetta, I've done my job here." Then he might've fallen over, for there was a noise, and one of the Harrell kids said, "Are you all right?"

I wasn't paying attention much. I'd come across a cache of Matchbox cars—vintage ones, though I didn't know the difference at the time. Someone had built a miniature Grand Prix road course of sorts, complete with barriers, army men onlookers, trees fashioned from those colored-cellophane toothpicks, and what appeared to be the Calloustown Courthouse that never existed in the first place. I might've said, "Hey, can we play down here later?"

Or I might've kept it to myself, thinking that if Mr. and Ms. Whalen ever die in a fiery wreck, I'm coming back down here to get some things before anyone else finds them. Again, my parents hadn't gone over those Ten Commandments at this point, especially the one about coveting your neighbor's 1:43 scale die-cast toy cars.

I walked into the circle of light and looked up at all the little Munson and Harrell blank faces looking down at me. I said, "What's going on up there?"

Mr. Whalen reappeared and said, "Hey, I got an idea. We might as well go through the whole nine-month process," and he told the boys to throw their hooks back down. To me he said, "Hey, Luke, do me a favor. This is going to be fun! Place all the hooks around your belt loops. Go ahead! I won't let you get hurt none."

Ms. Whalen's sixth-grade boys pulled me up through the hole in her den floor. I have no clue what kind of test line they used, or how the bamboo poles didn't break under my weight hanging there in the crawlspace, but Ben Whalen told me to start screaming like crazy, and I did. What else was I supposed to do? I couldn't see any of my unlikely deliverers, for they'd had to back down the hallway pulling.

Mr. Whalen stood there leaning against a bookcase that held a dictionary, a number of ashtrays, some candles, and framed photographs of dead deer. He yelled out, "Okay, y'all run back in here," as I gathered myself on the lip of the hole, surrounded by ice bags.

No one said, "Are you all right?" Ms. Whalen yelled from a back room something about how we needed to settle down so as not to fall back in the hole.

Ben Whalen said, "And that's how a baby is born, but without the ice or clothes that Luke is wearing."

My teacher's husband shoved what ice hadn't melted over the hole's lip. He slid the makeshift hatch over his own crawl-space, and covered the exposed wood with a rug that wasn't much bigger than the jagged edges it needed to hide. "I'm going to make a spiral staircase down there one day," he said, apparently to himself.

I said nothing about all the cool Matchbox cars my sixth-grade classmates and I would sleep directly over. I wanted to tell someone about it, but already understood that, if I revealed what I had discovered, somehow a Donnie, Lonnie, Gary, or Billy would label me a big baby for liking toy cars over the real ones that they swore they drove around all the time when their parents weren't home.

My teacher said, "Now, no horseplay tonight, boys. Y'all stretch out your sleeping bags in here and go to sleep. Mr. Whalen will be walking y'all up early-early-early. 'What Does Sherman Know?' is a long and tiring day. I made some special treats for tomorrow in the freezer, so don't go around snooping."

"Goodnight, Ms. Whalen," we said in unison. I have no idea what happened to her husband, but I heard the back door squeak open while our teacher warned us against cutting fool all night.

She turned off the lights. We made no noise. Then Stonewall Harrell giggled. He'd commandeered the flashlight at some point after I got birthed. Stonewall said, "I know what a woman's nookie looks and feels like for real. It ain't like what he told us."

I don't want to say that my organic-farming, ex-corporate-lawyering parents sheltered me. But I'd never come across this "nookie" term. I knew poontang, beaver, snatch, trim, twat, quim, muff, quif, box, cooter, and meat wallet, but not nookie.

Lonnie and Donnie said, "No you don't," and then there was a bunch of uh-huhs and don't neithers.

"I can prove it," Stonewall said. "Y'all cover me. I'm going into the bathroom."

I didn't mean to say nookie out loud, but I did just to get a feel for it. It's not the kind of word, I knew, that I could use daily, like when I said something about a box or beaver.

"Stonewall better not come back in here dragging along Ms. Whalen," Donnie said.

He didn't. No, Stonewall returned with a gigantic blue jar of women's nighttime facial cream. He said, "What I'm about to show y'all is something my cousin taught me last year. Now, everyone slop some of this stuff on your wiener, and then come stick your wiener in my armpit." He slung off his T-shirt and got down on his knees. "You got to close your eyes, though, for it to work best."

I'm not sure what happened after that. This isn't one of those "selective memory" occasions. I'm not being judgmental for what those Munson and Harrell children did the night before "What Does Sherman Know?" but I didn't join in—perhaps because I thought a joke was being played on me. I got up from the floor and grabbed the flashlight. I went to the bookcase and opened up the dictionary to find everything marked out by black Magic Marker. It's like an entire language disappeared, page after page. I turned to the Gs to see if maybe they'd left "God" there, but they hadn't. I turned to the Js, for Jesus, but it was marked out, too. I picked up the dictionary—this was one of those Thorndike-Barnhart red hardbacks, probably stolen from our classroom at Calloustown Elementary—and went out the front door with it. I walked without paying attention, as if on automatic pilot—which they say General William Tecumseh Sherman mastered above all else—and skirted the briars and next-door pit bull successfully. No noises emanated from the den at this point. I opened the door to beneath the house and found Mr. Whalen seated cross-legged, surrounded by his Matchbox car collection. He had a drop light hanging from a floor joist, and he didn't turn his head.

"You want to play a little game I like to call 'What Does Henry Ford Know?'" he asked me. "You want to play a little game I like to call 'What Does Detroit Got that We Don't?'"

I should've jumped, but I didn't. I should've either said yes or no instead of pointing to the floorboards above me and whispering, "They're fucking each other's armpits upstairs with your wife's Noxzema."

Mr. Whalen said, "Now, not everyone likes a tattletale, Luke. I do, though, so you came to the right place." He handed me his plastic cup, told me to take a drink if I wished—I did, only to learn that he partook of Pepsi and George Dickel, a combination I'd had before—and got up from the cement floor without grunting. He whispered, "Unfortunately, your teacher threw away all the boxes to these cars. They'd be worth a lot more money if I still had the boxes. Don't forget that, Luke. Sometimes a box is more valuable than what goes inside it."

Years later I would realize that he still worked on his sex lesson. I said, "Yes, sir."

"What're you doing with that dictionary?" he asked me quietly. I shrugged. He leaned in closer and said, "I blacked out every word in there except for 'desperation.' Go ahead. Turn to page 275. I keep waiting for Monetta to open the thing up. Maybe she already knows all the words inside."

I drank more from his cup, not thinking.

Mr. Whalen kept a stepladder in his crawlspace, of course. I took a theater appreciation class in college my freshman year and learned three things: If there was a pistol on the set, it would be fired at the end of the first act; if there was a telephone on the bedside, it would ring, usually not on cue. I learned, too, that most drama majors were obnoxious and insecure, and that if they didn't make it in a summer rep group they'd go off to law school, eventually get disenchant-ed should they have any sense whatsoever, then finally give it all up in order to farm berries, sing campfire songs sponta-neously, and teach their children most of the euphemisms for female genitalia.

So I wasn't surprised or shocked when my sixth-grade teacher's drunken husband said to me, "Let's stand this aluminum ladder up right under the hole where I'm going to eventually build a spiral staircase." He kicked it open, then tested the floor for balance. Ben Whalen held his index finger to his mouth for me to be quiet, then took his plastic cup of booze from me.

Here's the scariest segment out of the most freakish night in my life up until this time: Mr. Whalen offered no pantomime hand gestures à la high school ROTC members obsessed with semaphore. He looked at me once, didn't smile, and we simultaneously climbed up both sides of the stepladder—he on the "Do Not Use for Steps" side, and me on the traditional silver treads—like Olympic-caliber synchronized swimmers, or champion ax men at a logging competition in the Pacific Northwest, or adjacent geysers at a national park. Ben Whalen put his plastic cup in his mouth, we placed our palms up to the makeshift hatch, and shoved hard so mightily and fast that not one Munson or Harrell child had time to react. Listen, these guys never exactly reacted quickly most days—thus all the bruises during baseball season—but you'd think that an eruption of floor below a cheap throw rug might cause four prone Harrells getting faux-screwed in the armpits by Noxzema-slathered Munsons to yelp, run, or fight before their discoverers underwent sensory-based deductions, which could only end, later on, in blackmail situations.

"What the hell you boys doing?" Mr. Whalen yelled out, even before the circle of floor tipped over entirely against the useless bookcase. He emerged into his living space, took two or three determined steps, and flipped the light switch. By the time I came out of the hole all of my sleepover comrades rushed to find their pajama bottoms and hide both erections and tainted, compromised armpits. There would be talk of my being "born again," within the next six months, and—like an iconic unseemly act performed in public by a celebrity—by the time I left Calloustown for good it seemed as though everyone aged twelve to forty had been present and witnessed the occasion. "What the hell you boys doing to each other?"

Before anyone could answer—and I'll admit that I started laughing uncontrollably, which is why I don't play poker—our sixth-grade teacher flew into her own, now corrupted, den. She got that look on her face that meant "I'm calling your daddy," and without raising her voice much said, "Get your clothes back on, boys." She reached down to the floor, picked up her fouled jar of night cream, and said, "Where'd y'all get this?"

Oddly, she looked straight at her husband. Did I mention that he never set down his plastic cup throughout the spooky entrance, or how a pint bottle peeped out of his left back pocket?

"We was just playing a game," one of the Munson boys said.

I quit laughing long enough to say, "Playing Pin the Pecker on an Armpit," and, perhaps affected by a jigger's worth of good bourbon, lost my balance and fell back down the hole, half-sliding down the ladder's stringers.

You'd think that I'd've heard one of the adults say, "Uh-oh" or "Are you okay?" I swear, though, between terra firma and the cement floor I heard my sixth-grade teacher say, "No wonder Sherman swerved from this wasteland."

I regained consciousness with my head against a dirt mound built for Matchbox car coasting. Jefferson Davis and Robert E. Lee stood beneath my eyes, and Jeb Stuart covered my upper lip. Ms. Whalen held the three in place, delicately. What would've been our little surprise treats sometime between the Finger Museum and the Stuffed Wild Animals petting zoo—Kool-Aid frozen in ice-cube trays, with plastic confederate soldiers frozen into them to be used as handles—now worked a secondary mission, namely to keep the swelling down from the tumble I took down Mr. Whalen's imaginary ice hole/vagina.

I woke up and said, "What day is it?" like that, like I always had done in the past after getting knocked out.

My teacher shushed me and said, "You're a different kind of Calloustowner, Luke."

Upstairs, though I didn't know it at the time, all the Munson and Harrell boys had been locked up inside the Fresh Meat on Wheels refrigeration truck in order to keep them out of the way and unable to call their parents. Somehow, if I knew the parents of Calloustown, the entire Noxzema incident would be interpreted as the Whalens' fault. She'd get released from her teaching duties, and every Harrell and Munson would go back to eating non-fresh meat bought from a grocery store chain's amateur butcher.

"I called his parents but didn't get an answer," Ben Whalen said to his wife.

I sat up and said, "I like the ambulance best," referring to the Lomas Ambulance #14 Matchbox car that Mr. Whalen—during playtime—had backed beside a #57 fire truck, both of which were in front of a #13 Dodge wrecker, which seemed to be aiding the grenade-throwing army man who had just wrecked his #73 Mercury station wagon.

"You don't need an ambulance," Ms. Whalen said. "By the time an ambulance gets here you'll have healed these bumps and grown new ones." She took Jeb Stuart off my lip and put him in her own mouth. "You're okay, comparatively."

I said, "I think my parents drove down to Columbia to see a movie, that's where they are." I got up and said, "I'm okay."

Mr. Whalen didn't offer me another sip of George Dickel. He said, "I got a good mind to leave them boys in the truck for the rest of the night. We got any Pine-Sol? I need to go scour down the den from whatever emissions those boys made up there."

My teacher leaned in to look at my pupils. I thought she wanted to kiss, but she said, "What's the capital of Florida?"

Immediately I said, "Miami."

"He's all right," Ms. Whalen said, and her husband nodded.

We walked out the crawlspace door. When we passed Mr. Whalen's work truck he banged on the panels hard a few times. Inside the house my teacher put on some rubber gloves and covered the hole in the floor, then the rug, then scooted a table over the hole. She told me to try my parents again, I think just to see if I could remember the number. My mother answered on the first ring. She said she and my father had decided against going to a movie, that they'd been there all night, that the phone hadn't rung. I told her she needed to come get me, and when she asked why I didn't say, "Because I know anatomy," or "I don't fit in," or "There's a chance I'll turn to alcoholism if I stay here much longer," or "My teacher doesn't know state capitals." I said, "I hit my head when we were playing freeze tag."

Ms. Whalen took the receiver from me, finally, and said to my mother, "Luke was It," among some other things. Again, in retrospect, I think she might've been speaking metaphorically.

So I missed another ceremonial burning of the Calloustown Courthouse. I heard later that Mr. Whalen's minibus didn't start up the next morning and that he had to drive my classmates around in the back of his work truck. Those idiots said they were surrounded by hanging meat for the entire day, by carcasses meant to be bought by their kin. I shrugged a lot over the next six years and lied back at them. I told them my father let me take dates out on his cherry picker once a year to see our hometown fake burn, and it worked in regards to getting girlfriends amorous. When, finally, I told my parents the truth about that one night I had with the Whalens, my father made a point to order a gigantic box of sausage, though he only cooked the patties and set them out for crows to eat, then fly around our hometown fouling windshields and rooftops. My father believed that a modern-day Sherman might act likewise.

Gripe Water

I assumed that my wife's childhood friend, Dottie, never encountered an etiquette handbook, or never had the common sense and decency to consult any number of social skills experts who offered advice in daily newspapers or Internet web sites. How hard is it to take a deep breath, drop the knitting needles, and contact a grief counselor or birth consultant in these days of omnipresent bloggers? You'd think that the first half-dozen times Carol miscarried would've taught Dottie to stay home and wait for an all-clear. I don't want to accuse my wife of impatience, but maybe—with three early miscarriages behind her within two years, six or eight since we officially married—she shouldn't have told her friend Dottie, or my relatives, or even me. One time I got on the Internet and found a pregnancy authority who said that, until every childhood disease had a cure and car seats got deemed foolproof and failsafe, an expectant mother shouldn't announce her pregnancy until the kid enrolled in second grade. Maybe the specialist exaggerated. I'm beginning to think that a number of everyday bloggers like to show off their sarcastic viewpoints, that they sit back in their rooms alone laughing over what people might undergo in the realm of bad luck and poor judgment.

"You might as well leave now," Carol told me right before Dottie showed up the early afternoon after the last miscarriage. This was a Saturday. Two nights before, Carol went to the bathroom. We didn't go to the emergency room, or call an ob-gyn. I always said, "Do you want me to take you to the ER?" because it worried me. I would always say, "We need to see someone more specialized than a general practitioner." I think I stole that line from a husband character I saw one time in a made-for-TV movie.

She and I didn't even have regular GP doctors. It's not like we were Christian Scientists. Carol and I, it seemed, were the type of people who believed that bad news and worry caused sickness and premature deaths.

"It's nothing," my wife always said. "It's not even noticeable. There's not much difference than sitting down first thing in the morning and finding out your period started in the middle of the night."

I'd looked up some information myself, quietly. I ruled out some kind of Munchausen syndrome, seeing as Carol would more than likely deliver a child and then push it down a flight of steps if that were a valid diagnosis.

"Please don't let Dottie come over," I said. "She's an idiot, and you always get upset afterwards." I didn't say anything about how, on top of her initial stupidity, Dottie'd gotten "born again," and couldn't participate in a two-person conversation without Matthew, Luke, John, and Mark horning in and spouting off.

Here's Dottie: Carol announced her pregnancy, way too early—"A miracle, at age thirty-six!" or -seven, -eight, -nine, and Dottie got to work knitting an afghan. Two or three weeks later my wife would tell everyone about the miscarriage, and Dottie would show up with one square of the baby's afghan, announcing, "You can use it for a trivet," or oven mitt, or something to set down between a terracotta planter and wooden table.

Carol said to me, "Go to the bar for a few hours. Go watch football games. Call up Eddie and Albert and have them meet you down at the Side Pocket. I'll be okay with Dottie. She means well, really. And if you're here I'll get all nervous and either be mean to her, you, or both of y'all."

That's another thing that showed up in all my miscarriage research: certain women can't be left alone, certain women insisted on being left alone, some women preferred only the company of strangers, and others sought out old childhood friends in order to reminisce about middle school P.E. teachers that they later realized were lesbians. The percentage of those women who eventually left their husbands was pretty high.

What I'm saying is, there's an infinite number of possible ways each mourning near-mother will act. I guess if I should ever weigh in on the subject and leave a comment on some of those blog sites, I might add, "Certain women lose all rational abilities and force their husbands to go out binge drinking with Eddie and Albert," et cetera.

I left the house but didn't contact my friends. We worked together, the three of us, thirty miles away at Die-Co, the die-cutting outfit. Eddie and Albert were my best friends, but even after working together fifteen years, whenever I saw Eddie and Albert I thought "Eddie Albert," which made me think of the actor who played Oliver Douglas on *Green Acres*, which caused that theme song to play in my head for some time afterward.

Or I thought of the actress Eva Gabor who, from what I learned, got married five times and never had a child.

Eddie and Albert didn't know about Carol's other miscarriages. They never said to me, "When y'all going to have some kids?" even though Eddie had three daughters and Albert a son named Albert Jr. I don't accuse my friends of being inattentive or self-absorbed. Die-cutters, on the whole, think about protecting their fingers most of the day, and at night the severed fingers they've seen on the floor.

Maybe I didn't always feel like drinking outside the house when Carol's friends came over and my wife shuttled me out. Carol worked the cosmetics counter at a Belk department store thirty miles in the other direction of our Calloustown abode. Her coworkers—I forget their names, but they worked Fine China, Lingerie, Children's Shoes, and Handbags—showed up at times, always complaining about the store manager, no commissions, mothers who accused their kids of growing out of clothes on purpose, and the lack of basic human civility in general. Anyway, the coworkers drove all the way out to our house on occasion, and Carol requested my absence.

Like almost every time this occurred, on this particular day I drove into Calloustown, parked my truck, and found myself inside Southern Exotic Pets, a place that specialized in reptiles, tropical fish, the irregular chinchilla, and—according to rumor—trapped and shipped dingoes from Australia. If I know my canines, the dingoes were nothing more than pointy-eared thin dogs from the swamps down in the lower part of the state and southeast Georgia called, plainly, Carolina Dogs, and recognized by the AKC. For what it's worth, unlike typical, non-feral purebreds, Carolina Dog bitches underwent three estrus cycles in quick succession, much like my wife.

Southern Exotic Pets stood between the Side Pocket bar and Calloustown Grill. Across the street we had a pawn shop, a fireworks outlet, and a storefront long vacant and unrentable due to the ghosts living inside ever since Grady Dorn shot and killed his entire family and then hanged himself there inside what had been his Calloustown Florists business. It's not like a curious person couldn't wile away a good few hours, which often made me wonder why Calloustown never seemed to attract northern retirees and/or fugitives in need of relatively safe refuge.

I walked into Southern Exotic Pets and waved at Spence, the owner. He yelled out, "Sorry to hear about Carol!" too loudly. I nodded, held up my hand, and turned toward the stacked-up aquariums. I passed blue neon guppies, tetras, angelfish, the usual. I tried to stare down an apartment complex of Siamese fighting fish, but they seemed bored. On down the aisle Spence kept a couple piranhas and a slither of eels—which made me think that a sushi joint should open up in Grady Dorn's old flower shop, seeing as the chef could cross the street and get his fresh ingredients—and then I rounded a corner to a line of snakes, lizards, salamanders, and tortoises.

If a five-year-old boy had not mistaken me for his father—at least that's the original scenario I concluded—I might've leaned down to a ball python and thought about Dottie showing up and constricting all the air out of our house. But the kid, two terrariums down from me, tapped on glass and said, "Here's what I want. It's a corn snake, but I can tell everyone it's a coral snake. 'Red touch yellow, kill a fellow.' This has red touching black, so it's a corn snake."

I walked over and bent down to see. He looked up and said, "Hey, you're not..."

Growing up, I had mistaken strangers for my father too, a number of times. I never decided if I was the one who strayed off inside grocery and hardware stores or if my father wasn't the most conscientious guardian. To the kid in front of the snake I said, "How long will that corn snake get?" and hoped he wouldn't start screaming out, what with how modern parents implant fear and paranoia into their children's heads, rightly or not, to the point of it being impossible to approach any child aged two to nineteen and say, "Hello, kid, do you know anything about how that Kentucky Fried Chicken box you're holding got die-cut?" without a mother appearing out of nowhere, already punching 911 on her cell phone.

"Hey," the boy said. He didn't need to introduce himself, I thought. He wore a stick-on "Hello My Name Is" nametag on his shirt with REX written in block letters. Who let his kid walk around in public with a nametag? Now that was an unconscientious guardian.

"Hey back at you, Rex. I'm Duane." I said, "Do you want me to help you find your father or mother?"

Whenever Eddie, Albert, and I got together, Albert got stuck thinking nonstop about Duane Eddy, the guitarist who recorded the 1960s instrumentals "Peter Gunn" and "Rebel Rouser." Sometimes when Albert didn't respond to questions both Eddie and I knew he'd gotten those twangy notes stuck in his head.

Rex looked like he belonged in a breakfast cereal commercial. There weren't many children left in Calloustown—

occasionally someone over the age of forty might have an un-planned pregnancy—and I thought about how I'd never seen this kid before. Maybe he lived in a town even smaller than Calloustown, a place like Gruel or Level Land that couldn't support a store that specialized in pets other than calicos, Dachshunds, and minnows.

Rex said, "A coral snake's one of the most dangerous snakes in America. There's the rattler, and water moccasin, and copperhead. But the coral snake's better."

I'm not sure why I decided it was the proper time to tell this little innocent boy about a nonexistent mythical creature my crazy uncle Dillard told me about when I was Rex's age. I said, "Coral snakes are scary, but not like a pine gator. I doubt they sell pine gators here. They're too rare and vicious."

Rex shook his head sideways, then said, "What?"

"A pine gator," I said. "It's kind of like a regular alligator, but it has a monkey's tail. Pine gators are shy, reclusive an-imals that mostly live in the Appalachian Mountains. They hang down from tree limbs, you know, and wait for people to walk by. Or deer. Pine gators have been known to eat the heads off bears that aren't paying attention, or that are spend-ing too much time by a pine gator's personal tree sniffing around for honeybee hives. You can hardly even see them, they're so camouflaged. A pine gator's hide looks just like pine tree bark."

I felt sure that Rex wasn't from here, or even the state of South Carolina. It's not difficult to make out a stranger—the men have haircuts performed by professionals, the women pluck their eyebrows consistently, and the children don't squint, stammer, and wear long sleeves in summer to hide their scars and bruises. Strangers ask for directions back to

I-26, I-20, I-85, or I-95; they try too hard to use double negatives when talking to us; they leave tips at the Calloustown Diner.

Rex said, "I used to have a pine gator for a pet. I had one."

"You did?" I said. "I never had one. I've seen a couple, but I got scared and ran. I didn't want my fingers bitten off, seeing as I already work as a die-cutter."

"Mine's was named Gypsy," Rex said. The corn snake in front of him lifted up toward its cage's roof then dropped down.

"That's a pretty good name for a pine gator," I said, though I didn't mean it, seeing as we didn't live far from Irish Travelers, and I knew that the term "gypsy" wasn't all that right a thing to say. "I believe that if I ever had the good fortune of owning a pine gator, though, you know what I'd name him? Gypsy! I'd name him Gypsy, that's what I'd do, no doubt."

"Hey, that was my pine gator!" Rex said. He laughed and stomped his feet. "I just said that!"

He walked toward me, and then, without my having to take his hand or shoulder, followed me to the cash register where, I assumed, we'd find his parent. "I came across this little snake aficionado over in your snake section," I said to Spence.

"You did?" Spence looked over his drugstore-purchased reading glasses. "Nothing I like more than to have a herpetologist in the room."

The kid said nothing. Spence and I stood there looking at each other for too long, then we looked around to find no other adult in the pet store. I said, "Rex, was your father or mother in here with you earlier?"

He said, of course, "Why do you keep calling me Rex?"

We ran outside and yelled for help. We looked down aisles, behind aquariums, in the storage room, in the restroom. We did everything three times. In between I said, "What's your name?" and "How did you get here?" Looking back, maybe I didn't give the kid enough time to answer. When he started crying—wailing, really, just like any kid in a movie about divorced parents or not getting a toy—I didn't know what else to do outside of calling Carol and interrupting her sullen rendezvous with Dottie.

"We got this kid down here at the pet shop don't know his real name his father or mother seems to have abandoned him!" I yelled over the phone.

My wife said, "Try 'Jacob.' Try 'Jacob,' 'Jason,' 'Joshua,' or 'Jeremy.' Those are the most popular names right now."

I looked at him and asked if those were his names. He said, "I'm not supposed to say my name to strangers." He'd quit crying, but Spence needed to hold a Kleenex to the boy's nose. I wasn't going to do it.

"Just bring him home," Carol said. "We'll figure this out." She turned her head from the mouthpiece and said to Dottie, "You see any 'Lost Child' posters on your way over here?" To me she said, "Dottie says check his pockets and tags of his shirt and underwear."

"Good idea," I said, and hung up.

The three of us stood there at the register. Someone next door beat on the wall, either excited or upset with the football game being aired. I told Spence what Carol said. "I ain't doing that," Spence said. "Ten years from now Little John Doe here will have some questionable memories and the next thing you know you and me'll be sharing a prison cell with Father Fudgepacker."

The kid said, "I want the corn snake."

I pulled the back of his T-shirt and looked at the tag. His parents hadn't printed a name there. I said, "Is your daddy's name Rex? Did you get that sticker from your daddy?" I thought I'd come up with a good idea, logic-wise. My father always let me wear the paper bracelets they wrapped around his wrist at the hospital, back before drinking and driving was a sin and my father wrecked his car.

Spence said, "Who wants a corn snake?" and smiled.

"I do," the kid said.

"I don't know anyone named 'I.' You're going to have to be a little more specific, or Duane here's going to take you out on the sidewalk and pull your pants down."

I said, "Damn, Spence, shut up. You've already gone too far with the Father Fudgepacker thing." I said to the kid, "I'm not going to pull your pants down. Do you want a Tootsie Pop or something? Spence, you got any Tootsie Pops back there?"

"Who is it that wants a corn snake?" Spence said again.

"George Washington never told a lie," the boy said. To me, he no longer looked like a child actor who starred in cereal commercials. I kind of didn't like him—or his parents—and maybe thought about how lucky I was not to have to deal with a kid daily.

I wanted a drink something bad. I felt it necessary to go to the Side Pocket and pull for colleges I'd never heard about. It wouldn't've taken a gun to my head to drive home, shoo Dottie, and get to work impregnating Carol until she kept a baby to term.

Spence said, "No, you idiot, I don't have any Tootsie Pops. Does this look like a candy store? Why would you even get the boy's hopes up in such a way?"

The boy started bawling again. "I want a Tootsie Pop," he blurted out. Something flew out of his nose, then returned. It looked like a moray eel, I swear to God.

Spence said, "Who wants a Tootsie Pop? I don't know anyone named 'I.' Again, you have to be more specific."

I thought about how a five-year-old child wouldn't understand "specific." The child, though, said, "Wyatt Speight Jr. wants a Tootsie Pop."

"See?" Spence said. "That 'junior' part sure makes it easier."

I said, "I know that you can't leave the register, so keep an eye on him and I'll canvas the block looking for his parents." To the kid I said, "Did Wyatt Speight Sr. bring you here, or your momma? Or Wyatt Speight's parents? Do you know what your mother's maiden name is, in case I need to look for those grandparents?"

Little Wyatt shrugged his shoulders. Spence told me to shut up, go ask around, and look for a sucker for the kid while I was at it.

Because I've seen the news, *City Confidential, Cops, America's Most Wanted, 20/20, Dateline,* and those other television programs that delve into the uncompromising side of evil human beings, I knew better than to walk into the Side Pocket, stand on the bar, and yell out, "Is anybody in here looking for a little five-year-old boy?" I don't want to say anything about my Calloustown citizens during rough economic times, but there was the chance that some of them might want an extra kid around for cheap labor, and the others for possible ransom demands. No, I walked into the bar, ordered a beer from Pony Robbins, the owner, and looked around for unfamiliar faces. I seemed to know everyone, and if not by name I knew them enough not to be named Wyatt or Speight or Senior. I said to Pony, "You seen any strangers in here today?"

He wore a long ponytail, which I guess he grew what with his official, given name. Sometimes Pony Robbins got drunk and said, "I'm glad my daddy didn't name me Mohawk or Fu Manchu. I'm glad my parents didn't name me Beehive or Bob." Pony said, "You just missed Eddie and Arnold."

"There's a little kid next door who's lost his parents. You know anybody around here named Wyatt Speight?"

Pony shook his head. "Only locals and regulars today. You can pretty much tell if an out-of-Calloustowner's been in here by examining the bottom of this." He held up an empty tip jar. He handed me a glass of draft beer. "You look like you seen a goat," Pony said. He always told people how a goat's eyes scared him more than a wisp of specter crossing an empty street, say from the old florist's place over to the bar.

I drank my beer, ordered another, and placed a five-dollar bill on the bar. "I'll be right back," I said, and went to the diner and called out, "Wyatt Speight Sr.?" then repeated the process up and down the street, sticking my head in storefronts.

Nothing.

Somebody at Calloustown Diner said, "Wyatt Earp" immediately after my summons, evidently thinking I wanted to start up a bastardized game of word association.

When I returned to the Side Pocket fifteen or twenty minutes later, Carol and Dottie stood beside my empty stool. They had Wyatt Speight Jr. with them. The kid had a piece of yarn tied to his wrist, which, I learned later, originated from a potholder Dottie had knitted. My wife held the other end of the yarn.

"I told her you weren't in here," Pony said, "but she recognized the five-dollar bill you left."

I thought he joked. I said, "No one showed up at the pet store? We need to call the police." To Wyatt I said, "Did someone drop you off and leave you? Did you hit your head? Do you know your address?"

Pony said, "Your wife goes through your wallet and memorizes numbers on the bills. Then she can go to places you say you haven't been and trade money from the register in order to look through all the serials."

Dottie said, "How old are you, Wyatt Speight Jr.?"

He said, "Five and a half."

"Hey, didn't you have a miscarriage five years and eight months ago, Carol?" Dottie stomped one foot down and opened her mouth wide. "If you ask me, this is the Lord's way of giving you the baby back. And that's how good Jesus is! He's saved you from dirty diapers, vaccinations, a breast pump if you so chose that option, potty training. The list goes on! Jesus probably saved y'all'ses marriage, seeing as old Duane here didn't have to lie and sneak out of the house when he couldn't take the kid howling from colic anymore. Jesus saved you a fortune in having to buy gripe water."

I looked at Carol, hoping she'd be able to read my eyes, with which I tried to say two things: "We need to ditch Dottie somehow," and "Do you really go through my wallet?"

Wyatt Speight Jr. said, "Are you my new mommy?" Maybe he had some kind of wall-eye problem, but he appeared to be asking Pony.

———

Out of everyone involved, Spence—who may or may not have bought and sold cobras, inland taipans, black mambas, bushmasters, cottonmouths, and diamondbacks to questionable breeders and collectors—called up the sheriff's department and the Department of Social Services to report the situation. When Deputy Leonard Marder showed up to ask questions, we left the bar and returned to the pet store in case anyone—namely the kid and me—needed to reenact the scene.

We let Spence give the appropriate answers. In a place like Calloustown, die-cutters were considered much more reliable than housepainters, roofers, or pulpwood drivers, but not shopkeepers. There were a number of occasions wherein I allowed someone else to talk to an authority figure, mainly because Die-Co came out Dyke-o to most people's ears, and a cop or meter reader might be prejudiced immediately.

"What time did you first notice the boy?" Marder asked.

"I don't know. What time was it, Duane?"

Dottie said, "I come over at noon."

My wife said to Dottie, "Let's let them figure it out. Let's go get some coffee." I don't know if I said, "Thank you, Carol, thank you," audibly. To Marder I said, "Yeah, I'd say about noon."

The kid said, "I had Cocoa Puffs for breakfast."

I didn't think anything of the statement, but Deputy Marder might've had better training than I understood. He said, "So you're not from Calloustown, are you? We don't sell Cocoa Puffs around here."

I said, "What the hell's gripe water? Dottie—the woman who just left with my wife—said something earlier about babies needing gripe water."

Leonard Marder said, "Where you been, Duane? I thought you and your buddies took your bourbon with gripe water. Go on over to the Bag 'n Pay and look in the formula section. Or in Mixers."

He seemed unnecessarily adamant about his directive. Maybe I breeched the law enforcement officer/witness protocol.

Spence said, "Every minute counts, I'm thinking."

Wyatt Speight Jr. said, slowly, a series of numbers. It wasn't little-kid-trying-to-count numbers, either. He didn't go, "One, two, three, eight, fifty!" He counted out seven digits, which Leonard Marder wrote down while I concentrated on a defense strategy, seeing as that's how I ran my life daily with Carol and my boss.

Spence said, "You can use my phone here."

Leonard Marder said, "I don't know why they went and got us all cell phones. Got to drive out of the county to get a proper and reliable signal."

I learned later, on Monday, that everything worked out for little Wyatt Speight Jr. and his parents. There had been some disharmony in the family, evidently, and Wyatt Sr.'s father-in-law tried to scare his daughter. The old man kidnapped young Wyatt, young Wyatt escaped, and his grandfather chickened out and drove two counties away. Was he going to ask for ransom money? Did he plan on reinventing his life elsewhere, complete with very young son? Eventually,

I felt certain, Leonard Marder or the Department of Social Services caseworker or a minister would recognize the entire story.

My wife and I had returned home without saying much to each other. I don't want to say there was a tension between us, but something caused us both, I felt sure, to feel a need to be alone and with one another simultaneously. Perhaps it was guilt—I beat myself up for owning seed that couldn't grip for more than a month, and I got that Carol, too, underwent a sense of hopelessness in regards to our ever filling the extra bedroom with a crib, mobile, and stuffed animals reminiscent of what thrived in tiny cages at Southern Exotic Pets.

Carol sat down in the den and tried to teach herself how to knit.

I stared at her more often than not for the rest of the weekend, in hopes that should words come out of my mouth I wouldn't say something that might make her cry.

We didn't answer the telephone when a television news reporter called from fifty miles away. I kept the TV tuned to the Weather Channel and concentrated on a documentary about Hurricane Hugo, which had affected Calloustown peripherally twenty years earlier. Carol and I didn't answer the phone when a newspaper reporter called, or when Dottie called, or even when Wyatt Speight Sr. called and left a message of gratitude.

I said to my wife, "We would make the best parents ever, more than likely."

Carol's needles clacked out a noise that—if I remembered rudimentary Morse code well enough from back in Boy Scouts—spelled out either S-O-S or S-O-N.

Like I said, I learned the entire story on Monday. I had called in sick and figured it safe to go buy a newspaper to check out both Saturday and Sunday's scores.

I read where Wyatt Speight's father promised his son that corn snake, as it ended up. And right there on page 2A under Local News the father mentioned how his son really wanted a "pine gator," but a snake would have to do, after this ordeal. He said, "I want to thank all the people who helped bring my boy home," and said that he wouldn't be pressing charges against his father-in-law, a man who "fought some demons." Evidently the grandfather thought Wyatt Jr. liked dinosaurs more than snakes, thus the "Rex" ploy.

My wife and I ate Alpha-Bits for supper that night, as we had most nights, spelling out words to each other and waiting without complaint.

Is There Anything Wrong with Happier Times?

Harold Lumley needed to check out his mother's reported lapses in judgment. He had received a call from the executive director of the Calloustown Community Center—a place where Ruth Lumley had volunteered for the past six years reading to the children of migrants, offering English lessons to the workers, and basically being a joyful person in a variety of capacities. She'd refereed Liga Pequeña basketball games up until her hip replacement surgery and had taught a roomful of Latina women how to cook a number of Southern staples when it came to funeral foods, from potato salad to chicken pot pie. Ruth Lumley'd conducted seminars on how to open bank accounts, pass the DMV's written test, and talk to a child's teacher without having the teacher feel threatened. She had offered baton-twirling lessons so the little girls could one day feel good about themselves as majorettes.

The woman—Ms. Pickens? Ms. Pickering?—had told Harold over the phone that, although she didn't want to pry into the Lumley family's way of treating their elderly relatives, perhaps he should drive down and observe his mother's recent peculiarities. She said, "I don't want to judge you or nothing, but I believe your momma might be getting to that point where a retirement facility's the best option. When they start acting peculiar, it's a sign. I don't know for sure, but she seems to have befriended some puppets, and turned her back on the rest of us."

Harold cradled the phone to his ear. He needed to talk to his franchise owner about firing three people—one for ineptitude, one for stealing herbal Viagra, one for sexual harassment. He managed a place called Other Medicine—a small chain, a constant for Buddhists and Unitarians distrustful of pharmaceutical companies and reassured by the OM in the store's name. "Can you be more specific?" Harold asked the woman. "Say your name again?"

"This is Berta Parks. I'm the executive director of the Calloustown Community Center down in Calloustown."

Harold thought, "How did I get Pickens or Pickering out of this? Maybe I'm the one who needs to be reported for dementia." He thought, "Wasn't the old Miss America master of ceremonies named Bert Parks—man, how much crap did this woman get for her name?" He said, "Is my mother all right?"

Harold felt guilty about not visiting more often. Evidently his brother, Kenny, visited her two or three times a week. But with a divorce, two high school kids on weekends, and an ever-present rotation of minimum wage–earning high school graduates who confused Niacin with acai, vitamin B with bee pollen, and nickels with quarters, it seemed as though he spent eighteen hours a day outside of his own apartment. He brought his mother up for every other Christmas, for every other birthday. "I can't come down to spend two or three days in Calloustown," he used to say. "First off, it sends me into depression and flashbacks of growing up there. Two, I'd get stolen blind if I left someone else in charge of the store."

To Berta Parks he said, "Okay. Okay. I talk to my mother all the time—almost daily—and she doesn't sound any different to me. Kenny says she's doing well, too."

He'd not spoken to Kenny, who lived in Calloustown still after taking over their father's extermination business, since he didn't know when. Berta Parks said, "The elderly find ways of masking their frailties and insecurities. They find ways to adapt, you know. If you start talking to them about an open wound on their head, they can find a way to veer the conversation into something that happened to them in 1945 when open wounds were all the rage."

Ever the salesman, Harold said, "I can get you some ginseng, gingko biloba, gotu kola, yerba mate, and rhodiola rosea if you think it would be a good idea to have some on hand for any of the older people who frequent the community center. These are all fine herbal supplements. They're not necessarily approved by the FDA, but we all know the FDA is holding back the American public when it comes to valid, non-traditional antidotes to some of the more common ailments from which the public suffers these days. In our fast-paced modern world." He had taken a community college public speaking course, and the instructor had advised everyone to use "fast-paced modern world" whenever possible.

Berta Parks said, "I'm just saying. I've been taking notes, and I'm about to start tape-recording some of the things that your momma's saying. I tried to call your brother, but he got all choked up and said he couldn't deal with it. He also said he had enough going on what with the field rat infestation we got going all over here."

Harold tried to imagine a plague of rats overtaking the Calloustown Community Center, or Tiers of Joy Bakery, or

Worm's Bar, or the clapboard house where he grew up. He could imagine the fear that must have consumed a dwindling population on its way to attaining ghost-town status, and could smell the ammonia of a rat-infested abode, seeing as a teenager he'd been forced to exterminate with his long-deceased father. He envisioned his mother sitting in that La-Z-Boy chair in front of the TV—maybe one of those competitive cooking shows airing, or a *Green Acres* marathon—with rats flitting back and forth unperturbed.

"What's she doing that's so peculiar?" he asked Berta Parks. "I mean, Jesus, old people—sometimes they finally realize they can say anything they want to say. I hope I get to that point. I want to get to the point where I can look a customer in the eye and say, 'No amount of milk thistle is going to heal that enlarged liver of yours, ma'am.' You know what I mean?"

"I might as well go ahead and get to the point," Berta Parks said. "You can do what you will with it. Let me say right off that we appreciate the hours and hours Ms. Lumley's put in at the community center as a volunteer. She's done more than anyone else around here. That being said, she's started using a lot of profanity that we think is unnecessary. Somewhere along the line she became convinced that the little Mexican children should hear Br'er Rabbit stories in order to understand English better—you know those stories by Uncle Remus?—but she keeps adding all these curse words in between that aren't part of the original stories."

Harold didn't hear, exactly, all of Ms. Parks's complaint. He got stuck on the "that being said" part, which was another thing his community college public speaking instructor advised using whenever possible. Harold wondered if Berta

Parks might've been in the same class he took. He said to her, "I remember those old Br'er Rabbit stories. We used to have some kind of storyteller woman show up and tell those stories to us back at Calloustown Elementary. Something about Br'er Rabbit living in the briars all his life. Or Br'er Rabbit going down into a well, stuff like that."

"Uh-huh. But you probably don't remember Br'er Rabbit saying stuff like, 'I'mo blank your blank sister if'n you don't get that blank tar baby outta my blank field of vision, you son of a blank.' Ms. Lumley's saying those kinds of things to the little Mexican children. We have come to believe that—illegal immigrants or not—they don't deserve such lessons."

Harold said, "Oh come on now. Are you sure? Sometimes my mother has a speech impediment." He tried to think back to when she ever said a curse word. He said, "Well that doesn't sound all that great. At least Spanish-speaking muchachos might not understand what she's saying!"

"Like I said," Berta Parks said, "it's what we have before us. We just think it would be good if you could talk some sense into her, or see if there's a better place for her to be."

"I understand. Okay," Harold said. He thought about how he'd not fire anyone today. He thought about how he probably needed to visit his brother, too, if his car could make it through a roadblock of vermin on the outskirts of Calloustown.

Ruth Lumley's car isn't in the carport, and she's not home. The side door's locked, and Harold finds her extra key hidden in the same spot where his parents kept it when he grew up: in a conch shell sitting atop a clay flowerpot filled with playground sand, previously used as an outdoor ashtray when

Mr. Lumley held his annual "I Exterminated You" BBQ for the year's clients. Harold has thought often about how, in a strange way, he became interested in herbs and vitamins due to these yearly fetes, how in between sneaking drinks from the bar he thought of how all these people would one day suffer from the effects of even the lesser pesticides and insecticides his father sprayed beneath their abodes and how one day they might be in need of something like detoxifying herbs such as burdock and dandelion root.

"Why even lock the house?" Harold thinks. "Who would break in here?"

He unlocks the door and finds the familiar smell of his childhood: Pine-Sol, boiled cabbage, cigarettes, Pledge, coffee grounds. He would think something like, "My mother hasn't changed whatsoever," but he finds himself mesmerized and bombarded with what she's hung on the kitchen, then the den, walls. Ruth Lumley has, evidently, joined the computer age and—addicted to eBay—bought every available eight-by-ten promotional photo of TV and motion picture animal stars. Harold looks up at the nicely framed pictures of Lassie, Rin Tin Tin, Flipper, Gentle Ben the bear, Trigger, the Lone Ranger's horse Silver, that Jack Russell terrier Eddie from *Frasier*, Zorro's black stallion Toronado, Clarence the cross-eyed lion from *Daktari*, and Festus's mule. He walks into the den to find some of those same photos, plus ones of Tonto's horse Scout, Fred the cockatoo from *Baretta*, the fake shark from *Jaws*, Willy the Orca, a bundle of rats from *Willard*, and a snake from one of the snake movies that Harold doesn't know. She has three photos of Duke the bloodhound.

Then there are the animation cels: Heckle and Jeckle, Dino, Marmaduke, Scooby-Doo, Tom and Jerry, Astro, Tweety

Bird, Roadrunner, the Tasmanian Devil, Wile E. Coyote, Pepe Le Pew, Yogi and Boo-Boo. Harold's mother had gotten rid of a bookcase in order to fill the wall behind it with eight-by-ten framed cels of Deputy Dog, Droopy Dog, Goofy, Hector, Huckleberry Hound, Mr. Peabody, Odie, Pluto, Snoopy, Spike, and Underdog. He feels bad about thinking, "Good God, there goes the goddamn inheritance." Framed photos of Br'er Fox, Br'er Rabbit, Br'er Terrapin, and Miss Possum line the very top of the wall—all from *Song of the South*.

He calls Kenny and says, "Hey, man, where are you?"

"I'm on Mr. Reddick's roof because he has these rats stuck in his gutters running in some kind of race. You ought to see it, man! It's like a living river of smooth brown hide. It's like some kind of bizarre stock car race."

Harold says, "I'm at Mom's house. You been here lately?"

Kenny says, "If I'd've known it was this bad I'd've brought a Gatling gun up here with me. You ought to see these things go. Hey, come on over! I ain't but a mile away."

"What's the story with all these photos on the wall? Have you been by here? I don't know if I can even count as high as how many pictures she has on the wall."

"Jesus, I'm going to have to go get a flute and see if I can lead these things out of here. Hold on. Let me get down off this roof, which means we'll probably lose the connection."

"Did you give her all these pictures? I hope to God that's the case. Because if it's not, then we might have a problem."

"What pictures? Pictures like you look at, or pitchers like you pour tea out of? I might've given her one of each. Over time I might've given her one of each. I sent her a picture of me and the boys and Dora last Easter in front of that big cave opening."

Sure enough, they lose their connection.

Harold enters the hallway to find nothing on the walls except finishing nails sticking out a half inch each, apparently in wait for more publicity shots and/or animation cels. He enters his and Kenny's old bedroom, which appears untouched, then goes to the guest bedroom to find his mother's laptop turned on and stuck to a page that shows an eBay auction for a Quick Draw McGraw and Baba Looey cel, at the moment going for $99.99 with three hours left.

"A hundred goddamn dollars? Are you kidding me?" Harold says out loud.

He looks down to an old Calloustown Extermination notepad that his father gave to clients thirty years earlier and reads, "Password—ImNotOld81" and "UserID—ImNotOld81."

He locks the side door and places the key back in the conch shell. Harold thinks about going over to the community center and sitting down with Ms. Parks but realizes that—in a small town—sometimes people exaggerate the quirks of the elderly.

So he drives over to the Reddicks' place to talk to his brother first. Harold passes his mother coming toward him, a mile from his house. He waves at her, but she doesn't seem to see him. She wears oversized sunglasses handed out at the ophthalmologist's office, her eyes an inch above the steering wheel.

Harold turns quickly into an old logging road, backs out, and accelerates to catch up with his mother. She drives twenty-five miles an hour, so he meets up with her in a matter of seconds. He flashes his lights. He blows his horn and waves. She doesn't notice. He veers left and thinks about pulling up beside her on the straightaway. She has a number of dings and scrapes on the back bumper of the 1988 Lincoln Continental, the last model bought by Mr. Lumley after what he labeled the Great Bee and Bat Scare of 1987.

Harold's phone rings and he picks it up off the passenger seat without looking down. Kenny says, "I figured we'd get cut off."

"I'm behind Mom right now," Harold says. "I'm following behind her. I was calling you earlier about her house. When's the last time you went inside there?"

"I don't know," Kenny says. "It's been a while, now that I think about it. We meet for supper over at that Ryan's a couple times a week. She can almost eat for goddamn free if we get there by four thirty."

Harold watches as his mother sticks her left arm out for a turn signal instead of hitting her blinker. He thinks, "She probably thinks it costs money to use any of the electrical system. She'll spend ten thousand bucks on weird cartoons, but she won't use her blinker."

"You want to come on over and meet me at the house? I believe this might be one of those intervention kinds of things that everyone's talking about all the time. Is she drinking?"

Harold wonders if he's lost another phone call. He pulls in behind his mother in the driveway. Then he hears his brother going, "Rat in the truck, rat in the truck!" followed by brakes screeching.

In Ruth Lumley's mind, Harold should've taken over the family business. He was older than Kenny by four years, and he had the education and business acumen to turn Calloustown Extermination into a thriving chain throughout the lower piedmont region of South Carolina. But Harold went two states away in order to get an associate's degree in hospitality and tourism, received a job immediately at a resort down in Myrtle Beach, then turned his back on the entire industry in order to explore the burgeoning world of non-traditional herbs, roots, and panaceas amply supported by a number of medical personalities that provided free advertising daily on the talk shows—something both his ex-wife and mother always deigned snake oil salesman at best. He'd gotten into a conversation with the man who ended up hiring Harold away from Wild Sea Oats Resort and Spa, an entrepreneur of sorts named Bill Will who'd recently diversified from land development into what he explained to Harold as "making up for ruthlessness." This was at a tucked-away local hangout called He Just Left. They had an all-you-can-eat Fish Sticks Night on Friday, and before Harold needed more tartar sauce he'd become convinced that his destiny involved echinacea, St. John's wort, and garlic bulb tincture. It involved horny goat extract known as epimedium, though that word reminded him of "epicedium," a word that had to do with funeral dirges that Harold learned in an English class taught by an overeager instructor who insisted on vocabulary memorization. Bill Will said he had a feeling, and hired Harold immediately, right there at the bar. Within a month Harold learned from his own wife Mollyanna that he'd become irresponsible, that he wasn't thinking about the kids, that a place called Other Medicine didn't exactly provide his children with unlimited swimming pool usage or free driving range privileges. He learned, too, that she'd been seeing her chiropractor on the sly for over a year.

Parked in her carport, Ruth checks her rearview mirror and says, "What now?"

Harold gets out and approaches his mother's Lincoln. He bends down at the waist and counts all the dings—seventeen. After his mother closes her door and walks toward him he says, "You sure you should be driving?"

"Don't make me drive, don't make me drive! Law, whateber you do, don' thow me out into duh got-damn macadam!—Hey, I was born on the highway, Harold. Mind your own business." She reaches her face upward so he can kiss her. "I have never had a ticket or wreck in my life, for your information."

She smells like alfalfa extract, Harold thinks. She smells like a combination of baby powder, alfalfa, and chicken livers. "Well something's going on here. Maybe you're going so slowly down the road that deer are banging into the back of your car."

She says, "All right. Who died? Why're you here?"

"You want to go inside?" Harold asks. "Let's you and me go inside and talk about the community center." He knows that if she doesn't let him inside, then she's trying to hide all of the photographs and cels. If she appears unconcerned about her latest décor, then he might need to worry.

"I'm on my way to the community center right now, goddamn it," Ruth says. "Move your car, you're blocking my way."

"Wait a minute—if you're going to the center, then why'd you come home and park your car in the carport? That doesn't make much sense, Mom."

"It's a habit I have, that's all. Don't you have any goddamn habits that people don't quite understand? Like having a perfectly great job and leaving it in the dust so your wife leaves you and your children now don't have much of a college fund because you gave up a hundred K a year for thirty?"

Harold wonders about her blood pressure. He can't quite tell if she's red in the face, due to the foundation she wears that must've come straight out of a local embalmer's stock overrun sale. He says, "I've already been inside. I've seen what you have on the walls. I got summoned here to see what's going on over where you volunteer with the little migrant workers' kids or whatever. But now I kind of want to know what's happened to the kitchen and den walls."

The mail deliverer pulls in behind Harold's car and, even though it's obvious that his appearance is known, he honks his horn. Through the open window he yells, "Hey there, Ms. Lumley, I got you another delivery won't fit in the box without bending it." He holds out three flat cardboard boxes.

"Just set them down there, Elwin," Ruth says.

"On the driveway?"

"Oh, son of a bitch," Ruth says, stomping toward the mailman. "Here. Do I need to sign anything?"

"No, ma'am. That's it."

"Well make sure you're in reverse this time so you don't bang into my car again. Or I guess my son's car. Hell, keep it in drive and ram into his back bumper all you want."

Harold says to Elwin, "Hey, Mr. Patterson."

Elwin nods twice, grimaces, and backs out onto the road. Ruth Lumley's at the door, trying to fish keys out of her pocketbook and get inside so—Harold feels certain—she can lock him out. He runs up to her just as she's closing the door, gets his hand in, and pulls it back right before she slams his fingers in the jamb. "Go see your brother. Go visit your brother. There's a rat problem all around here and he could probably use some help."

"Let me in," Harold says. He bangs on the door, then presses the buzzer and holds it. Harold thinks, "I should let the air out of her tires." He thinks, "I can take the battery out of her car and that'll keep her immobile for a while." He begins laughing. "Come on, Mom, let me in. I'm having flashbacks of growing up and Dad wouldn't let me in the house until I hosed out the back of his truck."

Ruth Lumley doesn't respond at first. Harold says, "Well, fuck it then," and goes back to his car. She'll have to come out of there at some point, he thinks, driving down to Worm's, a place he'd not entered since high school. A couple beers, he thinks, and I'll come back when she's outside practicing her baton, or whatever she does.

He doesn't hear her yell at the closed door, "They make me remember happier times. Is there anything wrong with happier times?" He doesn't hear her tear open an envelope and exclaim, "Lamb Chop!"

When he enters the bar, Harold finds Kenny sitting on the first stool. The décor's not changed since about the time beer companies converted from pull-tabs to flip-tops. Half-naked women on auto parts calendars adorn the walls. There's a bumper pool table wedged uselessly in a corner, a jukebox that might offer the most selections of Conway Twitty, Ferlin Husky, and Jerry Lee Lewis on the entire Eastern seaboard. "I figured you'd be here sooner or later," Kenny says.

They do not hug. Worm, whose father went by Worm, says, "See no time long." He points to Kenny and shrugs his shoulders to Harold.

Kenny says, "That's enough of that. Worm's trying to break some kind of record for speaking everything backwards. He wants to be in that book."

Harold says, "Coldest whatever's me give," but it takes him a minute to say it in order.

"To get back to your question, yes, I know all about Mom's little hobby," Kenny says.

Harold says, "They never have invented a better-smelling cockroach spray? Man, you reek of that stuff. It's going to get in your pores, and the next thing you know you'll be happy you got a brother who knows a thing or three about detoxification remedies." He says, "I wouldn't call it 'little' hobby, by the way. She must have a hundred framed photos on her walls. It's kind of creepy. It would make a nice veterinarian's office, though."

Worm opens three Tall Boys and sets them on the bar, two in front of Harold and one more for Kenny. He says, "Here."

Kenny says, "When it first started happening—or when I first learned about it a year or so ago—she said she wanted to start up some kind of museum. She said she wanted to open up the kind of museum people would drive off the highway to go visit. Like those giant balls of string, or giant balls of tinfoil, or giant balls of rubber bands. We was all for it. We could use some visitors, you know."

Harold shakes his head. He doesn't smile. He says, "How's Dora and the kids?"

"Kids're fine. Dora don't want me asking Mom much about her museum, seeing as Dora thinks if we bother her too much she'll evict us from the will. You know what I mean? Dora thinks at least we'll get a bunch of pictures of Mr. Ed and Lassie when Mom dies, as long as we don't piss her off none. And Cheetah. Did you know Cheetah just died a month or so ago? He was eighty years old. Mom's got two signed photos from Cheetah, from the old Tarzan movies."

Harold stares at his brother but he's not listening. He wonders if perhaps he should've stayed in Calloustown. What if he'd taken over Calloustown Extermination, as was his father's plan? He'd be living in a regular house somewhere nearby—Kenny made enough money to buy an old farmhouse and a hundred acres he leased out to dove and deer hunters in season—and would've probably kept his mother's dream of an Animal Picture Museum from ever forming.

Worm says, "Back in go to have I," and waves his right arm out, ending at the cash register, in the international way of letting the brothers know that they're in charge of retrieving their own cans of beer and putting the money in the cash drawer should they so choose.

Harold says, "I guess there can be worse hobbies. Worse dreams."

Kenny nods. He finishes his first beer and opens the second. "Sometimes I have to hire out this old boy to help me out, you know. He's pretty good at cockroaches, fire ants, and termites. Name's Bobby, but I call him Cool Breeze 'cause I swear to God he comes in and the women around here fall for him so much they got him setting traps for badgers and mongooses in their crawlspaces just so he'll stick around. His momma ain't but something like fifty, and she's already showing signs of crazy, you know? Won't pay nothing but the minimum on her credit card each month 'cause God told her to be that way. Drives in reverse half the time thinking it'll turn back her odometer and keep her younger, I guess. Shit like that."

Harold says, "I miss my kids." He says, "Sometimes I kick myself for not taking over Dad's business, so my kids could take over mine. There ain't no promise they can become an Other Medicine manager just because I'm an Other Medicine manager."

"It sure makes it easy knowing what to get Mom for birthdays and Christmas and Valentine's Day. Me and Dora got her one of those publicity shots for that cat that used to do the cat food commercials. I think he's dead by now. Anyways."

Harold says, "Has a woman named Berta Parks called you up about her cussing a bunch at little Mexican kids, something about telling off-color jokes about Br'er Rabbit?"

"About Berta Parks cussing a bunch, or Mom cussing a bunch."

Harold looks at his little brother. He says, "Mom. We're talking about Mom. Has Berta Parks ever called you?"

"Yeah. She's called twice. She's got a bad rat problem too—at the community center, and at home. She called me up twice, and I went out to set out poison and traps both."

Harold thinks, Now I remember why I got out of my hometown.

Harold leaves his brother at the bar. He puts down money and tells Kenny to hold some cold-pressed sunflower oil under his tongue for thirty minutes, then brush his teeth with baking soda in order to detoxify. Harold says, "I'm going back. I don't want to leave here feeling bad about Mom." He doesn't say, "What if she dies and this is my last memory of her?" though he thinks it.

Kenny says, "I got me a sweat lodge I built. That's how I sweat out the poison."

Harold wonders what his wife and that chiropractor are doing at the moment. It's four o'clock in the afternoon, and he imagines that his children are now home, that his ex-wife is succumbing to an adjustment of sorts. He drives a back road to the house of his upbringing and plans to park up the hill in the direction his mother would never take upon leaving for anything Calloustown had to offer, unless she wished to view a swamp, the town dump, or Mr. Reddick's nursery that he'd surrounded with a five-foot-high fence made up entirely of grout and liquor bottles.

There, hidden halfway behind a live oak a quarter mile away, he calls his wife's new house, gets the answering machine, and says, "Hey, kids. I'm in Calloustown if y'all need me, but I got my phone. Can't wait to see you on Friday." He forgets to say "I love you," calls back, but it's busy. He waits five minutes—his eyes focused on the estuary made up of his mother's driveway and the ancient asphalt—calls again, but it's still busy.

Ruth Lumley backs out and points her Lincoln away from Harold.

He lights a cigarette—Other Medicine sells packs of additive-free tobacco products with Bible verses on the flip-tops—squints, pulls down his visor. He turns on the radio to find, as in his childhood, Calloustown only receives a gospel channel clearly. Harold hums along to "It Is Well with My Soul" and wonders how he knows the melody. "Wasn't there something tragic about the man who wrote this song?" he wonders. "Wasn't there something about a young son dying, and four daughters lost at sea, and some kind of relentless fire?"

He watches his mother weave almost indiscernibly, then reach Old Calloustown Road and turn left, toward what remains of the town. She drives in the direction of Worm's and the community center. She drives past Tiers of Joy bakery. Harold remains a safe distance behind her, crawling along at twenty miles an hour. He watches as his brother comes from the other direction and notices how Ruth doesn't seem to notice. Kenny waves at their mother, then blows his horn and swerves toward his brother, a big open-mouthed laugh on his face.

The ember falls off of Harold's cigarette right onto his lap. He brushes his pants quickly, flicking the ember, somehow, straight into a crease between the sock on his right foot and his loafer. In an attempt to toe the shoe off completely with his left foot, he steps on the accelerator and, not watching the road, rams into his mother's car. Harold's two front teeth, capped, break off on the steering wheel. The airbag doesn't deploy as it does on Ruth's car—Harold's father had bragged about the 1988 Lincoln Continental being one of the first vehicles out of Detroit to have driver's-side bags.

"Son of a bitch," Harold yells out, throwing his shoe across the road into a ditch. He holds his hand to his mouth, spits two teeth out, and then reaches down to take off his sock. By the time he reaches his mother she's already out of the car, her eyes shut tight from whatever chemicals or gases had released.

Ruth says, "What the hell are you doing, boy?"

He doesn't say anything about the cigarette. He doesn't want his mother to know that while she wasted money on cartoon characters he spent money on what would eventually kill him. He says, "I must've blinked. You stopped for no reason, and I must've blinked."

She says, "I didn't want to hit those rats crossing the road. Did you see those rats? There was a line of them, just like deer but smaller. That's bad juju to run over the helpless."

They walk together to view the damage. Harold's car's radiator spills antifreeze on the pavement. The Lincoln appears barely damaged, though several of the small dings have now transformed into one large dent. "Is there a dentist left in this town? Damn, damn, damn. I can't deal with customers if I look like this."

"Why are you following me?" Ruth asks. "Are you trying to kill me or something? Is that what this is all about? You out of money or something, son? Come down here finally to scare me to death, run me off the road, get you and Kenny what's left of the estate?" She holds the back of her neck. She opens one eye slightly.

"It's that song from Dad's funeral," Harold says. "That's how come I knew that song on the radio."

"Call yourself a wrecker, son," she says. "I got things to do." She walks back to her open car door, still holding onto the back of her neck. There are children waiting for her to tell stories, and single mothers who need to learn how to knit. At six o'clock she's supposed to teach a class on making wind chimes out of bamboo. Plus, she's promised to help Berta Parks speak in proper Southern dialect, should someone ever need to take over Storytelling Hour. Then there's the puppet show. Ruth bends down slowly and lifts her eldest son's compromised sock off the ground. She says, "This will work out just fine for a puppet, I'm betting."

Unraveling

Long after I moved away, knowing nothing but bad things could occur to me—bad job followed by no job, bad marriage followed by no marriage, painful lesions followed by death—my father continued to struggle with mysterious demons and/or the Opposite of Newton's Third Law. It need not be pointed out that my father, born Sinclair but known as "Sin" forever, owned a printing company until the remaining denizens of Calloustown discovered Kinko's, that my mother left him for a man down in Sumter who retired from the Air Force and opened up an oyster bar, and that boils/hives/shingles arrived simultaneously on Dad's torso, just like I'd warned him. Sometime after I'd moved away, my father swore, he would pick up the phone to call someone only to find that person already on the other line, and then when he hung up the telephone would ring. He'd fill up premium unleaded into his tank, get a mile down the road, and run out of gas. My father put worms on his hooks and caught nothing, then, in desperation, threw in a naked bronze Eagle Claw and immediately pulled out a palm-sized bream. He'd spray his live trap with apple juice and place carrots in the tray in order to catch rabbits so he could breed the things and sell them to locals, only to have a cloud of Mexican free-tailed bats roost in the chimney. One time he had a sneezing attack, took over-the-counter medicine, went to a certified allergist, and after a thousand pinpricks the doctors concluded that my father was allergic to Benadryl. This went on and on. I had moved off to college then stayed for fifteen years. My dad closed down Sin's Printing, my mother left, the lesions erupted, and I visited less frequently until I picked up the phone one day to call my father and he was already on the other end.

"I told you this kind of shit happens all the time to me. And listen—because I know you're going to bring it up—if I moved away, then it would be like letting my nerves win," he told me. "Where would I move? To Sumter, where I'd be stuck eating oysters and letting Soretta live the high life from her goddamn husband's profit? Fuck that. I know she's your mother and you probably love her still, but I can't make myself hope that she does well. As a matter of fact—and I hope there's nothing to bad karma, you know, wherein you wish bad things on a person and then bad things happen to you because of it—I kind of want her to die a miserable death. Well, no, I want her to think she's going to die a miserable death, but really live to a hundred always on the edge of thinking it. Does that make any sense, son?"

I said, "Hello?"

"Listen. I wouldn't be so pissed off if there was a goddamn reliable doctor in this town. Do you remember Dr. Stoudemire who used to be here? He was a great man. You know what he did when the town died? He decided to move and start up doctoring in New Ellenton, which is close to being a ghost town on the edge of the Savannah River Nuclear plant. Ellenton's under water, in case you didn't pay attention to South Carolina History in seventh grade."

I hadn't. I mean, I remembered something about slavery, and a nuclear bomb that accidentally fell through the bomb door hatch of a B-47 above Mars Bluff on March 11, 1958, and— although the uranium and plutonium core wasn't attached—it created a mushroom cloud and hole deeper than most freshwater lakes in the area. I remembered that Senator Strom Thurmond ran for president as a Dixiecrat and opposed desegregation, though he fathered a biracial daughter. I remembered that a man named Senator Brooks beat up Senator Charles Sumner with a cane back before the Civil War. There was some kind of mention of a slew of astronomical events predating the end of the Pleistocene epoch hitting right around Calloustown, things called "Carolina Bays" because of the holes in the ground that, oddly, looked similar to that bomb hitting Mars Bluff. The teacher made a big point bi-daily to say something about how a man named Ruple went off to embalming college, got a job in one of the more prone-to-die-early cities, and left her in Calloustown alone.

I said, "Okay. I think we've gone over all of this before. Why did you almost call me but didn't because I picked up the receiver to call you and you were already there?"

"There's more," my father said. "There's so much more. A lot more."

I looked over at my wife. She had taken up knitting and spent more time—from what I could tell—untangling knots than actually manufacturing a scarf or mitten or bootie for one of her friends who planned on having a baby in the next twenty-seven months. I said, "Do you want me to drive down there?" I should mention that as soon as my mother left, back when I was in college, my father insisted that I call him only "Sin." I said, "Do you want me to drive down there, Sin?"

He said, "It's gotten to the point where I go to sleep at six fifteen in the morning, and wake up at eight thirty at night. It's all backwards. It's not like I'm scared of dying, like that man in that famous story. It's not like I want to stay awake all night afraid I'm going to get murdered." He said, "I caught myself last week toweling off before I got in the shower. And then I got in the shower with my clothes on, goddamn it."

I looked at Patricia. She said, "Are you all right?" She unknotted more yarn. It looked like a stalagmite of reddish noodles at her feet.

I shook my head. To my father I said, "Tell me what I can bring down there that you can't get in Calloustown. I'll stop by the store and get it, and then see you in a couple hours."

Patricia said, "Here we go again," set down her needles, and walked to the bedroom.

I called out to her, "Hey, don't get mad."

My father said, "Pussy."

If you gave Sin laxatives, he'd become constipated. A diet of hoop cheese sends him sitting on the toilet non-stop. His eyesight has gotten better with age. His skin de-freckles when he sits out in the sun too long.

I drove down to Calloustown and got there at two o'clock in the afternoon, walked in the unlocked door, and found him sitting in his old half-stuffed chair with copies of the *National Enquirer*, *Star*, and *Sun* unfolded across his lap. He said, "How'd you get in?"

I said, "I thought you said you slept all day long. You aren't asleep." I looked at the end table to see if he had a bottle of bourbon set out, but he didn't. He drank either water or vodka.

My father got up from the chair. He let the tabloids fall to his feet. "Thanks for coming down here, Duster. You still go by Duster, or have you shortened it rightly to 'Dust' by now? Like Sin. Sin and Dust, father and son. We could go into business together doing something. Like a fucking oyster house. Too bad my daddy—that would be your granddaddy—didn't name me Dirt." He shook my hand, which seemed to me a little mannered and inappropriate. We'd not seen each other since National Boss Day—the only holiday he ever celebrated when I grew up, seeing as he was my boss, his own boss, the boss of everything other-mental. My father understood that he was the boss of his, say, triceps, but not of his psyche. So it had been two months. Patricia and I spent Thanksgiving with her parents, and they feigned amazement at the two trivets she'd haphazardly crocheted out of Nu-Grape bottle caps so that the sweet potato and squash casseroles wouldn't scald the dining-room table.

I said, "The door was unlocked."

Sin—at this point he wasn't but sixty-three years old—looked at the door. He said, "It used to be that the door locked when I turned that little knob up and down. Now up and down means unlocked. I don't like this one bit. I can't keep up. Where's Patricia? I miss seeing your wife."

I walked into the kitchen and opened the refrigerator, just out of nosiness. Nothing seemed unusual, except that he had an inordinate amount of fast food–acquired condiments stacked neatly on the top three shelves, categorized. There was no McDonald's, Burger King, Long John Silver's, Arby's, Sonic, Hardee's, Krystal, Jack in the Box, or Taco Bell within fifty miles of my childhood home. He had some from a place called Swensons, which I knew from my travels only existed in and around the Akron, Ohio, area, some six hundred miles from Calloustown. I got a can of ginger ale out and said, "What's with all the mayonnaise and mustard? What's with the horsey sauce, taco sauce, three pepper sauce, and ketchup?"

I walked back in. Sin said, "You still married to Patricia?" He said, "Listen, you should read some of the articles in these newspapers I've been reading. There's a shoe-hoarding man in South Dakota who owns a white slave, and it's legal! The slave even says he likes it! His name's Thompson, and he says he's working to be in the *Guinness Book of Records* for most shoes shined in a lifetime. There's a picture of them in here," he said, picking up one of the papers, "and the South Dakota guy has Thompson wearing a choke collar, on a leash. America!"

I didn't say, "Those stories are made up, Dad." I didn't say, "Don't believe everything you read, Sin." I said, "I bet the slave owner's got something on Thompson," because I didn't know what else to say.

"Kind of like your mother had something on me. Is that what you're saying?"

I shook my head. I grabbed the channel changer and turned on the TV, even though I knew intuitively that it wouldn't work. Sure enough, the radio came on. I said, "I'm allergic to shellfish."

"Back to the question," Sin said. "I have figured out a way to garnish my sandwiches without having to pay for it. It saves me a fortune. See, I'll drive to one of those places, go inside—that's where everyone makes a mistake, going to the drive-through—and buy the cheapest thing on the menu to go. Then I walk over and absolutely overload my bag with packets of condiments. I've been meaning to get me a few empty jars and spend one of my nights squeezing what I have into them so it won't take up so much space."

I said, "The price of gas, Sin." I said, "Why am I here again?"

My father shook his head. He reached up and pulled at a patch of gray hair that grew mischievously to the left of his crown. He walked over to the window and looked out at my car. He said, "I thought you were going to bring me some pussy. Hey, you want to go throw some tin cans at a BB pistol out in the front yard?"

I sat down on the couch. I looked up at the photographs my father had put on the wall since my last visit—all of them pictures of various birds one might find browsing a Yankee feeder: goldfinches, sparrows, cardinals, bluebirds, Carolina wrens. I said, "You mean take the gun out and shoot at cans, like when I was a kid?" There were also photographs of crows, hawks, blue jays, and woodpeckers, a lone osprey—birds that didn't visit traditional feeders.

"You're not a kid anymore, Duster," my father said.

"Why're these birds on the wall? Are you into birding nowadays?" I got off the couch and corrected a frame. I said, "Who took these photos? They look professional."

My father looked at the frames on the wall as if he'd never noticed them being there. He raised his eyebrows up three times, then squinted. He said, "I was hoping you'd bring someone with you. I always kind of liked Patricia's mother. She's classy, you know what I mean? I mean, Patricia's mother's classy."

My wife's parents had been married for forty-plus years and from what I could tell thrived unapologetically up in Wise, Virginia. They keep a sign in their front yard that goes VIRGINIA IS FOR LOVERS, like it was some kind of non-argumentative statement on par with Rain Falls Downward. I said, "I think Patricia's mom's out of your league, for one. And she's unobtainable for two. Three, Patricia's dad has never liked you, and he would kill you. He was a sniper in the old days, you know. He was a sniper in the Army, or whatever. He shot actual people. He didn't throw things at his own gun."

My father walked out the door without saying anything. He got in the passenger side of my car and sat there. Of course most people I would tell this story later would think, "That man is going through the first stages of dementia!" They would say, "He's the kind of man you read about for two days under the 'Editor's Picks' section of the MSN homepage!" I was used to it, though. I went out to the car, opened the driver's side, and said, "You want to go to Worm's Bar?"

"After," he said. "I didn't call you to drive all the way down here to take me to the bar. Hell, I can walk down there if I want to. Or hitch a ride. I can drive my own truck if I feel like the fucking cop is taking a nap. I can get on the riding lawn mower."

"After what?" I said. I went ahead and got in the car and cranked it. I didn't feel sad or indifferent or happy or excited. I'd been going through this routine for a while with Sin. I said, "Where we going?"

My father said, "I need to go see a doctor. I mean, yeah, after Worm's, I need to see a doctor. I'm afraid with the way things are going, I might live forever. I don't want to not die, Dust. Who wants to live forever?"

———

The hot-water tap turned cold, and vice versa. When he tried to quit smoking and put on a nicotine patch, it made him crave cigarettes more. One time he told me that his vices began at age seventeen with heroin, which led him to cocaine, which led him to marijuana, which led him to bourbon, which led him to the occasional domestic beer. My father swore he bought my mother a parrot that never learned to talk, and rescued one of those non-barking Basenji dogs that ended up howling all the time, then running off. His mousetraps worked better without peanut butter on the little tray.

I don't like to think of myself as a bad son, but I drove my father straight to one of those emergency care clinics out off Highway 78 instead of the bar. I had called up Patricia from the driveway, for my father said he needed to go back inside and apply layers of black bloodroot salve on his torso and limbs before hitting daylight for too long, what with the lesions and hives and shingles that arrived like bad cousins, one after the other. To my wife I said, "I don't know why I'm here."

She said, "Yes. That's one of the great existential questions. Sometimes when I'm unraveling, it's the only thought that goes through my mind."

I told her how my father seemed listless and depressed, that he looked like he could no longer take the world, that he'd given up on fighting. "He wants to go to a bar, so I told him we could go there for a while. But in reality, I want to take him to see a dermatologist. Can you get on the Internet and Google something like 'Dermatologist/Calloustown, South Carolina/unexplained neurological disorders/ex-wife married an oyster shucker,' and find out if there's any kind of medical center within a fifty-mile range?"

Patricia didn't answer immediately. Then she said, "I think it's you who wants to go to Worm's Place, but that's another story." I heard her clicking away on the keyboard, and imagined her there in our den, a cell phone cradled to her delicate neck, enough merino wool yarn surrounding her to fashion a car cover.

My wife clucked her tongue, which sounded exactly like knitting needles clacking together when she was on a roll of knit-pearl-knit-pearl maneuvers for more than a couple minutes. I said, "No, I only want to drink all day long when I'm in my hometown, Patricia," hoping that she'd think, "Because of me, is that what you're saying, because of me?"

She said, "There's a veterinarian who's still in business. Dogs get mange, and that's more or less what your father has. Why don't you go see the vet?" I didn't say, "Ha ha ha." I didn't answer until Patricia said, "There's one of those doc-in-the-box places, and that looks like your only choice without driving all the way to Columbia or Charleston."

I said, "I might have to spend the night here. I brought along my gym bag, just in case." She got on Mapquest and gave me the directions. "If you've gotten to some kind of golf ball driving range, then you've gone two hundred feet too far."

Anyway, my father said nothing when I pulled into the parking lot, but I could tell from the look on his face that he felt betrayed. He said, "I wasn't making a plea for help, Dust. When people make pleas for help, they take a bottle of aspirin, or cut their wrists in the wrong direction."

I pulled right up to the front door—you'd think that an ersatz emergency room of sorts would have a handicapped parking spot or two, but this place didn't—and turned off the ignition. I said, "I could hear it in between the lines of your voice, Dad. Plus, once we get you diagnosed for real and get proper medicine, then we can go to the bar and drink without worrying so much about the future."

"Right-o," my father said. "I knew there was a reason why your mother and I paid for all that education." He reached for and extracted his wallet. "I got my Medicare card with me. You going to sit out here in the car or are you coming in?"

I said, "What do you want? Of course I'm coming in."

"Right-o," he said.

I looked over at a man and kid hitting golf balls at the Calloustown Practice Range next door to the emergency clinic. The sign out front of the driving range had gigantic CPR letters out front, and I wondered if people in mid-heart attack ever got confused with which parking lot to enter. I said, "Why do you keep saying 'Right-o'? Are you watching a bunch of British sitcoms or something? Let me guess, your TV only gets British stations."

He got out of the car and said, "To be honest, what I'd rather do to save some time is have you let me go in here—I know you have to get back home—and while I'm talking to the so-called doctor or nurse practitioner or whatever they're calling these people nowadays, I'd appreciate it if you'd run into town and see if Tree Morse has any aloe plants for sale at his nursery. I've been reading up. Even if they don't work medicinally, it wouldn't be a bad thing to have something around that needed me, water-wise."

"That sounds like a plan," I said. I didn't mean it, of course. I knew my father just wanted me off the premises, that when I came back he'd be standing in front of the clinic after never checking in, and so on.

He shook my hand again for some reason and entered the building. I started my car and backed out of the parking lot, then put it in drive and returned to my spot. Then I reached beneath my seat and pulled out a squeeze tube of hand sanitizer, just in case my father's skin supported a contagion from which I could never recover.

A snake caught and ate his cat. Back in the old days he got drunk one night, got a tattoo that read "Sin + Soretta" and it faded invisible a week later. One time he bought a recapped tire and it ended up gaining tread. I talked him into driving all the way down to Myrtle Beach to take part in a speed-dating extravaganza one time after my mom left for the retired Air Force colonel, not knowing that there was a convention of stutterers in town who'd pretty much clogged the sign-up sheet. It went on and on. Back when he actually set up appointments with Dr. Stoudemire, he was told he needed to eat more hot dogs and processed meat, seeing as his sodium levels were dangerously low.

I sat in the parking lot a good hour. I mean, I waited twenty minutes, got out of my car, opened the door to the clinic, looked inside, and saw only a receptionist behind the desk, no one else in the waiting room. I thought, "Good." I thought, "My father's in one of the examination rooms with a man or woman who probably half paid attention in medical school, more than likely in one of the Caribbean-nation medical schools."

It doesn't take a brain surgeon who went to the Medical University of South Carolina to figure out what I couldn't: that there was a back door of sorts and my father sashayed his way straight through there without seeing a valid epidermal expert. The fucker. I waited my hour, I went inside the clinic and sat down for five or ten minutes, no one showed up with an accidental shotgun blast to their torso, and I said to the receptionist, "Are you doing a crossword puzzle, or a sudoku?" I said, "This isn't such a bad place, out here in the middle of nowhere. Let me guess: most of the people you get in here suffer from snake bites."

She didn't look up. She said, "I know you. Do you remember me? Say. Say."

I looked hard and tried to run a Rolodex of faces through my mind. I said, "Oh, Jesus, I haven't been back to Calloustown for so long."

She looked anywhere between forty and sixty years old. I thought, "Was she an old teacher or something?" I thought, "Have the schools gotten so incapable of offering teachers a paycheck without a furlough—what with the idiot governor—that people have quit in order to be paid-by-the-hour receptionists inside virus-filled cement-blocked buildings?" I thought, "Did I take this woman to the prom, and then she had no other choice but to age mercilessly like some old dug best known to Appalachian photographs?" I said, "I'm sorry. I'm consumed with my father's well-being."

She tilted her head hard to the back corner of the building. "Well, your daddy seems to be consumed with not caring about his bank account."

I looked at her hard, for I didn't know what she meant, then looked at the door that led to the examination rooms. A woman came out of there wearing a standard white frock. She said to the receptionist, "Sometimes I wonder why we even have to show up here, Hannah."

I looked at the doctor and said, "Hey."

"Of course," I thought to myself, "Hannah Hannah Hannah?" I said to the doctor, "Is it leprosy? Is it just a case of hives or shingles gone bad? Does it have something to do with fire ants, or nerves?"

Hannah said, "She ain't seen him." She said, "Back to what we were talking about, you asked me out one time I was in tenff grade you was in tweff and you never showed up. It wasn't anything like the prom or nothing but it was enough to make me know I should like girls the rest of my life."

The doctor stood there staring at me. I didn't remember any of this at all. I said, "What?" I said, "Hannah, I'm sorry."

The doctor said, "What are you talking about?"

I said, "My father."

"He paid me twenty dollars to show him the back door out," Hannah said. "Sorry."

I said, "I don't think I called you up for a date. Are you sure it was me? I dated one girl the whole time I was at Calloustown High. Her name was Vivian. You remember Vivian? And then we broke up and I went to college, and then I met a woman I ended up marrying."

Hannah stood up. She grunted. She shook her head sideways. "I knew you'd end up no good, even back then, cheating on Vivian like you done."

The doctor said, "I don't know what you're talking about," and retreated back into the examination rooms. I could see in her eyes, though, that she didn't believe my story, and that she felt sorry for her receptionist.

I said, "Someone played a joke on you. Or on me! On top of that, my father's telephone doesn't work right anymore. Maybe it didn't back then, either. Did you pick up the receiver and I was there already?" I looked in her face and tried to recognize anything. "Where's my father?"

Hannah said, "Search-a-Word. I'm doing Search-a-Words."

My father swore that his doors changed overnight from opening in to opening out. All of them. He said he'd put his hand on a Bible and tell the story about how one morning, maybe six months after my mother left for the oyster entrepreneur in Sumter, he got up to go put black oil sunflower seeds in the Yankee feeders only to pull and pull on the door knob, thinking someone had come along post-midnight to shove silver slugs between jamb and lock prankster-style. He said he tried the front door, the back door, and a side door that went off to a sunroom of sorts. Understand that this was a good decade after I'd lived in the house, so I couldn't remember if doors went in or out in the first place. I didn't even remember a sunroom in my house of training.

I went back outside from the clinic thinking about this—I accidentally tried to pull the door toward me, then pushed it out—and wondered where my father might have gone. I tried to think backward. Would one leave a doctor's office and light out for the funeral home, or the maternity ward of a hospital? Would he hitchhike back home because he figured I would never think of him doing so, or toward Sumter, or to the opposite of Calloustown—which happened, in my mind, to be Asheville, North Carolina. Would he go to a wedding chapel?

"I'm over here, Freckle-dick," I heard my father yell out. I looked at the CPR driving range and saw, still, that man and child standing there with three-woods in their hands.

The man took his club and pointed down to the opposite end of the wide fairway. My father stood three hundred yards away and appeared to have a ball teed up to hit in the woods beyond the Calloustown Practice Range's perimeter.

And he had his shirt off so that, from where I stood, he looked like a man with a thousand ticks on his back. I started walking his way. I entered the driving range's boundaries and kept looking behind me in case the man and kid wanted to tee off in my direction, which is exactly what I would've done. My cell phone rang, I pulled it out of my pocket, and I noticed that Patricia was on the other end.

"Hey," I said, breaking into a trot. My father addressed the ball. Where did he get the club? I wondered. Did the CPR hand out drivers to people who showed up clubless and unprepared? I said, "I'd be willing to bet I'll be staying here tonight."

"I might've found a dermatologist in Calloustown, or someone who's a specialist," Patricia said. In the background I could hear her yarn whispering down to the wooden floor of our den. "What's a dendrologist?"

I said, "No. That has to do with trees."

"Well they have one of those people in your hometown."

My father reared back and swung at the ball. He hit a beautiful tee shot over the scrub pines that edged Calloustown Practice Range's property. Behind me, a ball landed from the kid teeing off like a normal person perfecting his swing. I didn't want to say, "It might be time to look for a psychiatrist," so I didn't. I said, "We got it all under control here. I'll see you tomorrow," and punched End.

Sin teed up another ball. As I reached him he said, "Was that Patricia? Did you tell her I said hello? I don't want any shit from you about this. Listen, if I got my skin cleared up, then I'd end up being perfect. Can you imagine what it would be like being perfect? And then everyone around here would hate me all the time. People around here would kill a perfect person just so they wouldn't come up so short at home daily."

"Why're we out here at the end of the range?" I asked him. I looked back. We were too far away to be in possible danger from anyone, unless they pulled out a modified potato gun and shot Titleists our way.

"I can't think up there. I can't think teeing off from where everyone else tees off. Listen to this idea, Dust. Listen to what I came up with just before you showed up: it's a commercial for either a golf club or a golf ball. The camera shows a man at a par three hole, you know, like 150 yards from the tee box. So he pulls out his gigantic driver, and his playing partner says, 'What're you doing?' and the dude turns around with his back to the green. Then he rips one and—I think they can do this now, what with all the fancy cameras and computers—it goes around the world, like a meteor, and then plops down on the green and rolls in the hole. Can you see it? The ball goes 24,901 miles, and then he gets a hole in one."

I had to admit it seemed like a viable and worthy television commercial for a dimpled ball or oversized clubhead. I said, "Put on your shirt and let's go to Worm's." I said, "Do you have any other ideas for commercials? I have a buddy in Charlotte who works at an ad agency."

My father hit one more ball into the woods, topping this one so that it never reached knee high, then ricocheted off a pine tree and nearly came back to us. "So what did you think of Hannah?" my father said.

I handed him his shirt and tried not to make eye contact with those lesions. "She was kind of abrupt with me. Who the hell is she? I don't remember her whatsoever."

My father left his driver on the ground. He didn't pick up his tee, which hadn't moved through any of his swings. We walked on a veer toward my car. He said, "One day gas will be solid, and the Earth will be gas." At the unlocked car my father said, "That Hannah woman used to call me up every day, thanking me for the way I brought you up. She says she wouldn't have become the woman she is if it weren't for you. She used another word for 'woman.' I forget it. Hell, she called so much your mother got to thinking that we were having an affair. I kept telling her—your mother—that everything was backwards."

I drove to the bar, but I didn't pay attention to Sin's constant monologue. I thought, how many times have I unwittingly caused someone to choose a path in life? I thought, I wonder if there's a woman out there that I should've married—one who never had to unravel yarn, or who never attempted to manufacture mittens in the first place. And then I got stuck thinking, what if my mother met the retired Air Force colonel before he retired, and he became my father? What would I be doing now? Would I be working in the restaurant, shucking oysters for the hungry masses? Would I be delivering shells to people who wanted crushed driveways? Would I encounter some kind of shellfish allergy and break out in hives?

Sin said, "I kind of miss her." I didn't ask him if he meant my mother, my wife, or the woman at the clinic. I even thought that, perhaps, by "her" he meant "him."

We got in the car and Sin picked up my cell phone from the console. I got on the two-lane to drive into Calloustown proper. He pressed the receiver icon as if to make a call, then said, "I knew it would be you." Was Patricia on the other end? Did that Hannah woman somehow retrieve my number, maybe through my father having written it down under Emergency Contact during another visit to the clinic?

Sin listened—or feigned listening to a made-up caller—and I thought about all the things that hadn't turned backward in his life: The trees in his yard didn't lose leaves in May, for example. His plates didn't come out of the dishwasher dirty. His clothes didn't appear to become dirtier straight out of the washing machine.

I pulled into a parking space in front of the bar. My father said over the phone, "An oyster-shucking knife isn't sharp, but it can still cause harm. I met a hand doctor one time who invested in oyster-shucking knives."

I turned off the ignition and said, "That's not Mom."

Sin said, "Hello?"

After School

Later on, in the parking lot waiting for bulldozers, we thought back at how a young girl—no one remembered her name—transferred from either Arizona or North Dakota, suffering from allergies we couldn't comprehend. This was 1970 or thereabouts. Her parents brought along what appeared to be a certifiably genuine prognosis from an ear, nose, and throat specialist. Ragweed, goldenrod, dandelions, crabgrass, centipede, pine bark: this girl seemed to be pretty much allergic to everything the South had to offer. Back then we were all young, and we thought things like poor thing, et cetera. This was a time before charter schools and school choice and private schools and home schools. Our custodian, Mr. Willie, wasn't pleased, but there seemed to be no choice but to kill all the shrubbery, cut down trees, gravel over every inch of the school grounds, spray DDT on the ball fields, and remind each other that no roses could ever be delivered on anyone's birthday, Valentine's Day, Secretary's Day, and that all future proms would be corsage- and boutonniere-less. No one argued about it—we wanted to make this little girl and her parents feel welcome in the community.

She graduated. She matriculated to Arizona State or the University of North Dakota, as I recall. I'm not sure why someone on the school board never piped up, "Well, now that that's over, we need to replant some azaleas out front." We just remained barren. I still taught only biology and chemistry back then and even kept nothing but plastic and/or ceramic accessories in my classroom aquarium, or the little habitat I sketched out for box turtles that Mr. Lawson constructed with his third-year Advanced Shop students.

It took another decade before—again, this was a child who transferred from northern Minnesota—we found ourselves liable if anyone brought peanuts, walnuts, or pecans onto the school grounds. I remember this particular case only because the tenth grader, Marty Mortensen, had an hourglass-shaped head. I'm saying, it looked like a peanut rested atop his shoulders. I wouldn't be surprised if his parents—I think they moved down here because the whole family suffered from that depression that supposedly sets in from short days and long nights—acquired a questionable medical professional to make up Marty's allergy, as an attempt to thwart likely and subsequent days when they served boiled peanuts in the cafeteria and one of our more observant students yelled out, "Hey, my plate's filled with little Marty Mortensen heads!" like that. Sometimes children throbbing with hormones don't think about how words can echo in a fragile peanut head right on up until about the twenty-year reunion when he returns to the Moose Club with an automatic weapon.

So there we were in a school that looked plopped down in the center of a wasteland, forever wanting nuts in our brownies or cookies. Plus the Snickers, Payday, Almond Joy, Reese's Cups, and Baby Ruths disappeared from the vending machines and we opted for either plain Hershey's bars or plain M&Ms.

As an aside, how come blind people don't have that seasonal disorder all the time? I never heard about Stevie Wonder or Ray Charles or Helen Keller moaning around how they needed more sunlight.

Anyway, it might've been 1984 when more than a few children realized they were allergic to cigarette smoke. There went the outdoor smoking area, there went teachers smoking in the lounge. Deep down I understood that everyone should quit anyway. I showed a filmstrip that involved healthy lungs compared to coal/asbestos/glass dust/cigarette-damaged lungs. But goddamn. We got to where we took turns being late to our own classes. One day I'd pretend to need to check oil in my engine block between second and third periods, just to stand outside and smoke while Mrs. Allen looked in on my class. Other days Mrs. Allen feigned forgetting her extendable pointer in the trunk of her car and I told her history class stories that weren't in the textbook. Our P.E. teacher flat out took showers at the end of every class and smoked in the stall.

I think it took almost six years before we had a child so allergic to dust mites that our whole home ec division got wiped out mid-semester. Soon thereafter we had a couple students show up with medical forms saying they couldn't be within a hundred feet of anyone wearing perfume or cologne. This included deodorant, pomade (Mr. Willie's), hairspray, and acne cream. I didn't bother taking down precise notes to all of this—I had enough to worry about, seeing as kids needed to dissect frogs, the district couldn't afford ordering the things, and I spent many a Saturday night/Sunday morning gigging—but this seemed to be when our school really started to deteriorate.

A whole knot of tenth graders, out of nowhere, learned that they were allergic to both paint fumes and alumina, one of the central ingredients in glaze. So we quit offering art classes and the two part-time teachers got laid off. On top of this, Mr. Willie couldn't paint over graffiti. "General upkeep" vanished from our work environment.

I kind of liked one of those art teachers. She let her students paint still lifes and imagine what a walnut would look like resting atop a pear, banana, orange, or mango. Call it passive aggressive, but she always hung her students' canvases in the hallways.

Mr. Lawson couldn't take it anymore. He smoked and had a hard time waiting for the three o'clock bell. His students—in the past they'd been best in the state for their cabinetry skills—could now only wish to gain employment at Naked Furniture, what with the "no paint" directive. Lawson, on one particularly bleak winter day when he caught his students firing nail guns at one another, walked over to his miter box, placed his arm down, and cut off his left hand.

Gary Doherty sprang into action, evidently because he'd almost made it up to Webelo in the Boy Scout hierarchy. That kid ran directly to the first-aid station, extracted gauze, a compress, surgical tubing, and those gloves. He staunched Lawson's bleeding long enough for the EMTs to show up, take the shop teacher down to the emergency room at Graywood Emergency Regional Memorial, and not connect his hand back on like they do at regular hospitals filled with doctors who paid attention in med school.

When everything settled down, that's when we learned that Doherty had a latex product allergy.

From what I heard, his doctors told him he could never use a condom. From what I heard, Doherty succumbed to a number of sexually transmitted diseases by the time he almost finished his associate's degree in pulpwood management at one of the technical colleges.

And then—perhaps a geneticist or eugenicist could explain this—everyone became allergic to something. Maybe a clinical psychologist, or that absurdist playwright I read back when I thought I wanted to be a big-game veterinarian and came across a book called *Rhinoceros*, has something to say about how no one wants to be left out. We had students coming in with doctors' notes saying they couldn't be around PVC pipes, copper tubing, plaster, Styrofoam cups, everything. A swarm of young girls were afflicted with migraines due to fluorescent lights. The offspring of the Perfume People decided they couldn't be near hand soap of any type, from GoJo to Ivory. By this time one of the many right-wing governors of ours had made it so anyone could call him- or herself a certified teacher, open up a certified charter home school, and let the kids play video games and read the Old Testament all day in order to make them better soldiers.

The school pretty much emptied by 2010. I had planned to retire in another year. We dropped from a student population of 1,200 back about the time Nixon took off on a helicopter all the way down to one student: Tony Timms. We wondered how come the school district didn't shut us down. Tony Timms could be bused to another district, we all thought, for a cheaper price than keeping biology, algebra, remedial English, Spanish Uno, and history teachers on the payroll, not to mention the cost of electricity and the Department of Health and Environmental Control sending out inspectors tri-weekly.

It's because our school board members didn't believe in busing, and hadn't since 1970—coincidentally the year when our allergy-prone students' parents became so protective, holy, and litigious.

I won't say that it wasn't great having one student for ninety minutes every other day because of that A/B schedule. Tony Timms had me fourth period, after lunch, but I still clocked in at 7:45, stood around front as if I had bus duty, went to my room and played around with my collection of Bunsen burners. Sometimes I stood in the cafeteria and pretended I needed to break up a food fight on tater tot day. Mostly, though, I sat in my room and wished that over the years I had paid more attention to all the latest student-friendly lab experiments they'd developed that didn't involve baking soda and vinegar.

Finally, in what seemed like the school's final days, Tony Timms came into my class without his book or calculator. He didn't have the slide rule I'd let him borrow either. He said, "Have you talked to my parents yet?"

I looked up to see him standing in the doorway with a plastic Bi-Lo bag over his head.

I said, "No. Was I supposed to? Did I miss a PTA meeting? Do they want to discuss your grade in here? Are they concerned that my trying to teach you how to master a 1964 Pickett No. 120 Trainer-Simplex slide rule is on par with our old home ec teacher years ago teaching her students how to darn socks and cobble shoes?" Perhaps I spent so many hours in silence at the school that, when asked to speak, I released all of my trapped thoughts. I said, "Did they watch that television program aired last night on NBC about the history of inappropriate teacher-student conduct? Is this about my saying I couldn't offer you a strong recommendation to Harvard, Princeton, Stanford, Yale, the University of North Dakota, or Arizona State because you've not recognized the difference between helium and hydrogen on the Periodic Table of Elements?"

Tony Timms lifted the bag. I saw, per usual, his mouth open enough to view his uvula. He said, "Here they are," and moved closer to the doorjamb.

I turned to find his parents, dressed—oddly, I thought—in what appeared to be the latest swimwear. They wore scuba masks, too, and had those diving cylinders strapped to their backs. I said, "Hey. Y'all please don't stand next to the Bunsen burners." I said, "Is this one of those days when parents come in and tell everyone about their jobs?"

Even before real and imagined allergies took their toll on the student population, I dreaded Bring Your Parent to School Days, seeing as most everyone's parents started up their employment descriptions with, "Well, I used to be a loom fixer over at the mill, but now I'm a..." whittler, small engine repair fiend, jockey lot entrepreneur, birdhouse maker...

Mr. Timms handed me a signed document from his son's doctor. I read it twice. "He's allergic to air?" I said. I looked at Tony, my final student. "That's why you're such a mouth-breather, because you're allergic to air?"

Mrs. Timms said, "This air. Not all air. This air. It's got too much argon. Tony's allergic to argon, as are we. It's a congenital condition."

I didn't know how to respond. Well, I knew enough to say, "Get the fuck out of my classroom, you idiotic people." Then I ripped the mouthpieces away from their faces and chased them away. I screamed out, "This is what you get for naming your child after an adjective," because I'd been thinking about kids named Tony, Misty, Merry, and Randy.

As it ended up, those were my last official words in my teaching career with American students. Later on, standing there with my five or six colleagues, waiting for our brick-and-cement-block school to become dust for the townspeople to breathe in and sneeze out, I imagined what my last words might've been had I taken a job at a less sickly and paranoid school district. Would I have said, "I've enjoyed every minute" or "There's forty years I'll never get back"? Would I have shaken hands with administrators even though I believed them to be a cross between weasels and newts? Would I have felt as though I made a difference in some teenager's life?

The principal, whose name I never learned and who hadn't shown up since we dwindled down to ten students, drove up on his new Harley-Davidson. He yelled out, "Good news! I've been hearing the rumors, but I didn't want to let y'all in on it until it was official. They've postponed demolition! We've been chose by the government to be a Special Ambassador School. We got us forty children showing up tomorrow from a Chinese leper colony."

He said that even Mr. Lawson would return to teach woodworking, no longer embarrassed to reveal his nub.

I shook my head. "Don't count me in," I said. "This has all been sad, confounding, and miserable enough. Do you know what happens right after all these new students die off? I'll tell you. Amphibians from the sky. Fire everywhere. Winds we've never imagined. I don't believe much in the Bible, but I do believe that Revelation section."

The principal forgot to put down his kickstand and the motorcycle toppled over. He said, "There will be a need for extra grief counselors, if you're right. What's your name? I'm going to see if I can get you promoted to vice principal. If the end of the world's coming like you say, then we need more vice principals with similar farsighted thoughts."

As if I'd arranged it beforehand, three claps of thunder sounded. Everyone ran inside except for me. I righted the principal's Harley, started it, and rode off in search of a high bridge with low guardrails. Speeding down the corrupted road, though, I understood that I didn't have what it takes to end my own life. Being a scientist of sorts, I needed to view firsthand what happens after lepers.

What Could've Been?

Take a left out of the driveway. Take a left at the stop sign. Drive to the first convenience store—which used to be a 7-Eleven, or Pantry, or Quick-Way, but now offers scratch cards and Fuel Perks—and take another left-hand turn. Get in the slow lane.

Drive past the elementary school that looks nothing like the one you attended. A row of brick ranch-style houses. Maybe a set of clapboard mill village houses. At the light—there will be a McDonald's here—take a right. Pass the Dollar General, or the Dollar Tree, or the Dollar Store. Look to the left and see how the pawnshop sells guns and buys gold, as always. Pass the grocery store that used to house a different chain, that used to house a different chain, that used to house a different chain—Publix, Bi-Lo, Food Lion, Ingles, Winn-Dixie, Community Cash, IGA, Piggly Wiggly. You'll try to remember the succession.

The same will occur at the Bank of America. Nationsbank, FirstUnion, C&S, that other longtime local savings and loan where you started a checking account in high school.

Drive past a barrage of fast-food restaurants that includes a Burger King, Hardee's, Dairy Queen, Sonic, Chick-fil-A, Zaxby's, Pizza Inn, Pizza Hut, Papa John's, Little Caesar's,

KFC, Bojangles, Captain D's, et cetera. Outback, Chili's, Ruby Tuesday, Applebee's, Moe's Southwestern, TGIF. Subway, another McDonald's, Firehouse Subs, Taco Bell, another Bojangles, Ryan's, Red Lobster, IHOP, and so on. Huddle House, Waffle House, Cracker Barrel, Shoney's. This will take about two miles. In between there will be a Walmart, a vacant Kmart, Lowe's, Home Depot, and Big Lots. Exxon, Texaco, BP, Citgo, Shell, Kangaroo, Sunoco—none of which have full service, or mechanics available who can fix a flat or check transmission fluid.

Take another right onto the four-lane road that used to be a two-lane country road forty years earlier, where you and your friends drove around smoking cigarettes, drank Miller Ponies, pulled over with the overhead light on into rusty-gated pasture entrances so someone could fumble with Zigzag rolling papers. Drive past the dilapidated wooden building that housed the little store where your father bought Nehi grape sodas, or NuGrape—it's the place where the owner got murdered and the police never caught a killer. Or it's the place that the owner's children didn't want to operate, seeing as their father sent them off to college. Or it's the place where the owner had diabetes so advanced that the doctor said a leg needed amputation, and the owner felt as if he had no better choice—what with all the grocery stores nearby—than to put a shotgun in his mouth behind the ancient tree behind the property. One of your friends used to claim that a man got hanged from the lowest branch of that tree. One of your friends carved his initials, plus the initials of, say, Ann Guy, in that tree. Years later—twenty years later—you figured out that the "A. G." really stood for a boy who didn't smoke cigarettes, roll joints, or drink from tiny beer bottles: Alan Gray, or Alvin Gillespie, or Aaron Giles. He was the boy who got accepted to a college where no one from your hometown went, and he made a mark on the world before dying in a tragic manner, not much different from the owner of the store where your father bought bygone classic sodas, which made him smile.

Pass a junk shop that holds as much merchandise outside as inside the cement block building. There's a sale on drive-in speakers.

You're not that far away. Pass a subdivision of lookalike houses wherein all the roads are named for British monarchy. Pass a subdivision of lookalike houses wherein all the roads are named for famous golf courses of the world. Pass a subdivision of lookalike houses wherein all the roads are named for Ivy League colleges. Pass a subdivision of lookalike houses wherein all the roads are named for Native American accoutrements.

You will reach the land where the drive-in movie theater once stood. The screen's structure remains, though the front of it peels away. Metal posts stand without their speakers, like the headless parking meters at the beginning of *Cool Hand Luke*, which you probably saw here. You should park your vehicle and walk these grounds—already scoured by men and women with metal detectors, already used for a makeshift flea market that somehow failed, already surveyed for a three cul-de-sac subdivision called Hollywood Hills that will offer nothing but drainage problems for the houses built closest to the screen.

Go to the back row—or at least where you think the back row might've been. Forget about the snack bar/projection booth. Weave through high weeds to the back row and think about how the windows fogged up. Think about how you never, through all of the pre-planning, imagined what difficulties a steering wheel might offer, or how the seats might nearly concuss both of you after pulling the levers, or how you tried to maneuver into the backseat as if you'd had experience as a rock climber and high hurdler. Think about the difficulties both of you encountered, brought about by a triple row of brassiere metal eye hooks there on your first real date, or at least the first date remembered. Think about the bad acting, the car chase, the unreal setting, the chainsaw, the shark, the blob, the giant insect, the monster, the seemingly normal neighbor with the unruly, untoward, and despicable urges. Think about tires on gravel and how you hoped the driver continued on, that it wasn't anybody you knew, that it wasn't your parents.

Were there swing sets down by the screen, where children played before the movie? Did you think to yourself, "Those poor idiot parents, bringing their children to a place like this on a Saturday night?" Was there some kind of Coming Attractions? Did you say to the person next to you, "I got your 'coming attractions'" and think it was the wittiest thing ever said?

Stand on that spot.

Stand where you think your Opal, Datsun, Ford, Chevy, Buick, Toyota, MG Midget, or parents' Lincoln or Cadillac might've stood. Look at the compromised screen. Go ahead and say, "Fuckin' A—how did I make it this far?" Say, "Jesus Christ, all that bad living. All those close calls. What could've been? What could've been? What could've been?"

Then there's the mother or father standing there, thirty minutes after curfew, and the story you have memorized. You have twenty lies, all of which you'll recycle for the rest of your life, though you didn't know it then, in the driveway, looking at your hand on the gear shift, thinking about putting it in reverse.

Acknowledgments

I am happy and proud to work with editor Guy Intoci. Thanks for putting up with our quirky dialect down here. Thanks to Steve Gillis and Michelle Dotter at Dzanc. I hope that my students and colleagues at Wofford College know how much I cherish their hard work and relentless esprit de corps. Bless you, Glenda Guion, for moving from one Calloustown to another.